PRAISE FOR MELANIE DICKERSON

"*The Piper's Pursuit* is a lovely tale of adventure, romance, and redemption. Kat and Steffan's righteous quest will have you rooting them on until the very satisfying end!"

—LORIE LANGDON, AUTHOR OF *OLIVIA TWIST* AND THE *DOON* SERIES

"Christian fiction fans will relish Dickerson's eloquent story."

—*SCHOOL LIBRARY JOURNAL* ON *THE ORPHAN'S WISH*

"*The Goose Girl*, a little retold fairy tale, sparkles in Dickerson's hands, with endearing characters and a charming setting that will appeal to teens and adults alike."

—*RT BOOK REVIEWS*, 4¹/₂ STARS, TOP PICK! ON *THE NOBLE SERVANT*

"Dickerson is a masterful storyteller with a carefully crafted plot, richly drawn characters, and a detailed setting. The reader is easily pulled into the story. Does everything end happily ever after? Read it and see! Recommended for young adults and adults who are young at heart."

—*CHRISTIAN LIBRARY JOURNAL* ON *THE NOBLE SERVANT*

"[*The Silent Songbird*] will have you jumping out of your seat with anticipation at times. Moderate- to fast-paced, you will not want this book to end. Recommended for all, especially lovers of historical romance."

—*RT BOOK REVIEWS*, 4 STARS

"A terrific YA crossover medieval romance from the author of *The Golden Braid*."

—*LIBRARY JOURNAL* ON *THE SILENT SONGBIRD*

"When it comes to happily-ever-afters, Melanie Dickerson is the undisputed queen of fairy-tale romance, and all I can say is—long live the queen! From start to finish *The Beautiful Pretender* is yet another brilliant gem in her crown, spinning a medieval love story that will steal you away—heart, soul, and sleep!"

—JULIE LESSMAN, AWARD-WINNING AUTHOR OF THE DAUGHTERS OF BOSTON, WINDS OF CHANGE, AND HEART OF SAN FRANCISCO SERIES

"I couldn't stop reading! Melanie has done what so many other historical novelists have tried and failed: she's created a heroine that is at once both smart and self-assured without seeming modern. A woman so fixed in her time and place that she is able to speak to ours as well."

—SIRI MITCHELL, AUTHOR OF *FLIRTATION WALK* AND *CHATEAU OF ECHOES*, ON *THE BEAUTIFUL PRETENDER*

"Dickerson breathes life into the age-old story of Rapunzel, blending it seamlessly with the other YA novels she has written in this time and place . . . The character development is solid, and she captures religious medieval life splendidly."

—*BOOKLIST* ON *THE GOLDEN BRAID*

"Readers who love getting lost in a fairy-tale romance will cheer for Rapunzel's courage as she rises above her overwhelming past. The surprising way Dickerson weaves threads of this enchanting companion novel with those of her other Hagenheim stories is simply delightful. Her fans will love it."

—JILL WILLIAMSON, CHRISTY AWARD–WINNING AUTHOR OF THE BLOOD OF KINGS TRILOGY AND THE KINSMAN CHRONICLES, ON *THE GOLDEN BRAID*

"Dickerson spins a retelling of Robin Hood with emotionally compelling characters, offering hope that love may indeed conquer all as they unite in a shared desire to serve both the Lord and those in need."

—*RT BOOK REVIEWS*, 4^{1}/2 STARS, ON *THE HUNTRESS OF THORNBECK FOREST*

"Melanie Dickerson does it again! Full of danger, intrigue, and romance, this beautifully crafted story [*The Huntress of Thornbeck Forest*] will transport you to another place and time."

—SARAH E. LADD, BESTSELLING AUTHOR OF THE CORNWALL NOVELS

The
PEASANT'S
DREAM

ALSO BY MELANIE DICKERSON

Court of Swans (available January 2021!)

YOUNG ADULT FAIRY TALE ROMANCE SERIES
The Healer's Apprentice
The Merchant's Daughter
The Fairest Beauty
The Captive Maiden
The Princess Spy
The Golden Braid
The Silent Songbird
The Orphan's Wish
The Warrior Maiden
The Piper's Pursuit
The Peasant's Dream

A MEDIEVAL FAIRY TALE SERIES
The Huntress of Thornbeck Forest
The Beautiful Pretender
The Noble Servant

REGENCY SPIES OF LONDON SERIES
A Spy's Devotion
A Viscount's Proposal
A Dangerous Engagement

The PEASANT'S DREAM

MELANIE DICKERSON

THOMAS NELSON

Since 1798

Published in Nashville, Tennessee, by Thomas Nelson. Thomas Nelson is a registered trademark of HarperCollins Christian Publishing, Inc.

Interior design by Phoebe Wetherbee

Thomas Nelson titles may be purchased in bulk for educational, business, fund-raising, or sales promotional use. For information, please email SpecialMarkets@ThomasNelson.com.

Scripture quotations are taken from the King James Version. Public domain. Also from the Holy Bible, New International Version®, NIV®. Copyright © 1973, 1978, 1984, 2011 by Biblica, Inc.™ Used by permission of Zondervan. All rights reserved worldwide. www.zondervan.com. The "NIV" and "New International Version" are trademarks registered in the United States Patent and Trademark Office by Biblica, Inc.™

Publisher's Note: This novel is a work of fiction. Names, characters, places, and incidents are either products of the author's imagination or used fictitiously. All characters are fictional, and any similarity to people living or dead is purely coincidental.

Library of Congress Cataloging-in-Publication Data

Names: Dickerson, Melanie, 1970- author.
Title: The peasant's dream / Melanie Dickerson.
Description: Nashville, Tennessee : Thomas Nelson, [2020] | Summary: Frederick, a peasant farmer's son who dreams of earning a living using his God-given talent as a woodcarver, falls in love with Adela, a duke's daughter who yearns to prove herself as an artist. Includes discussion questions.
Identifiers: LCCN 2020006414 (print) | LCCN 2020006415 (ebook) | ISBN 9780785228332 (hardcover) | ISBN 9780785228349 (epub) | ISBN 9780785228356
Subjects: CYAC: Nobility--Fiction. | Wood carving--Fiction. | Social classes--Fiction. | Love--Fiction. | Middle Ages--Fiction. | Christian life--Fiction.
Classification: LCC PZ7.D5575 Pe 2020 (print) | LCC PZ7.D5575 (ebook) | DDC [Fic]--dc23
LC record available at https://lccn.loc.gov/2020006414
LC ebook record available at https://lccn.loc.gov/2020006415

The
PEASANT'S
DREAM

CHAPTER 1

~

Adela stood watching her brother Steffan marry his true love, Katerina of Hamlin, memorizing how the autumn sun bathed everything in warm light and made the stained glass windows of Hamlin Cathedral spark and glow. She would begin to capture this moment with her paints and brushes as soon as she went to her room in her brother and sister-in-law's home.

The scene was perfect—a lovely wedding on the steps of the Cathedral. Katerina's violet gown brought out the rich color of her chestnut hair, and even Steffan looked handsome, in spite of the fact that he was her irritating older brother.

The two stood on the steps of the Cathedral and smiled at the townspeople of Hamlin, who loved them very much, judging by their teary-eyed gazes and cheers.

And no wonder they loved Katerina. She had saved her town from a nefarious mayor. Steffan, who had always been so contentious with Father and so teasing with her and her sisters, had needed to mature in order to be worthy of her.

But perhaps Adela shouldn't be so smug about Steffan's former bad behavior. After all, she was the youngest of her family, besides Toby, and she'd heard the servants' whispers once or twice about

1

her being spoiled. Perhaps they were right. She was a duke's daughter and therefore accustomed to getting whatever she needed—and usually what she wanted as well.

What she truly wanted was adventure and a chance to prove herself as a great artist. Each one of her siblings had done something striking, courageous, adventurous—and then they married and their lives had become uneventful. They'd set up homes, had children, and every day seemed much the same, from what they told her. Before settling into a mundane life such as that, Adela longed to prove herself, to have her own adventure, though one different from her siblings, who had found themselves in some very perilous situations. Adela didn't crave danger. Instead, she longed to travel around the region painting scenes, painting portraits, making a name for herself, and showing that a woman could be just as talented as any man.

If Steffan could find his own adventure—and true love— surely Adela could as well. Steffan had to leave Hagenheim to find those things. Adela needed to do the same.

As the daughter of a duke, Adela was expected to obey her parents, who would hardly let her out of Hagenheim Castle. Convincing them to allow her to leave Hagenheim to wander the region, painting landscapes and portraits, would be difficult, but they might allow it if she were accompanied by her father's guards.

She glanced around at the townspeople of Hamlin who had come to celebrate the wedding. They were not waited on by servants. They took care of themselves, as did the people of Hagenheim. Adela had always had servants to take care of her. Would she be able to manage without them? She could take a female servant with her, and the guards would find places for them to stay. She could also sleep in the outdoors. She'd done it before when traveling to visit her siblings.

If she wanted to prove that she was a capable painter, then she would have to take matters into her own hands. And now was the time to do it, because once she was married, she'd be trapped in the dullness of daily life.

After all, her nobleman husband, whoever he turned out to be, would never let her wander the countryside painting.

❧

Frederick used the rough side of the chisel to smooth an uneven spot on the wood door he'd been carving. He'd worked on it for months.

Now, as he stared hard at it, he imagined how he might paint it, what colors he'd use to highlight the shapes. But he realized he liked it as it was, natural, the grain of the wood giving the piece character and beauty.

He blew out the candle and opened his window. The sun was up.

He jumped to his feet and hurried into the kitchen to grab a bit of food before rushing out into the field to tend the cows.

Two hours later he was helping a mother cow clean her newborn calf, using an old piece of coarse linen to rub the rest of the afterbirth off its hindquarters as the mother vigorously licked her baby's face. After what he'd had to do to get the calf, which had been turned the wrong way, out of its distressed mother, he was surprised the cow wasn't lowing and kicking him. But she seemed to understand that he'd helped her and did not object to him touching her calf.

Frederick smiled as the calf stood up on its own, wobbled, then immediately tried to suckle. The cow gave up her attempts at cleaning her new calf and let him eat.

Looking down at the mess on his hands and arms, Frederick's

smile turned to a grimace. He used the cloth to wipe himself off the best he could and started back toward the house to change his shirt and wash up.

"Where are you going?"

Frederick's father stood propped against a tree, a straw clenched between his teeth, which were a yellow brown from all the wine and ale he drank.

Frederick stretched out his hands. "Breach calf. Going to get cleaned up."

"You're not courting a lady. Go finish raking the hay. You can clean up when the work is done."

Frederick's chest tightened. "When have I ever not finished the work?" He continued on his way to the house, passing by his father and refusing to look back at him.

Once inside the entryway of the kitchen, he quickly poured some lukewarm water into the basin, then dipped a cloth into the water and scrubbed his hands up to his elbows to rid himself of the slime. Good thing he had not been wearing sleeves, even though it was a cool late autumn day. Unless the air was cold, he wore his sleeveless tunic when he worked.

As he dried his arms, he heard voices in the house. He couldn't make out any words, as the two buildings were five feet apart, but the tone let him know that something was wrong.

He hurried through the empty kitchen, crossed the pathway to the back door in two giant steps, then burst into the house. He passed through the empty back room and into the entryway, where Mother stood embracing their neighbor, Christa, who was sobbing.

"What's wrong?" Was there something he could do to help? Her tears made his chest ache.

Christa looked up at him with wide eyes rimmed with red. "The baby is sick."

"How bad is it?"

Even his stalwart mother had tears in her eyes. It must be bad. Poor Christa. She and her husband had three previous babies, and all had died before they were a month old. This one, baby Jaspar, was six months old—he knew because they'd celebrated the half-year mark last week.

God, don't let this baby die too.

"He's struggling to breathe. He's turning blue. I don't know what to do." Tears slid down Christa's face and her lips trembled.

"I'll go get a healer."

"The nearest one is in Hagenheim." She said it as though the situation were hopeless.

"I can get there in half an hour by horse."

Christa's eyes brightened for the first time. "But I have no money to pay a healer."

"Let me take care of it." Frederick rushed down the narrow hallway to his bedroom. Thankfully, he had not built a fire this morning, so he reached barehanded into the back of the fireplace and pulled out the loose brick. He dug the leather pouch out of the hiding place he'd made, took out some coins, and shoved the pouch back in. He carefully replaced the brick, then ran out of the house and headed for the stable.

His father had not moved from where he'd last seen him, now whittling a stick with his knife. He looked up as Frederick entered the stable, grabbed his saddle, and readied his horse. Frederick mounted his steed inside and ducked low as he rode out through the stable door, urging his horse to a fast trot before he was even on the road.

Was that his father calling to him? He didn't look back.

As his horse increased his speed, Frederick gave him his head and leaned forward, the wind blowing his hair into his eyes—perhaps it was time for a haircut. He said a prayer that the sick baby would not die.

His horse was fast and loved to gallop. His hooves ate up the road to Hagenheim. Frederick slowed him down at the town gate so as not to look suspicious and to let the horse rest. The animal still had to carry him all the way back, and Frederick was not a small man, being both tall and muscular from all the work he'd been doing on the farm since he was a small child.

Did he look like the rough farmworker that he was? It didn't matter. He needed to get to the healer and help save Christa and Johannes's baby.

Thank goodness he'd cleaned up after the birth of the calf.

He rode at a fast trot through the cobblestone streets. Hagenheim Castle rose above the town on a hill surrounded by another wall, the gate guarded by Duke Wilhelm's men. Frederick had once thought if he ever became desperate for work—or desperate to get away from home—he could offer himself as a soldier. The duke needed guards who were large and could fight. Frederick fit that description well.

As he walked his horse up to the castle gate, a man stepped out of the guardhouse and held up a hand.

"Halt. What is your business?"

"I need the healer. That is, my neighbor's baby is sick, and I've come to fetch the healer."

The guard exchanged a look with the soldier next to him. Had he said something wrong?

"Frau Lena is the healer, and she will perhaps give you a remedy, but a person does not 'fetch' Frau Lena."

"Very well. May I pass?"

"Go to that tower there." The guard pointed to the castle tower closest to the gate, then stepped out of Frederick's way.

Frederick hurried forward, dismounted when he reached the door of the tower, and went in.

A young woman about his own age was talking to a woman of forty or fifty, who looked up at Frederick.

"May I help you?" The older woman's hair was a pale rust red streaked with white.

"My neighbor's baby is very sick. He can barely breathe."

Though he was more focused on the healer, he couldn't help but notice that the young woman with the healer was beautiful. Her skin was pale and delicate, and her features were perfect. And she was staring at him.

"How old is the child?" the healer asked.

"Six months."

"You say he can barely breathe. Is he laboring to breathe? Or is he too weak to breathe?"

"I don't know. He has been sick, and his mother said he was struggling and turning blue, and she was afraid he was dying. Won't you come with me? It is only half an hour's ride from—"

"I cannot leave, but I can give you something for the child." She turned and went toward the back of the round tower chamber.

"You don't understand. This woman has lost three babies already. She needs your help." He took a couple of steps farther into the room.

The young woman was still looking at him. When he met her eye, she didn't glance away. Her eyes were a pretty blue, her lashes thick and black, while her hair was long and blonde and hanging unfettered over one shoulder. But it was the expression on her face, the depth of her gaze, that made him want to talk to her.

He shouldn't be thinking about this young woman. He had to get help for baby Jaspar.

Frau Lena emerged from the back room. "Here are some herbs

for better breathing. Put them in a bowl of water that has just been boiling and let them steep for a few minutes. Put it as close to the child's face as you can—but see that you don't burn him. Once it is cool enough, dribble some in his mouth and have him drink it. Do you understand?"

"Yes." Frederick took the pouch of herbs from her.

"And rub this salve on the baby's chest." She handed him the smaller pouch in her other hand. "Boil lots of water and try to get the baby to breathe in the steam."

"Won't you come with me? I'm sure you could help—"

"It is not difficult. Just do as I said—should I repeat the instructions?"

"No, that is not necessary. I have it."

"Shall I go with him, Frau Lena?" the young woman asked.

"You, Adela?" The woman's eyes went wide and her mouth fell open.

"Perhaps I could help."

"No, no. Besides what I have told him, there is nothing more anyone can do. And your father . . ." She scrunched her brows down low over her eyes in a severe, almost scolding look.

Frederick could think of no reason to take the girl with him— though he wished he could—so he said, "Thank you, Frau Lena," then nodded to the girl. "Thank you." He dug in his pocket and presented two coins to the healer.

The healer stared at the money in his hand. She shook her head. "I do not accept payment. You can put the money in the poor box, if you wish."

He had never heard of someone who did not accept payment for a service or goods. Did she think him too poor? But perhaps Duke Wilhelm paid her for her healing work.

He nodded to her and took one last glance at the pretty young woman, then left, hurrying to get on his horse and get back to Christa and her baby.

❦

Adela watched the young man go. Though he was obviously a peasant, she was sure she'd never seen anyone so handsome. With his muscular frame and his strong jawline, chin, and cheekbones, he reminded her of a knight who'd been training his body for war. His brown hair was thick and hung down on his neck, and his eyes were a clear dark blue. He looked back at her in such an honest way, as if he had nothing to hide. As if he felt the same strange desire to speak to her as she did to him.

Adela's cheeks heated as she remembered how she'd offered to go with him and how horrified Frau Lena looked. But she longed to go tearing out of the town gate on her horse with this stranger to help him however she could with his neighbor's sick baby. That would be an adventure, something useful and not dangerous. But Father would not have approved at all, would have thought it very foolish. Yet, in her opinion, the only thing that made it foolish was the fact that she knew nothing about caring for a sick baby.

It was not just that she found this young man handsome, or that his passion to help save his neighbor's baby compelled her to want to help. She needed a purpose, some way of contributing to the world. She didn't want to always be the spoiled daughter of the Duke of Hagenheim who never did anything but stay locked up in the castle waiting for her father to marry her off.

Would she ever see the young man again? By the looks of his clothing and his muscular frame, he was accustomed to hard work. He must be a farmer or some other kind of laborer, but one who cared enough to come rushing all the way to Hagenheim to get help for a neighbor's sick child.

She didn't even know his name. But the memory of when their eyes met filled her with a wistful longing.

CHAPTER 2

Frederick rode hard and arrived at Christa and Johannes's small wattle-and-daub house. He dismounted and rushed through the door, almost in one single motion, without knocking.

Christa was holding the baby and crying, while Johannes was leaning against the wall, his face buried in his arm. They both looked up as he entered.

"Boiling water. We need boiling water." Frederick proceeded to tell them what the healer had instructed him to do.

They put the salve on baby Jaspar's chest, which smelled of mint leaves. He did not react. Soon they had a large pot of boiling water and were holding a bowl of the dried herbs and hot water near the baby so he could breathe in the vapors.

While Christa and Johannes were both hovering over the baby, Frederick took the large pot of boiling water and poured it into various containers and set them near the child. The air in the room became steamy and moist. He then fetched another bucket of water, poured it into the cauldron, and set it back over the fire to boil. "I think the herb water is cool enough for the baby to drink now. Do you have something I could use to strain out the dried herbs, a cloth or sieve?"

Christa told him where she kept her cheesecloth, then Frederick and Johannes strained out the herbs and put the water in a cup. Christa tried to coax the baby to drink it. Was it Frederick's imagination, or was the baby looking less pale? His lips were no longer blue gray but were now pale pink, and he was breathing a little easier.

She managed to get some of the water into the baby's mouth, but he soon screwed up his face and started to cry.

"Maybe it tastes bad," Frederick offered. "Could you put a little honey in it?"

"Yes, good idea." Christa instructed her husband to get the honey, and he put a little in the water and stirred it. Soon the baby was drinking the water.

"His breathing has improved, I think." Johannes looked hopefully at his wife.

"I think so too."

Certainly the baby was better than when Frederick had first arrived.

There didn't seem to be anything else Frederick could do. He made sure Christa and Johannes saw where he was leaving the herbs and salve, then said, "I should go. But I'll come back later and see how he's doing."

Christa and Johannes both thanked him, their eyes wide, as if they were fearful to trust that the treatment was working. He left quickly, afraid Christa was about to start crying again.

He headed to a thick copse of trees that grew between his neighbors' property and his father's, where he often went when he needed a bit of time to himself. He sank to his knees and started praying. But while he prayed for baby Jaspar, his mind kept going to the girl he had seen in Frau Lena's chamber. He pushed her face from his thoughts and concentrated on his prayers. After he concluded his prayers, he got up and went back to his work.

While he forked hay onto a cart and hauled it to the horses and then the cow pasture to feed the animals, his thoughts wandered again to the young woman. Frau Lena had said her name. What was it? He strained to remember. Was it Anna? Anya? No, that wasn't it. Adela? Yes, Adela. What a pretty name.

But it little mattered what her name was. He'd never see her again. By her dress she was a wealthy burgher's daughter. And he—he was little more than an unpaid servant, working on his father's farm. But he was a man with a dream, a hope of being able to make his living carving wooden doors, decorative timbers for houses, and furniture with intricate carvings. He was good at carving. It was his gift from God, and he wanted to use it as God intended.

And yet here he was, mucking out stables, forking up hay, hauling and chopping and milking.

It wasn't that he minded working on the farm. His father had a lame leg from when a horse threw him fifteen years ago, and his back and hip had not healed well. Frederick was glad to help out and would always help take care of his mother, but his father's ridicule, criticism, and contempt were heavy weights. His disapproval held Frederick back from taking samples of his work to the market in Hagenheim.

When Frederick finished spreading the hay on the wooden rack, he started back toward the house, as it was midday and his mother would have a meal prepared for him. But he noticed his father was standing against the same tree he'd been leaning against when Frederick went inside to wash up after delivering the calf. He prepared himself for what his father would say as he passed, and realized he was clenching his teeth.

"I heard you went over to help Johannes with his baby." Father narrowed his eyes at him.

"I did."

"Are you a nursemaid now, along with being a craftsman?"

Frederick's hands tensed into fists. He refused to reply and kept walking to the house.

"Honor thy father and mother. That's what the Holy Writ says. And yet you play nursemaid to the neighbor's brat when the winter wheat still hasn't been sown . . ."

Frederick entered the house and closed the door on his father's voice.

"How is Christa's baby?" Mother greeted him with a look of concern as she put some bread on the table.

"He was a little better when I left a few hours ago."

"That is good to hear. I'll go and take them some bread and frumenty and see if there's anything I can do. Your father was asking where you were. I told him you went to Christa and Johannes's house, but I didn't tell him you went to Hagenheim. I hope he didn't get angry with you about it."

"Father is always angry, but all is well. Don't worry."

Frederick sat down and ate his food, but his father's words and face loomed in his mind. He focused instead on the door he'd been carving. It had sixteen panels, each with a different scene. He'd been working on it for months at night when his chores were done. He'd done many smaller pieces, but this one would show what he truly wanted to do, to tell a story with pictures, the way a cathedral's stained glass windows told stories from the Bible. Large and bold, this door was a part of himself that he could never express in any other way.

His father would ridicule that kind of sentiment, as he had often ridiculed his carvings, mocking his son for believing he could make a living at it. "You're a peasant farmer. That's what I was born to be and that's what you were born to be, and you'll never be anything else." That's what his father had said to him on his twelfth birthday when he'd told his mother he was going to live in town and be a famous wood-carver someday.

Frederick's mother had glared at her husband, the first time Frederick had ever seen her give him such a look. Then she'd said quietly, "God determines what a man will be, and who's to say that God has not given him a talent for His purposes."

"God has determined he will be a farmer, or are you too daft to see that? Huh?" His father had knocked over a large cup of wine that he'd been drinking. Then he'd ordered, "Clean that up!" and managed to stomp with his one good foot, slamming down his walking stick, out of the house.

From that day on, Frederick understood that his wood carvings did not please his father, and he learned to hide them from him—or at least not to bring them to his father's attention.

Mother slipped out while Frederick was eating. When she came back she was smiling.

"Baby Jaspar is much better! And Christa and Johannes are so grateful to you. They say if you had not gone to the healer and brought back that help . . . They are sure you saved the baby's life." Mother's eyes filled with tears.

Frederick's heart seemed to expand in his chest. How good God was to allow him to help save the baby. He cleared his throat and said, "I am very glad to hear it."

She sniffed and took a deep breath, dispelling her tears. "I am very proud of you."

"Thank you, Mother." He stood up to go back out to work, and his mother wrapped her arms around him. He embraced her and patted her on the back. "I'm very glad God healed Jaspar. I have to go now, to plow the field for the winter wheat."

She stepped away from him and shooed him out the door, smiling.

❦

Adela rode alongside Lord Barthold, her newest suitor. Several eligible men had come to call on her, and she had rejected them each in their turn. But Barthold was the handsomest, with his dark brown hair and blue eyes. Would he be her future husband? So far she did not have any loving feelings toward him. Mother said love should come gradually, not on first sight, because until you truly knew the person, you couldn't truly love them. That made sense, although it did not seem very exciting.

Unfortunately, she could easily imagine what a boring, unadventurous life she'd have if she married Barthold.

Barthold smiled at her as he rode his black gelding beside her and her chestnut mare. He wasn't much of a talker, and he smiled as if someone had told him, "If you want a woman to like you, smile."

"Have you had your horse for a long time?" Adela asked. Men usually liked talking about their horses.

"I've had Edelstein for a couple of years. I don't like having to break in a new horse. A man depends on his horse to know instinctively what to do in any situation. Edelstein is adequate but not as clever as my last horse. I heard you have some very good horse trainers here in Hagenheim. Your father has approved of me extending my stay so that I can look for a new horse, and perhaps I can get your father's men to help me break him in."

Adela smiled back. Those were the most sentences she'd ever heard him utter together at one time. But was she supposed to express gratitude that he was extending his stay for a horse? Perhaps she was being too hard on him. After all, he was a good man, or Father would not have allowed him to pursue her. Although, her father had made a terrible mistake when he allowed Lord Claybrook to come courting her sister Margaretha. She was a young child when Margaretha's suitor Lord Claybrook had tried to take over Hagenheim Castle by force.

She looked askance at Barthold. He couldn't possibly be like Lord Claybrook, could he? Father had looked into his family and background and had known his father all his life, so it seemed very unlikely.

"Your father insists on you taking guards with you when you go riding outside the gates, does he not?" Barthold was looking at her.

"Yes, of course."

"More than one?"

"Sometimes only one, but usually two." Today one of Barthold's father's guards and two of her father's rode with them. They were ready for anything, it seemed. "But nothing bad ever happens in Hagenheim."

"Nothing? There was that kidnapping, if I remember . . ." He raised his dark brows at her.

Her stomach sank at the remembrance of what had happened to Kirstyn. How could she have forgotten, even for a moment?

"You are thinking of what happened a few years ago to my older sister. That was terrible, but Kirstyn is well now. But that is why my father always insists on guards going with me everywhere I go. I seldom go far. I'm not much of a horsewoman."

"You are doing very well." Barthold smiled. "My sisters don't like horses either."

She didn't like being compared to his sisters. She had met them, and they were haughty and unfriendly—two things Adela could not abide. But they'd been married off and gone to live far away, so if Adela married Barthold, she wouldn't have to see much of them.

"I didn't say I didn't like horses. I just don't ride very often. My sister-in-law Gisela is quite a good horsewoman. My nieces and nephews were better riders than I am when they were five years old."

"What do you enjoy, Lady Adela?"

"I spend a lot of time painting."

"I have seen many of your paintings in Hagenheim Castle. They are very good. Very colorful."

Adela smiled at the almost-compliment. "I like color. I also like to embroider belts and dresses and tapestries. I especially like embroidering flowers so that I can use bright colors. But you probably think painting and embroidering are silly. My brothers do."

"Your brothers know nothing of what's silly if they think that is. My sisters would rather stop breathing than do something useful. And even creating art is too much work for them."

She didn't want to say anything against his sisters, but she imagined what he said was very true.

Adela had always felt as if no one understood her desire to create things, to embroider beautiful flowers, or to paint scenes from real life on paper or canvas. Barthold was defending her, but she suspected he wouldn't understand her thoughts and feelings about her art either. Even her mother, who was kind and understanding, did not share her deep desire to create beautiful things. Although Mother was very good at making up stories to entertain Adela's nieces and nephews.

"Toby doesn't tease me about it as much as Steffan and Wolfgang used to. They would tease me and say I should be out climbing trees and practicing archery and swordplay with them, but I would just tell them, 'I don't want to be a daft boy like you.' But Toby is my shield if anyone wants to tease me now."

"Your brothers all seem like useful and intelligent men."

"Oh yes. I love all my brothers. Even Steffan has turned out to be admirable and good." She only hoped she could marry a man as honorable as her brothers.

Her horse moved a bit too close to Barthold's as they were

entering a thick copse of trees that narrowed the path in front of them. She managed to force the horse back to his side of the path, but not before her leg brushed against Barthold's. He wouldn't think she did that purposely, would he?

Neither of them spoke as a guard led them through the leafy overhanging branches and two guards followed behind. Kirstyn had been seized from a narrow street, but this would also be a good place for someone to attempt something nefarious.

Why would she think such a thing? She'd ridden down this path many times before. She normally thought it quite pretty. It must have been their talk of guards and Kirstyn's ordeal. When she glanced at Barthold, he was looking at her from the corner of his eye.

What did he think of her? And what did she think of him? She kept waiting for something, a "spark," as she'd heard her sister-in-law Sophie describe how she felt when she met Adela's brother Gabe. So far there was nothing like that. But she'd only known him for a few days.

Oddly, her thoughts flitted to the young man she'd seen a week ago in Frau Lena's chamber. She wished she knew how his neighbor's baby had fared. But there was no way to find out. He lived about half an hour's ride from Hagenheim Castle. Beyond that, she knew nothing of the man whose earnest face kept appearing in her thoughts, even when she looked at Lord Barthold.

❧

Frederick used the hem of his tunic to wipe the sweat from his forehead. He'd finally finished sowing the wheat seeds when he heard horses' hooves thundering down the road. Then he saw them—the Eselin brothers.

Ditmar, Everwin, and Gerhard guided their mules off the road and rode straight toward Frederick. He hurried to meet them to keep them from riding through his plowed field, even as he felt his hands clench. The Eselin brothers were almost always cooking up some kind of trouble. Sometimes they even managed to talk him into helping them. In the past, when he was more child than man, Frederick had sometimes been persuaded to join with them in their foolish schemes. He still struggled to say no to someone who told him they needed his help, but he'd learned to distance himself from the Eselins.

Everwin Eselin was grinning, as usual, and he and his brother did not dismount from their mules as Frederick greeted them. He waited for them to tell him what was on their minds, as they surely would, without his having to ask.

"I don't think you know who is visiting Hagenheim Castle," Ditmar began.

Frederick stared back, remembering the time the Eselin brothers had stolen his parents' milk cow and driven her into the neighbor's field. It had taken Frederick two days to find her, and when he confronted them about it, they just laughed uproariously.

Frederick didn't answer. How would he know who was visiting Hagenheim Castle? And why would he care?

"It's the Duke of Grundelsbach's son. The heir."

"I wish him a good visit. I would like to stand and talk with you, but I have work to do, animals to feed, fields to pl—"

"And did you know," Everwin said, as if Frederick hadn't spoken, "that he has sent word back to Grundelsbach for a large gift to be brought to Hagenheim, a treasure trove to bribe the Duke of Hagenheim to let him marry his daughter?"

"I did not know." Frederick frowned and spat on the ground, turning his body partially away from the men. But even as he tried to show disinterest, a tingle went down his spine as he guessed what they must be scheming.

"Do you not want a portion of that treasure, Frederick?" Gerhard interjected.

No, Frederick did not want something that did not belong to him. But he had to choose his response wisely. The Eselins knew things about Frederick's father that they would not hesitate to use to manipulate him into helping them.

Frederick held up his hands, palms out. "This is your idea. You and your brothers should keep the treasure for yourselves. You can depend upon me to stay out of your way." He couldn't imagine they would actually succeed in attempting to steal from someone as powerful as the Duke of Grundelsbach.

"We need your help, Frederick. Three men aren't enough, and you're the best horseman. We need you to keep us from getting caught. No one will get hurt. Those rich noblemen will never miss that money, but we can use it to feed our families."

Ditmar knew just what to say to play on Frederick's weakness.

"Yeah, Frederick," Everwin added, "don't you want to help your family with your share of the gold coins?"

"No. I don't want gold coins that I did not earn." He said the words, knowing it would not make any difference to them.

"Did we not help you and your mother when your father was drunk and chasing your mother with an ax?" Ditmar raised his brows. "And have we not kept it secret that your father, on occasion, steals a deer from the king's forest?"

Frederick's stomach clenched. Yes, his father had killed a deer a couple of times, and he could possibly be hanged for it. But it was a devious thing to use to manipulate him. Everyone killed a deer, secretly, on occasion. There was no one to enforce that law out here, so far from the king's foresters.

Everwin leaned closer to him. "We're your friends, Frederick. We help you. Now it's time for you to help us."

Frederick weighed his options. He could flatly refuse to have anything to do with their schemes, or he could pretend to go along with them, and then, if they actually came to the point of action, of thievery or violence, Frederick could make sure to be far away.

"Do you have a plan?"

The Eselin brothers grinned and guffawed, congratulating Frederick.

"We'll be rich!" Everwin said. "We'll be able to buy all the meat and wine we want!"

"You can buy your own house in town," Gerhard said to Frederick.

"Yeah, join the wood-carvers' guild and sell your carvings and do what you want," Ditmar said. They'd known since he was a boy that wood carving was his dream.

"No more slaving on a farm," Everwin said.

A cold fist tightened around his heart. It was exactly what he might wish for—a house in town—and he imagined his mother with him, far away from his cruel father. But could such a thing ever be? His father would never allow them to go, and he wasn't sure his mother would ever leave him.

Besides, Frederick could never be content to live off someone else's wealth, wealth he had stolen.

He was surprised, though, at how tempting the thought was. After all, the money was a gift from one wealthy man to another. Aristocrats who were so rich they would never feel the loss of it. And with his share, Frederick could save his mother from poverty and oppression, and he could improve the lives of his sisters as well.

"We have someone at Hagenheim Castle who will let us know

when the money is coming. We can lie in wait for it on the road between Grundelsbach and Hagenheim."

Lie in wait? No, Frederick was not about to be a party to this scheme. Besides, he knew nothing good could come of joining with the Eselin brothers. But he also didn't want the trouble the Eselins could cause if they accused his family of stealing the king's game. Perhaps he should pretend to go along with these troublemakers for a little while. In the end he would never help them rob anyone, no matter how rich, but they didn't need to know that. Yet.

More than likely, their plans would fall apart before anything happened.

"So you will tell me when you need my help?" He felt a niggling of guilt just saying those words. Was it because he was being deceptive? Or because even the pretense of wrongdoing agitated his conscience?

Everwin was grinning. "It may only be a few days from now."

Ditmar said, "You'll need a long knife and a sword. Do you have a sword?"

"I'm a farmer. I don't have a sword."

"None of us have swords either," Gerhard said. "But we'll all have knives and bows and arrows."

"Frederick was always good with a bow," Everwin said.

"Better than you." Ditmar laughed at his brother.

"Just bring some weapons when we fetch you," Gerhard said.

Frederick's heart sank. He wanted to tell them no, to say that he'd changed his mind and would not be a part of this harebrained scheme. But they would never be able to find out when the treasure was coming. The plan would fail and Frederick wouldn't have to do anything.

"We heard they only have three guards bringing it," Gerhard said.

"The four of us can take three guards, don't you think?" Ditmar added. "We can pick off at least one or two with our arrows."

Sweat formed under his arms and trickled down his back the more the brothers talked.

"I have to get back to planting." Frederick turned to walk away.

"We'll tell you more when it's time," Gerhard called after him.

Frederick just waved his hand in the air and kept walking. Daft Eselin brothers. Always scheming something but never clever enough to pull it off.

CHAPTER 3

Baby Jaspar was well and Frederick was restless. He wished there were some other urgent needs he could help with. He was a man now, twenty-one years old, little more than a peasant farmer scratching out an existence for his family on his father's land.

Mother watched him as he buttered his bread and took a bite. "Today is a market day in Hagenheim."

"Market day?" Frederick looked at his mother. Her face was brighter than usual, and a small smile graced her lips.

"Your father is sick in bed." She gazed at him over the rim of her cup. "He drank himself into a stupor last night and won't be up for hours."

"You may as well tell me what you're thinking." Although he had an inkling already.

"If you had no work to do and your father didn't know," she said softly, "wouldn't you take your carvings to market?" She arched her brows.

He always had work to do, and Mother knew that. But if Father was too sick to know . . .

Frederick jumped up from his stool so fast he knocked it over with a loud clatter. He went to his bedroom to fetch his smaller carvings.

Less than half an hour later he had his cart loaded and the horse hitched to it and was headed down the road toward Hagenheim at a fast walk.

❧

Adela stared out the window of her bedchamber and watched all the people milling about the *Marktplatz* of Hagenheim. She put down her paintbrush, no longer excited about the picture she was painting.

From her window, she was too far away to make out any faces—not that she would recognize anyone. The only people she knew were her family members and the servants who worked in Hagenheim Castle. Her sisters and brothers and the female servants were her only friends as a child, and now that her sisters had all left home, she was often lonely for someone to talk to. She could have talked to Barthold, but he was off riding with her father and brother Valten.

She'd always imagined falling in love with someone the way her sisters had—unexpectedly, with someone brave and good. Unfortunately, her sisters had fallen in love amid dramatic, even perilous, circumstances, and that part of their stories she did not wish to emulate. Adela wasn't fond of danger. Still, she did relish the idea of adventure and independence.

Her mind went back to the conversation from the night before when her mother had been brushing out her hair, then braiding it.

"I don't feel anything when I look at Barthold." Would he have to save her from some kind of danger for her to feel something for him?

"That doesn't mean he is not the right man to marry, Adela.

26

It just means you haven't gotten to know him in a way that reveals his character. You cannot look at a man and see his best attributes, and you shouldn't expect to fall in love with him right away either."

"Then how will I know whom I should marry?"

"You should choose a man with good character, someone you can trust to love you and always do what is best for his wife and children. And it isn't easy to know that about a person. You have to observe his behavior, learn what is important to him, and that is revealed over time, not in a day, or even a month."

Her thoughts went to the man who had come to Frau Lena seeking help for his neighbor's baby. Did he have good character? Surely he couldn't have had some nefarious reason for seeking help for the child. But then she remembered Lord Claybrook.

"Margaretha's suitor, Lord Claybrook—his character was very bad."

Mother finished braiding her hair. "Yes, exactly. And we did not know until weeks after he came here . . . although your father had suspicions about him right away."

"He did? Does he have suspicions about Barthold?"

"No, I don't think so, but he is still getting to know him. That is why he and Valten have taken him out riding. But don't worry, *Schätzchen.*" Mother squeezed her shoulder. "We will help you make certain you don't marry a man with bad character."

Now, as Adela stared out her window, she wondered if other young women's parents helped them choose a husband. Adela wanted to think she would simply fall in love and choose for herself, but there was some comfort in getting her parents' opinion on the man.

What if Adela did somehow manage to find someone to marry who was not chosen by her parents? To find someone herself— and have a grand adventure in the process—that seemed ideal. But Adela could hardly do that without leaving the castle.

The market looked so interesting, so colorful, as she stared at it out her window. She'd gone a few times with a servant and a guard, but what would it be like to go to the *Marktplatz* by herself? Her parents were always so careful to send a guard with her everywhere she went, but she would be much better able to observe scenes she might want to paint if she weren't drawing attention to herself with her father's guards. However, it wasn't safe for her, the daughter of a duke, to wander about by herself. But if no one knew who she was—if she dressed like a poor girl with no money . . .

Adela jumped from her seat by the window and went into her servant's small room where she slept and kept her clothing. Erma was about the same size as Adela, and surely she would not mind if Adela borrowed her clothes.

She found Erma's rough linen dress and quickly put it on. Then she slipped on a pair of Erma's sturdy street shoes. Adela checked her reflection in the looking glass. No one would imagine that she was the daughter of Duke Wilhelm. Her outer dress even had a small tear, showing a bit of her underdress. There was no adornment, no embroidery at all on the rough dress besides the lacing in the front. And if she put a kerchief over her head like the ones the servants wore . . .

Adela went back through Erma's things and found one of the white head scarves that all the female house servants wore. She put it on, tied it under her braid, and pulled it low over her forehead. Checking herself in the mirror, she was sure that even the guards would not recognize her.

She hurried to her door and looked out. No one was around. Adela ran down the hall and then down the stairs, her heart pounding as she watched and listened for people.

As she neared the bottom of the steps, she saw a guard walking past. He was looking the other way. Then a maidservant came through the hall. Adela pressed herself against the wall of the staircase. This girl might recognize her, even though she wore the kerchief. Thankfully, she walked by without seeing Adela.

She rushed the rest of the way down the steps, her foot slipping on the last step, making her stumble. She laughed at herself and hurried out the door of the castle.

As she was walking down the path toward the castle gate, the sun was shining on her head and shoulders, and a giddy feeling bubbled inside her. She was going into town and could speak to whomever she pleased, do anything she wanted. Not a soul would know who she was or that she was the daughter of the duke. Unfortunately, she had not thought to bring any money with her. But she didn't dare go back inside.

No matter. She would not be gone very long, and if she saw something in the market she wanted, she could send a servant later to get it for her.

She was getting close to passing the guards at the gate. Her father made sure all his guards knew all of the family, so she kept her head down as she passed them and even tried to slump her shoulders. She held her breath as she walked by, feeling their eyes on her. But as she went two feet, four, ten feet past them, they didn't call after her, so she raised her head and hurried to the *Marktplatz*.

Finally, she would have an adventure.

❧

Frederick reached the *Marktplatz*. His family came once or twice a year, but he'd never been here alone before.

As always, vendors were set up in rows up and down the town square. He finally found a place and quickly set up his makeshift stall, with a trestle table for a counter on which to lay his wares.

Next time he'd bring a tarp to stretch overhead, but for today, he was just content to be here.

He began laying out his carvings, smaller pieces that would show his craftsmanship. A woman came by and stared at his work.

"Did you make these?"

"Yes, I did."

She looked for a few minutes, then, without another word, moved away and bought some leeks and garlic from a vendor a few feet away.

He finished displaying his pieces and surveyed them. One with a relief of a unicorn that he had painted white. Another a sun and a flower, with vines entwined around them.

A man dressed very simply in a long black houppelande came by and paused. He drew near and carefully examined each piece. "Are you the carver?" He picked up a medallion with a lion's head and trees in the background.

"Yes."

"Whom did you study under?"

"No one."

"Self-taught, then? Very impressive." He nodded and smiled. "You have a gift."

"Thank you. Would you know any builders who might need my services, by chance? Maybe someone building a house?"

"I do not. I am sorry. But I do know someone who might be interested in your work."

"Oh? Who is this person?"

"He is the Bishop of Hagenheim."

Frederick's mouth fell open. He had a sensation, similar to the one when his eyes met those of the pretty girl, Adela, in the healer's chamber. He'd never imagined speaking with someone as important as the Bishop of Hagenheim. But he needed to say something. "And you are . . . a priest?"

"Yes." The young man's smile widened. "I am Thomas. I happen to know that the bishop is looking for someone to carve new doors for Hagenheim Cathedral."

Frederick sucked in a breath, swallowed, and said, "I could show the bishop my work. I have carved a panel—it could easily be made into a door—that I would be honored for the bishop to use. *Ach*, I did not bring it with me, but I could do another, another door for the bishop, with anything he liked."

Thomas was smiling. No doubt he thought Frederick a bumpkin as he stumbled all over himself in his eagerness.

"I will speak to the bishop. He may send for you, to bring your carvings for him to see. How long will you be here?"

"As long as I need to be."

"I will speak with the bishop this morning. You should hear from us before noon if the bishop wishes to speak with you and see your work."

"Thank you, Brother Thomas. God be with you."

"And with you. What is your name?"

"Frederick."

"Well, Herr Frederick, it is good to meet someone of your talent."

"Thank you, sir."

Frederick watched as the man walked away. Could this be the beginning of the fulfillment of his dream of getting away from the farm, of making a living by carving stories into wood, using his hands to do the work of his heart instead of sweating out in a field? Not that farming was a bad occupation. Some men enjoyed it. But it left his soul empty and longing, while carving pictures into wood fed his spirit.

Frederick stared up at the castle on the hill, then looked around him at the buildings surrounding the *Marktplatz*. He loved everything about it—the stalwart beauty of the crenellated castle towers, the varied structures encircling the cobblestone market, and especially the butcher's guild house. It was the most ornately carved of all the half-timber buildings of the square. Not only were there carvings of flowers, animal heads, Bible verses, the builder's name, and the date it was built, but the carvings were all painted bright colors, the letters and numbers highlighted in gold paint. He could stare at it all day. In fact, before he went home, he hoped to take a closer look.

Frederick sat down on the stool he'd brought. He'd arrived a little late to market, so already the crowd seemed to be thinning.

A young woman was smiling and examining some flowers across the row from him. Something seemed familiar about her. She wore a kerchief on her head, but her long golden-blonde braid hung down below it, reaching almost to the small of her back. She had a graceful way about her, and he found himself smiling at how she seemed intent on smelling every flower the vendor had. Then she turned to the side and he could see her profile.

His heart jumped, missing a beat.

It was *her*. The girl from the healer's chamber. His heart took off at a gallop.

She was dressed in much less wealthy clothing than before. Could it be that she was not so far above him, that she was also from a poor family?

Would she see him? What could he do to get her attention? What would he say?

She was still talking with the flower vendor. She laughed—such a lovely sound—then she turned around and looked straight at him.

Her face froze. Then her eyes widened and she smiled.

God was good. And for Frederick, this was obviously the day of His favor.

CHAPTER 4

~

Adela's heart was enraptured by the beautiful flowers. So much color. She questioned the vendor as to what each flower was called so that she could instruct her servants to buy the exact ones she wanted. Wouldn't her bedchamber look lovely with these flowers?

But as she finished talking with the woman and turned away, she realized she was being selfish. She should send flowers to Frau Lena and let them cheer whoever came today needing her help . . .

Her eyes caught sight of a handsome young man staring at her. *Dear heavenly saints.* It was *him.* The man who had come to Frau Lena's chamber to get help for his neighbor's baby.

Her heart jumped into her throat and stole her breath. She was afraid to blink lest he be gone. And he was starting to walk toward her.

She stepped toward him as well, like a moth moving toward a candle flame.

He was smiling, a gentle lifting of the corners of his mouth.

"*Guten Morgen,*" she said.

"*Guten Morgen.* Adela—is that your name?"

"Yes." Did he know she was the duke's daughter? Her heart stuttered. She didn't want him to know. She wanted him to judge her as he would any woman from town. "How did you know?"

33

"I heard the healer say your name."

"Oh."

"Do you live near here? In town?"

So he did not know she lived at the castle. The air rushed into her chest in relief. She could pretend to be just an ordinary young woman talking to an ordinary young man. This was like a dream she often had, of being seen for herself, not for being the duke's daughter.

"I do live in town. Where do you live?" She gazed up at him, captured by his blue eyes.

"Oh, I live on a farm far from town."

"Oh yes. I remember you said it was a half-hour ride on your horse."

"That's only if I ride fast." He smiled sheepishly.

"But you are here now."

"Do you come here a lot on market days?" His eyes seemed eager for her to say yes.

"I come . . . when I can."

His questions were making her nervous. But before she could think of something to say to change the subject, he asked, "Do you work somewhere in town? Is that why you aren't often in the market?"

"No, but my parents don't like me to come to the market alone." She wouldn't lie to him, but she could still conceal the full truth.

"Well, you are not alone now. You are with me." He frowned as if in apology. "That is, I will look after you, take care of you, if you wish."

Her heart tripped over itself at his words and the intense look in his eyes, focused completely on her. He had such a masculine jawline, and his shoulders seemed muscular, but not obnoxiously broad like some of Father's knights. His hair was light brown and wavy, almost curly. She couldn't remember ever seeing a handsomer man. His features were a bit more relaxed now than when he'd come searching for help for the baby.

"Oh, how could I forget to ask you! How is the baby, the child who was so sick? Did he recover?"

"Yes, thankfully." He gave her a smile. "He is well. Please thank your healer, because the child's mother and father believe her herbal remedies and instruction saved his life."

"That is so wonderful to hear." She peered around his back at the wood carvings on the trestle table behind him.

"What is it you are selling?" She moved around him and picked up a beautiful little wood carving of a sheep standing in a field of flowers and trees entwined with leafy vines. "These are lovely!" She drew in a breath as she ran her finger over the intricacies of the design carved into the wood, so perfect but realistic.

He was an artist! One who was sensitive enough to notice the petals of a flower, the shape of the leaves, and had the patience to carve them into wood.

He reached around her, brushing her sleeve with his arm.

"Here is my newest piece."

He picked up a round medallion, carved with filigree designs around the outer edge, and in the middle was a scene of an old man holding a knife high in the air, and an angel above and behind him, reaching for the knife. On a stone altar was a boy holding up his hands, pleading for his life.

"Is it Abraham and Isaac?"

He nodded.

"Your talent is wonderful. Is this what you do as your work, to support yourself?"

"No, though I hope someday it will be."

She turned to look up into his face. He was so close. She'd never been this close to a man who wasn't in her immediate family and wasn't a nobleman suitor. But this was no nobleman; he was a humble craftsman who worked with his hands, looking at her openly, with no formality or distance.

A shiver ran across her shoulders, and she wished she could move even closer.

But the next moment she was struck by the sadness in his expression.

"I would think anyone who could carve wood with so much artistry would be wealthy."

"I only carve wood when I have spare time—mostly at night. I work on my family's farm, growing wheat and oats and barley, milking cows, tending the animals."

"Oh. But . . . would it not be more profitable to work in town carving for the builders?"

He shrugged. "I don't know if I could leave my mother"—he cleared his throat—"and father. There's no one else to work the land. My father has a lame leg and cannot work."

What a travesty for a man of his talent to be forced to work as a laborer. Her heart ached as she stared into his face, with those blue eyes that softened the hard look of his square jaw and masculine chin.

"But that is why I'm here. Perhaps I could make enough money from carving to hire a man to take my place on the farm."

"Oh yes! That is an excellent plan."

His expression softened at her words. He gazed into her eyes.

"Would you like to walk around a bit? I cannot go far. I am waiting for someone who might be interested in hiring me for a wood-carving job."

"Is it a builder?"

"It's the Bishop of Hagenheim. He needs someone to carve a new door for the Cathedral."

"That is perfect! You could do it so well. I'm sure there is no one better. I don't want you to miss meeting with him, so let's not go out of sight of your place."

"Thank you. You are a very kind maiden."

And he looked truly thankful, heartfelt emotion shining from his eyes. Her heart seemed to stop beating, then thumped harder than ever.

She had no idea what the future held; she only knew that she had never felt so many different sensations as when this man spoke to and looked at her.

❧

Frederick's heart seemed determined to beat right out of his chest. Could Adela hear it? The way she looked at him made his heart beat harder than when he'd delivered his favorite horse's foal.

"I saw you looking at the flowers. Which ones are your favorites?" he asked as he walked her across to the flower vendor.

"Oh, I love them all, but I think my favorites are the poppies."

"But those grow wild in the fields." He could easily pick her a hundred.

"They do? I don't leave town very often, I'm afraid."

"Are you not allowed to? I assume your father is protective of you."

"Oh yes, he is. Very protective." She pointed to another flower. "I also love these peonies. They're so large and bright, almost like a face, don't you think?"

She held up the big pink flower, thick with petals.

"It does look like a face." He turned toward her with a thoughtful expression. "Are you an artist?"

"Well . . . yes. What made you ask?"

"I can't imagine anyone else I know saying that a flower looks like a face. And no one else I know is an artist."

She understood what he meant. When she painted ordinary things like flowers and trees, she found herself noticing the way they looked, from both far away and near. A dandelion suddenly looked like a puff of smoke with a burned charcoal center. A forest looked like a group of soldiers in the dark, marching straight and tall. A cluster of wildflowers on a distant hill became a mass of color and texture that she contemplated how to duplicate with a brush and paint.

None of the rest of her family seemed to think that way.

Adela had always felt as if no one understood her. Did he feel that way too?

"What kind of art do you do?" He leaned closer to her.

"I paint—landscape scenes and people working. I was hoping to get some ideas today. I'm also trying to get better at painting portraits."

"I would love to see your paintings sometime."

"Oh, and I also like to embroider scenes on tapestries, or flowers on clothing, which I suppose is art. In a way."

"Of course that is art." He looked thoughtful again, gazing into her eyes. "You are the first artist I've ever met."

"You are the first artist—and the first wood-carver—I've ever met." Then she remembered her sister Elsebeth who liked to paint, but she rarely saw her sister, and she didn't think she painted much anymore.

"I would very much like to see your work."

Unfortunately, she wasn't wearing her own clothing. Most of the time she wore something that had her embroidery on it.

"I like to embroider belts and cushion covers and tapestries, and make my own designs."

"You could use that skill to make some extra money, perhaps."

"Oh, well . . . Yes, that is true. I would very much like to paint scenes for other people, portraits of families, even."

"Yes. The wealthy would probably pay very well for a good portrait. You should inquire whether the duke would allow you to paint him and his family members."

Her heart stuttered. If she told him she was the duke's daughter, he would think her very odd for coming out to the marketplace in a servant's clothing. He also might not want to talk to her anymore, and he would certainly look at her differently.

"I don't know if I am skilled enough to paint the duke's family. I need more practice."

"You should not doubt yourself. Who in Hagenheim could paint their portraits better than you? I would dare to say that you are the only artist in town. Leastways . . . I would like to see your paintings for myself."

If only she could take him to the castle now and show him all of her paintings. But she couldn't, not if she wanted to keep her secret.

❧

Frederick and Adela moved to the next vendor and admired the leather goods being sold there. Adela kept glancing over her shoulder at his trestle table.

"I don't want you to miss your meeting with the bishop," she said.

They stayed near his table and continued to talk and look at the things being sold in the market.

"Did your mother send you to purchase anything?" he asked her. "Some vegetables or herbs?"

"No, no. And I should probably get back soon. Oh, there is the person who was coming to speak with you, I believe."

A man was indeed approaching his table, and it looked like Thomas the priest.

Frederick and Adela hurried back and arrived just behind Thomas.

"Oh, there you are," Thomas said. "The bishop wishes to see some of your work, so I have been instructed to buy one of your carvings." He studied the round medallion closely, with the scene of Abraham getting ready to sacrifice his son Isaac. "How many marks will you allow me to pay for this one?"

"Since it is for the bishop, please take it as my gift to him." Frederick picked it up and handed it to him.

"Oh no. We will pay what is fair for it. Here are five silver marks. Is that enough?"

It was enough money to take care of his family for at least half a year.

"I cannot possibly take so much."

"Of course you can. It is worth it." The young priest smiled and pressed the coins into Frederick's hand. "And how can we find you if the bishop wishes to hire you?"

"I can come again to the market."

"One week from today?"

"Yes, if you like."

"Very good. I shall tell the bishop. Good day to you." Thomas held the medallion to his chest and moved away, walking purposefully down the row of vendors.

Frederick stared down at the coins, then placed them in the pouch at his belt. Certainly today was a highly favored and blessed day.

❧

Adela listened closely to the exchange between the young priest and the handsome young wood-carver while keeping her head down and standing a few feet away. She was afraid Thomas would recognize her.

As soon as Thomas left, she stepped forward.

"Are you pleased to have sold your beautiful carving?"

"Yes." But when he met her gaze, he did not look very happy. "I've never sold anything before. I hope the bishop will like it."

"Oh, I am sure he will. It was perfect. The bishop will want you to carve the doors."

"Thank you. It is very kind of you to be so certain."

"It isn't kindness. It is the truth. You will see." She playfully touched his arm and smiled. He smiled back. Was this what it felt like to flirt? Was she being irresponsible? After all, this man was a farmer, a wood-carver, not an eligible suitor.

The Cathedral bells started to strike the noon hour. Anxiety suddenly made her throat tight. How long had she been gone? Was her mother worried? Had her father sent out guards to look for her?

"I must get back home." Adela touched his arm again. "I think I may . . . That is, I will probably be at the market next week."

"Please promise you will come and see me. I will be disappointed if you don't."

Her chest filled with air. And he wasn't even saying that because she was the daughter of a duke, because he didn't know she was. How glad she was that he didn't know.

"Fare well," she said and ran away across the *Marktplatz*.

This was surely the best day of her life! No one suspected she was the daughter of a duke, and though nothing dangerous had happened, it felt like an adventure.

Just as she hurried through the castle gate, she realized she had not asked him his name. Her heart sank a little. All would be well. She'd simply come back in a week and find the wood-carver with the beautiful blue eyes and a manner and temperament that was as gentle and engaging as any duke's son.

What would he say when he eventually discovered she was the daughter of the Duke of Hagenheim? But they were only friends. She could be friends with him, could she not?

❦

Frederick's heart was so full he thought only of Adela and the Bishop of Hagenheim and the Cathedral doors as he made his way home with his horse and cart and all but one of his carvings. He said several half-finished prayers and did not even remember to plan his response to his father in case he was angry at Frederick for leaving and traveling to Hagenheim instead of doing the farmwork.

He unhitched the horse, rubbed him down, and was putting the cart in the barn when he heard someone behind him.

"Where have you been?"

Frederick's sister Eulaly was standing with her arms crossed over her chest, tapping her foot. Frederick didn't want to lie, but he also couldn't tell her the truth. His sisters always told Father everything.

"Well?"

"Why do you want to know?"

"Because if you don't tell me, I'll tell Father that you were gone all morning." Eulaly set her jaw in that stubborn way of hers. Were all sisters so irritating, or only his?

"You must truly hate me."

Emotions played over Eulaly's face, as if she were at war with herself.

"He probably knows anyway, so go ahead and tell him." Frederick hefted the saddle from where he'd left it on the fence rail and carried it into the stable.

"He doesn't know. He's still sleeping." Eulaly followed him into the stable. "And I won't tell him—if you promise to take me with you the next time you go."

He stared hard at his sister's face. "Why would you say that when you don't know where I was?" Had his mother told her where he'd been?

"Because wherever you went, it must be more pleasant than here, and I need to see people." She stuck out her bottom lip. "If I have to stay here another day, I'll go completely moonstruck."

"No one wants that." Frederick retrieved the brush and went out to take care of the horse.

"Well, that's my offer, Frederick. Either take me with you, somewhere, anywhere, or I'll tell Father that you shirked your work all morning."

The last thing he wanted to do was take his prattling, mean-spirited sisters—for she would certainly bring her twin sister, Ursula, with her—when he was going on such an important mission next week. Besides that, he couldn't trust either one of them to keep her mouth shut and not tell Father. But what choice did he have?

"Very well. I'll take you with me next time, but you must not breathe a word about it to Father. If you do, I won't take you."

"Of course." Her smug smile almost made him change his mind.

"And you have to be ready to go at a moment's notice."

She nodded. "Can Ursula come along?"

"Mother will stay home. Why can't Ursula?"

"Well, I cannot vouch for how angry she will be if we sneak off without her."

"What is this?" Ursula appeared behind her sister as Frederick looked up from his brushing. "Are you two trying to *sneak away* somewhere without me?" Her eyes were mere slits as she fisted her hands on her hips. "You would leave me in this place of torment—"

"No one's leaving you behind, dear *Schwester*-wester." Eulaly made a pouty, placating moue, then smiled. "Frederick is taking us somewhere fun so we can have an adventure, see people and places, away from here."

"He is?" Ursula's face lit up. "Oh, where are we going, Frederick?"

Frederick let out a growl from deep in his throat, then sighed. "I will not tell you until the morning we are to go."

"Will we like it?"

"Yes, you will certainly like it." The market was his sisters' favorite place, full of things for them to beg for, full of people and interesting sights. "And I will sneak away without either of you, while you're still sleeping, if you ask me any questions or tell anyone about it. Now let me get my work done."

The girls went away giggling, clasping each other's hands.

He still struggled sometimes with forgiving them for all the times they had garnered him a beating from Father by exaggerating something he had done. For the hundredth time, at least, he crossed himself and said a quick prayer of forgiveness.

Perhaps it wouldn't be so bad. They would no doubt go off on their own as soon as they arrived at the *Marktplatz* and leave him alone to talk with the bishop and Adela. If he were fortunate, he might not even have to introduce Adela to his sisters.

CHAPTER 5

A dela slipped back into the castle and ran up the stone steps to her room. She took off her servant's dress and kerchief and put them back where she'd gotten them. Had no one even realized she was gone?

A knock sounded at her door.

Adela glanced down to make sure she was fully dressed. Thankfully, she had put on an overdress that laced up the sides instead of one that laced up the back.

"Come in."

A servant opened the door. "Pardon me, Lady Adela, but your mother wishes to know if you want to take a walk around the gardens with her before the midday meal. She's waiting downstairs."

"Oh yes!"

She did it! She'd gone to the market as a Hagenheim townsperson and no one was the wiser.

She hurried down, grateful her mother had not been worried about her.

Mother was sitting on a bench amid a cluster of red rosebushes. She smelled a bloom, holding it close to her face.

"Good morning, Mother." Adela sat on the bench beside her.

"I believe it is after noon. What did you do with your morning?"

"Oh, I . . . tried on some clothes . . . went for a walk." Her mind went to the young wood-carver. How she wanted to tell Mother about him. "I enjoyed myself."

"That is good to hear. I wanted to tell you that Lord Barthold has asked your father for your hand in marriage."

"Oh." Adela pressed a hand to her chest. A thrill went through her heart. Was it a thrill because she was flattered he wanted to marry her? Or a thrill of anxiety because she wasn't sure she wanted to marry him at all?

"Oh, Mother, I don't know . . ."

"It is too soon to decide." Mother reached out and patted her hand.

"Thank you, because I do not know if I will ever want to marry Barthold." Again, she wanted so much to tell her mother about the wood-carver she'd met that morning in the *Marktplatz*. She'd only talked with him for a short time, but already she felt as if she knew him better than she knew Barthold. But perhaps she was being foolish. After all, she could never marry a wood-carver. She was expected to marry someone wealthy and powerful, just as her sisters had. And she was not accustomed to being poor. And yet . . . she already liked the wood-carver so much more than Barthold.

"Perfectly all right." Mother smiled. "And Father told him we were not ready to give him an answer. He was very reasonable and said he understood, but that he wanted us to know the offer was good for as long as we were willing to consider it, which I thought showed a lack of temper and admirable maturity."

"Yes, of course. He is . . . pleasant enough."

Mother was staring hard at her, probably wondering if Adela would ever fall in love with Barthold.

Adela had never been in love. She loved her father very much—

was there another man on the earth who was as good as he?—and she knew she was a very fortunate girl indeed, even a little spoiled, as she honestly liked getting her way. At least she was well aware of how blessed she was, and she was very grateful. Even her brothers and sisters were good and kind and would never allow anyone to hurt her.

"What are you thinking about?" Mother leaned closer, gazing into her face.

"I was just thinking how good my family is, but I don't think Barthold's family treats him as well as mine does."

"Why do you say that? Has he been mistreated?"

"No, but he rarely speaks of his mother, and he once told me that he didn't see her very often when he was a child. He was mostly raised by nursemaids and servants. He didn't seem sad about it, but I thought it would be very sad if I had not seen very much of you when I was young."

"Was his mother sick?"

"No, I don't believe so. He never indicated she was. It seems as though she had always been very healthy until just before she died a few months ago. But he has said very little about his mother or anything else very personal or intimate. I simply don't know Barthold very well, and I am not ready to agree to marry him."

"That is very wise. I am proud of you for not being impulsive."

Impulsive was another thing Adela had been accused of once or twice, and she'd been told she was headstrong as well. But being impulsive and headstrong was not always bad, was it? After all, if she had not been impulsive and headstrong, she might not have met the handsome young wood-carver whose face was etched in her memory.

"Mother, is it very important that I marry a man who is wealthy? Someone who belongs to the aristocracy like we do?"

Mother opened her mouth, then paused. "Why do you ask?"

Her heart skipped a beat. She had to be careful not to reveal her secret. Mother might be upset with her for sneaking away to the *Marktplatz*.

"I always imagined I would marry someone like Father, a duke's son or maybe an earl, but . . . what if I fell in love with a man who was not wealthy, a man with no title? Would it be very difficult for me to live as an ordinary person, without money or position?"

"First of all, I don't know how you would meet such a man." Mother smiled as if she might laugh. Her expression turned sober, and she said, "I don't know. It would depend on several different things, I suppose."

Thankfully, Mother didn't question her, probably thinking there was no possibility that she had met someone like her wood-carver. She was already calling him "hers." Were her feelings getting the best of her?

"But it is difficult to be married to a poor man, I would imagine, when one is accustomed to being wealthy."

"I am spoiled, I suppose."

"Spoiled?"

"I am used to having everything I need and almost everything I want."

"You aren't spoiled. You are loved and blessed. And love is much more important than wealth. If you have to live without wealth, you might have some difficulties, but living without love . . . that would be tragic indeed."

"You don't think I am too spoiled to be content to live a simple life, without wealth?"

"I think you have a very loving heart." Mother reached out and pressed her hand against Adela's cheek. "Do not worry. I don't think you will have to live without either wealth or love, not as long as you have family. But I do want you to be in love with whomever you marry. So do not agree to marry Barthold unless you are sure."

"I won't." She was sure of one thing—she wouldn't be able to marry Barthold until she could get a certain handsome wood-carver out of her thoughts.

❧

A week had passed and Frederick arose before the sun.

He dressed more carefully than he normally did, wearing his best clothes and combing his hair. He'd bathed the night before, and his hair was a bit wavier than usual.

He hurried out to the stable, tempted to sneak away without his sisters. His father wouldn't be awake this early, as dawn was barely even a pale grayness in the sky. And he'd never known his sisters to awaken anytime close to dawn. But if he didn't take his sisters with him, they'd cause him as much trouble with Father as they could. Besides, he'd promised them they could go with him. And his father would be angry no matter what.

Even though his sisters were sometimes cruel and calculating, he did feel a bit sorry for them because they so rarely ever went to town. Eulaly used to beg Father to take her and Ursula, but the last few times they went, he humiliated them so badly with his behavior, falling down drunk before they could get him out of the alehouse, that they no longer asked to go.

He readied the horse and was hitching up the cart when he heard someone behind him.

"Trying to get away from us?" Eulaly smirked while Ursula yawned, rubbing a hand down her cheek.

There was no use in arguing with her, so he merely glanced at her and went on with his work. Thankfully, he had thought to put his carvings in the back of his cart the night before to save time. Now he wouldn't have to risk revealing his hiding place to his sisters.

"How are we supposed to sit on all that junk?" Eulaly groused.

"You can fetch a horse blanket out of the sta—"

"Ack! A horse blanket?" Ursula scrunched her face in a look of disgust.

"We can't sit on a horse blanket," Eulaly said in a tone that suggested he was stupid. "We'll get to town smelling like a horse."

Frederick offered no other solution as he tightened his horse's girth.

"You wait here for us, Frederick, do you understand?" Eulaly pointed a finger at him.

Finally finished and ready to set out, Frederick glared at her. She turned and ran back toward the house, while Ursula stood with her eyes closed and her chin resting against her shoulder, as if she were sleeping standing up.

It wasn't long before Eulaly came running back with the blanket from her bed and threw it with a triumphant smile onto the cart. The two girls clambered on and they set out.

They'd been traveling for an hour when Eulaly said, "Frederick, we couldn't help noticing that you're wearing your best shirt. Are you going to town to meet a girl?" She laughed.

"How would I know a girl in Hagenheim?" It wasn't a lie, just a deflection. Besides, it was none of their business. "Are you and Ursula going to meet men in Hagenheim?"

"We wish we were." They both broke out in hysterical giggles.

Frederick shook his head but couldn't help smiling as he lightly slapped the reins on the horse's back to keep him moving. His sisters were not very kind, but they were his family. He did hope they would marry good men—but men firm enough not to let the women bully them. Although . . . it was difficult to imagine them living apart from each other, with their own husbands in their own houses. Perhaps they could find twin brothers who wouldn't mind living together.

This thought almost made him laugh.

As he drew closer to Hagenheim, his heart thumped harder. Would Adela be there? He probably wouldn't be able to set up in the same location in the marketplace. Perhaps she wouldn't be able to find him.

They passed through the town gate. The towers of Hagenheim Castle were visible on the hill above town. The spires from the town's three churches, with Hagenheim Cathedral's spire the one closest to the castle, Saint Andrea's Church to the east, and Saint Michael's Church to the west, rose above the homes and various half-timber and brick buildings. He had visited the Cathedral on occasion, but he'd never visited the other two churches. Perhaps today he would be able to see them. Churches were some of the most beautiful buildings in all of Hagenheim. He imagined that was true of other towns in the German regions, though he'd never been to any other large town.

"Oh, look at that shop!" Eulaly cried. "Frederick, let us off here."

"I need you to come to the *Marktplatz* one hour after noon, no later, and find me. Listen for the church bells to chime the hour."

"We will!" Ursula scrambled out of the cart behind her sister, and they disappeared through the door of a fabric shop.

They would, but only if it suited them. He sighed. No matter. Father might be a little less wrathful since he had taken his sisters with him this time. He was much more lenient with them than with Frederick and would occasionally humor them.

He made his way to the *Marktplatz* and found a place very near where he had been the week before and set up his booth, displaying his carvings.

"Frederick?"

He turned and found Thomas.

"I know I'm early, but I thought you might already be here. Will you accompany me to see Bishop Werner?"

"Yes, of course."

"Perhaps the other vendors will be willing to look after your things."

Frederick turned and asked the vendor beside him, who agreed to keep an eye on his booth.

Frederick found himself walking beside the priest, who set a brisk pace. His heart thumped again, this time concerned that he might miss seeing Adela. Would she come while he was gone? If so, would she wait for him?

They were soon in sight of the magnificent Hagenheim Cathedral, with its massive nave and colorful stained glass. The honor of carving a new set of doors for this holy place would be overwhelming. King Charlemagne himself, hundreds of years ago, had witnessed a miracle here, as he and his men had been on their way home from a battle. They stopped and slept at this very place, and the king awoke to find a wild boar charging toward them. An angel appeared and slew the beast, and Charlemagne and the pope declared this holy ground and ordered that a cathedral be built on the spot.

The wooden doors on it now were impressive in their enormous height and breadth, but they were old and cracking and plain, with no carving or decoration besides the massive metal hinge plates reaching across them.

The thought of carving such a large area, of all the scenes he could create, sent his spirit soaring, air rushing into his lungs. His hands twitched as his fingers wrapped around an imaginary chisel.

Thomas opened the door and went in before him. They made their way behind the chancel to a narrow passageway, so dark he couldn't see his own feet, until they came to a wider corridor. Thomas knocked on a door.

A voice, muffled through the thick wood, came from the other side. Thomas opened it and led Frederick inside.

The bishop did not smile, but there was a benevolent look on his face as he stared hard at Frederick.

"Your Excellency, this is Frederick, the wood-carver."

Frederick had never imagined meeting a bishop before a week ago. He was so aware of his lowliness that he wondered if he should even raise his eyes to the bishop's. Too late. He'd already done that. He quickly lowered his head and bent his body in what he hoped was a decent bow.

"My son, are you the man who carved the medallion there?"

Frederick had to raise his head to see where the bishop was looking. Frederick's carving of Abraham and Isaac was on the altar, hung on the wall of the opulent room.

"Yes, Your Excellency. I am only a lowly farmer. I carve at night when my work is done." He also carved on Sundays, but he wasn't sure if that was considered a sin, so he decided not to mention it.

"Son, you have a gift, a gift only God could give. Do not call lowly what God has consecrated for His own purposes."

Did he mean that Frederick himself was consecrated? "Yes, Your Excellency." He bowed his head again.

"Sit down." He indicated a small wooden chair. "Tell me about yourself, Frederick."

Frederick sat. Unsure what to do with his hands, he clasped, then unclasped them, and rubbed his palms on his leather leggings. Sweat tickled the back of his neck and between his shoulder blades.

"I am the only son of a farmer who owns farmland between Hagenheim and Ottelfelt. I work the land, as my father is lame in one leg and cannot do hard labor. I did learn to read and write under my priest, who taught the children in the closest village. I have two younger sisters." Why was he telling him all this? The bishop surely wasn't interested, but what else could he say? "There isn't much to tell." He gave a slight shake of his head.

The bishop continued to stare at him. Frederick stared back, noting the bishop's large forehead, square face, and jutting jawline. But staring might seem disrespectful, so he looked down at the floor.

"I believe it is God who sent you to us now, Frederick, to carve the new doors for the Cathedral. Are you willing to serve God with your talent?"

"Yes, Your Excellency. I am willing. It would be my honor and pleasure, sir." He tried to force away the smile that was making his lips twitch.

"To serve God?"

"Yes, sir. To serve God."

The bishop stared silently at him again. Finally, he said, "You are confident in your abilities but humble enough to understand the honor of this undertaking."

Frederick held his breath. Was this truly happening? Would he be allowed to carve, to get away from the farm and from his oppressive father? It was almost too good to be true.

"Will you be able to begin the work soon? Next week?"

"I can begin tomorrow if you wish it. Today if you want."

"You will need to hire someone to take your place on the farm, I assume. And you will need money."

"Yes, sir, that is true. I cannot leave my mother and father and sisters without someone to work the farm, with no way to provide for themselves."

Besides the five silver marks the bishop had already paid him for the medallion, Frederick also had a small amount of money he had been hoarding. But how long would that money last?

"I will of course pay you for your work, and you may have a portion now."

"You are very generous, sir. I thank you."

Bishop Werner waved his hand at Thomas, whom Frederick had forgotten was even there. Thomas went to a chest in the far corner of the room, unlocked it, and took out a small pouch that clinked as if it was filled with coins. He brought it to Frederick.

The pouch was heavy and felt like freedom in the palm of his work-calloused hand. His heart swelled. *Thank You, God. You are so good.*

"I thank you for this opportunity. I will do my very best for you. For God."

"I would like to meet with you and hear your ideas, perhaps draw out a plan for the doors. Is that agreeable to you?"

"Yes, of course. I've never drawn my carvings first, but I can certainly make a plan and . . ."

"A plan, to hear your ideas, that is all I am wanting."

"Of course. I shall be glad to do that."

"Next week, same day and time. Just come into the church. You can find your way to my office, can you not?"

"Yes, thank you, sir. Thank you." Frederick stood and backed his way to the door, bowing.

Once he was outside, Thomas stood beside him, smiling. He put a hand on Frederick's shoulder. "The bishop likes you."

"I am very grateful."

Thomas smiled, looking as though he might laugh. "Go in the grace of God, my brother."

"Thank you. Until next week?"

"Until next week."

CHAPTER 6

Adela rose early in the morning on the day she was supposed to meet her wood-carver in the market. She confessed to her maidservant, Erma, that she'd taken her clothing the week before and asked permission to wear her dress again. Erma's eyes went wide and her mouth fell open.

"Lady Adela! It is not safe for you to leave the castle alone."

"Do you leave the castle alone?"

"Of course, but—"

"Then it is just as safe for me to leave when I'm mistaken for a maiden like you." She laughed, so happy with her own reasoning.

"I suppose, but if you are caught, I shall say I knew nothing of it."

"And I shall say you knew nothing of it, because I shall not tell you when I will take your clothes. So you will be blameless."

"I do not understand why you wish to go out. You are a duke's daughter. You have everything you need inside the castle. It is a comfortable, good life, is it not?"

Erma thought her foolish, probably. She did not comprehend this desire to see more, do more. Adela needed to see the world to paint it, did she not? But no one seemed to grasp her longing to paint, to recreate life and people and things using paint and canvas. The wood-carver was an artist. He recreated life in wood. He would understand her.

"But truly." Erma grabbed Adela's hand. "You must be careful. Do not go anywhere except the market. Stay in plain view of people. No side alleys. Promise me."

"Of course, I will."

"I would never forgive myself if something happened to you."

"Nothing is going to happen to me." She shook her head and gave Erma a hug. The wood-carver was a good man. She was sure of it, and he'd never let anyone harm her.

"You are not going to meet a man, are you?" Fear shone out of Erma's eyes.

Adela's breath hitched. She forced a smile. "What a thought! Indeed, Erma. Where would I have met a man?" She shrugged and shook her head at the same time.

"You must remember that you are the duke's daughter." Erma's voice was hushed.

"But that is exactly what I do not want to remember."

Erma's look of horror caused Adela to laugh. "Do not worry so much. All shall be well, and no one will recognize me."

Erma shook her head and left to attend her duties, and Adela hurried to don Erma's clothing again.

Erma seemed to think Adela very strange and even ungrateful to leave the castle alone, against her parents' wishes. No doubt she believed Adela should be content with staying inside, amusing herself with her family's companionship.

Adela's stomach sank. Surely God wouldn't condemn her for wanting to keep her word to the wood-carver, who seemed so kind and noble. But she didn't only want to go so that she could keep her word. She wanted to explore, to see, to do—and to talk to the wood-carver.

Erma had seemed so frightened for her to go outside the castle, but Erma went out alone all the time. She would not allow her maidservant's concerns to frighten her. She would simply stay in the open market among the townspeople of Hagenheim. She was perfectly safe.

It was such an innocent meeting. She only wanted to know if the bishop would offer the wood-carver the job of carving the new Cathedral doors, and she . . . What else did she hope to gain from seeing him again? To know more about him, to discover what kind of person he was, to hear about his life's story. But then what?

She wouldn't think that far ahead. Besides, was it not a good thing to learn about the townspeople of Hagenheim and how they lived? She might discover something valuable and find new scenes to paint.

Adela smoothed down her hair and hurried out of her room wearing Erma's clothes and kerchief. Again, she kept her head down as she made her way through the corridor and down the stairs and out of the castle. Still nervous as she passed through the gate, she realized it was easier this time. Was that always how it was when one did something wrong? Easier each time they did it?

She shook off any off-putting thoughts and kept up a brisk pace all the way to the *Marktplatz*. Her wood-carver might even be there waiting for her.

How fun it was to be so close to—to be amid—all the bustle and activity of the market, among the people and their booths and wares. But instead of pausing to look at the brightly colored fabrics, ribbons, or belts, she scanned the rows for the wood-carver and his display.

She made her way to where she thought she remembered him

being the previous week, but instead, there was a farmer who had put out bunches of carrots, leeks, beets, and cabbages. She went down the rest of that row, but her handsome young wood-carver was not there. She went down the next row and the next, but still no sign of him. She went back to the place where she'd seen him before and went one row up.

There was his table and his wood carvings, which were laid out the same as the week before. But no one was standing behind the table. He was nowhere in sight.

Perhaps he was meeting with the bishop—but he wouldn't leave his carvings unattended, would he?

The person sitting beside his table of wood carvings—a woman with a makeshift covering over her stand—was talking to a man who was buying some of her candles.

On the other side was a man with leather saddle bags displayed across a trestle table.

"Sir," she said, approaching the man, "may I ask where the wood-carver has gone? Do you know?"

"Him?" He pointed to the setup across from him. "He asked if I would keep an eye on his things. Went off with a priest."

"Thank you." Her heart soared, and she said a quick prayer that all was going well with the bishop.

"Did you want me to tell him something?"

"No, thank you. I will wait for him."

The man eyed her a little too knowingly. But she turned away and pretended to examine the woman's candles, then the scarves on the other side of her. Her heart had calmed, but now it thumped again. He could be back any moment. She couldn't help glancing up constantly at his table.

But as she wandered up and down, and after she had looked at every vendor's goods, she began to wonder if he would ever come back.

She fingered a particularly lovely belt, studying the embroidery, marveling at the skill, taking note of the design. Then she glanced up and saw that the wood-carver had passed behind her when she wasn't looking and was slipping behind his table.

Her heart fluttered. *Breathe. He will hardly think favorably of you if you lose your senses and can't speak.* But was it not strange she would have such a reaction to him? He was handsome, to be sure, but she would never be interested in him as anything more than a friend.

She forced herself to walk slowly and breathe deeply. Was it possible he was even handsomer than he had been a week ago?

His eyes met hers when she was still several feet away. His expression changed from thoughtful and serious to smiling, and he came out from behind his table and moved toward her.

"I'm glad you are here." His voice was gentle.

"Were you afraid I wouldn't come?"

"I was afraid I would miss seeing you while I was talking to the bishop."

"What did he say? Does he want you to carve the new Hagenheim Cathedral doors?"

The corners of his mouth rose. "He does."

"Oh, that is wonderful! I am so pleased for you. Are you pleased?"

"I can hardly believe it yet. It does not seem possible. But yes, I am very pleased."

"With God all things are possible."

"That is true."

Even with one corner of his mouth quirked up, his full lips slightly parted, his blue eyes shining, the best thing about him was the gentleness in his manner, the goodness in his expression. She hoped he married a kind and sincere girl, someone who deserved him.

"Did you know that is in the Holy Writ?" he asked. "I mean, have you read it yourself?"

"Yes. Have you?"

"Only the parts the priest allowed us to read when I was learning to read and write. But I wasn't able to go to the school anymore after my father's accident." He looked down at the cobblestones under their feet.

"That makes me sad for you."

He met her eye, and she couldn't read his expression. He shook his head. "People have to work so their families don't starve. I was fortunate I had the opportunity to learn to read. My mother was the one who insisted on it."

"You are very responsible. Your family is fortunate to have you taking care of them."

He smiled out of one side of his mouth again. "That is kind of you to say."

"It is true. I am sure." And it reminded Adela of something. How was she a blessing to her family? Did she serve them in any way? But they had servants. They didn't need her to serve them. She did go with her mother to the orphanage sometimes to read to the children or help them with their studies or celebrate festivals with them. But that was not really a sacrifice, for she enjoyed it. This young man had given up his childhood and his opportunity to learn more at the priest's school in order to work for his family.

"Shall we walk? If someone will look after my carvings?"

Adela turned to the vendor she had spoken to before. "Would you be so kind as to keep an eye on his carvings again?" She smiled but then realized how much she sounded like a duke's daughter. By the way the man looked at her, he probably resented her request. She took a step back, feeling the blush coming over her cheeks.

"Thank you so much. We won't be gone long," the wood-carver said, giving the man a big smile. He nodded.

The wood-carver turned his smile on her, and they walked down the row toward the fountain, which was in front of the Rathous.

She felt so safe with him as he walked close beside her but did not touch her. He seemed protective, not intimidating or overbearing.

Something her new sister-in-law, Katerina, had said flew to her thoughts. Adela had asked her the morning before the wedding, "What was it that made you fall in love with my awful brother?"

Katerina had smiled wryly, then said, "I did not like him at first. I thought him arrogant, and I knew of his bad reputation. But it was his protectiveness that made me trust him. That was why I fell in love with him, I think. He made me feel safe and protected when every other man made me feel threatened."

And now, staring up at the wood-carver, even though she barely knew him, Adela felt as safe as if she were with her brothers. Even the tilt of his head spoke gentleness, while the bulk of his arms gave testament to his strength, should she need him to defend her.

"You are very quiet," he said as they approached the fountain near the town hall. He reached for the communal dipper and filled it with the water that came from the underground spring, then offered it to her.

Adela took a drink of the cold water, then handed it back to him. He drank from it as well, closing his eyes and draining it, drawing attention to his neck, which looked quite strong and appealing. Then he hung it back up for the next person.

"I am sorry for being quiet. I don't talk as much as my sister Mar—my older sister." If she told him her siblings' names, he might eventually recognize them as the duke's children's names, and she did not want that. "Do your sisters talk a lot?"

"Yes, they do. They are twins."

"Twins? How unusual. Do they look exactly alike?"

"No. They are quite different in appearance, though similar in temperament."

"I've never known any twins. Were there problems with their birth?"

"No, all was well, or so I was told."

Her hip was propped against the top of the fountain, and the wood-carver stood in front of her. She wanted to put her hand on his arm, but that might be too forward.

"They were born only a year and a half after me. But my father doesn't allow them to help with the farmwork. He barely allows my mother to make them help her with the housework."

"Oh." If Adela lived in a poor family, she would help with the work, would she not? Actually, she found it difficult to imagine doing household tasks.

"You might even meet my sisters and decide for yourself. I had to bring them with me today."

"Oh. That would be interesting. I would like very much to meet them. What—" She was about to ask him their names, then suddenly exclaimed, "I don't know your name! I forgot to ask you! Can you believe it? How ill-mannered am I?"

"You are not ill-mannered." He smiled. "My name is Frederick."

"It is a very strong name. It suits you."

"Strong?"

"Yes. Masculine and solid."

He smiled. "And your name suits you, Adela. Very feminine and beautiful. Like a troubadour's melody."

Adela's breath caught in her chest. Did he mean it? "Such pretty words. You must be a poet."

"I used to make up rhymes when I was a boy."

"Rhymes? Truly? Tell me one."

He coughed and wouldn't look her in the eye. "You will think it's childish."

"No, I won't! You must tell me one."

"Very well, then." He cleared his throat again.

> "Suzy Slew
> fell in a shoe.
> She couldn't get out.
> She began to sprout,
> and she grew and grew and grew."

"I like that rhyme. I shall remember it and tell it to my nieces and nephews. Tell it to me again?"

He repeated the rhyme, and then she recited it back to him.

"It is easy to remember because it rhymes so well. I should embroider a tapestry to hang in my niece's room to go with it."

Frederick's smile was gentle and sincere. His eyes locked on her face.

"I shall make a girl sitting in a giant shoe, with a plant growing out of her head."

They both laughed. Some people walking by turned to look at them. Adela quickly stifled her laugh and turned her head away from the onlookers.

"Why are you hiding your face? You have a very pretty laugh."

Adela wasn't sure what to say. She just shook her head. "I'm a little shy, I suppose."

He just stared at her, a strange look in his eyes, a tiny smile on his lips. Finally, he said, "I would like to see your tapestry when it's finished."

"I will embroider the words of the rhyme at the bottom. But

I shall have to make more than one, as I have several nieces. My brothers and sisters have many children."

"Oh? How many brothers and sisters do you have?"

"Eight. I am the youngest, except for my adopted brother." She should stop. She'd soon reveal her parents' names, and then he'd surely guess who she was.

"If I had such a large family, I'd have more help with my work."

"I am sorry you don't have more siblings. I love my large family. We enjoy each other very much." She sighed. "But they are all grown up and have left me."

"I am sorry."

"No, I don't deserve your pity. I am very fortunate that they are often visiting us, and I go to visit them as well. But what about your farmwork? What will you do, now that you'll be working for the bishop?"

He looked down at the cobblestone street. "I will need to hire someone to work on the farm. I suspect I'll have to hire two men, as hired workers aren't as diligent as a man working for his family. My uncle Laurentz told me that once."

"Your uncle?"

"Yes, my father's brother. He . . . Well, to be truthful, he has been a bit more of a father to me than my father has."

"Oh?"

He sighed, still not looking her in the eye. "We don't have to talk about that." He shrugged. "My father has a bad temper and drinks too much."

"I am sorry." She had heard of men like that. There was one in the Bible, named Nabal, who was so evil and abusive that God struck him dead and gave his courageous wife to King David.

Frederick gave her a gentle smile, finally looking her in the eye. "I'd like to bring my mother and sisters to town to live while I am here."

"Oh, that sounds like a very good idea. But what about your father? How will he react to you and your mother and sisters leaving him?"

"He will be furious. But I have decided to do it anyway, if they will come."

"Do bring them. You can find a house for you all to live in, I am sure. In fact, I know of one that is empty, and I even know the owners." She clasped her hands over her chest at this realization. It was perfect!

He raised his brows at her.

"It is a very good house, in the middle of town—a good location. And it will not cost you very much, I wouldn't think." She would make sure of that.

"That is good to know. Thank you. If I do need the house, how can I find you? Will you tell me where you live?"

Ack. What should she say? Oh heavens and saints! She must think of something, but her mind was empty as she stared into his eyes.

"Perhaps I am presuming too much to ask you that."

"No, not at all. It is only . . . I do not know if my father would approve . . ."

"Forgive me—"

"I can find you at the Cathedral, can I not? I'm sorry."

"No, I was presumptuous."

"No, you weren't. But I have a specific reason . . . for not telling you where I live. I shall tell you one day. One day I promise I shall."

He looked at her thoughtfully. She wished she could tell him the truth. But he would understand why she didn't when she finally told him. It would make things awkward between them if he knew who she really was, and he might not wish to be friends with her.

When she went with her mother to the orphanage, or when she'd gone to the marketplace with guards or servants, people always treated her differently. They'd get that certain look on their faces—almost frightened, wary, nervous—and they didn't talk to her the way they talked to their friends. Their equals. She very much wanted Frederick to see her as an equal, to talk to her as a fellow artist.

"So, when do you start carving?"

"I am to come back next week with a plan for the doors. I want to do scenes from the Bible, but . . . I have not actually read the entire Bible." Frederick's mouth twisted slightly into a frown.

"You probably know many stories. You depicted the one of Abraham and Isaac on the medallion."

"I do have several stories in mind that I would like to do. Perhaps I will again use the story of Abraham and Isaac, the angel stopping Abraham from sacrificing his son, the lamb on the altar, and then, beside that I will have Jesus on the cross to show that, just as God provided the ram in Isaac's place, so Jesus is the lamb God provided for us."

"Oh, that is beautiful." Her heart skipped and stuttered in her chest, not only at his words, but at the way he said them. A man who was sincere and deep and spiritual? And tall and handsome. But he was not an eligible suitor.

Sad thought indeed.

CHAPTER 7

Adela watched Frederick, his face intent as he gazed at her.
"Will you tell me your favorite stories from the Bible?"

Adela had to think for a moment. "I love all of Jesus's healings—healing the blind men, the woman with the issue of blood. I love when He saves the woman caught in adultery from the men who wanted to stone her." She looked down when she realized what she had said. These were awkward stories to be discussing with a man.

"I know that one," he said, his gaze fixed on the ground.

"And there's the story of Adam and Eve."

"Everyone knows that one."

"It's not one of my favorites."

Frederick shook his head in agreement.

"And I love the stories of David, especially the one where he slays the giant, Goliath."

"Oh, that is a very good one."

"And the story of David slaying the lion and the bear to save his sheep."

"Also very good. I also like the story of Solomon judging between the two women about who the baby belonged to."

"Oh yes! You could certainly carve that story too."

"Do you have another one?"

He gazed at her face with such attention that it made her feel warm all over, like a longing was being satisfied. For attention? For being seen and known and valued? Strange that a poor wood-carver could make her feel something so deep. Perhaps it was because he was an artist like her. Then she remembered her favorite story.

"Do you know the story of Joseph?"

"The coat of many colors and the dreams that made his brothers jealous?"

"Yes, but my favorite part is when he went to Egypt."

Frederick's brows drew together, as if he was having trouble remembering.

"Remember, he was thrown into a cistern, then his brothers sold him to slave traders."

"Oh yes."

"They took him to Egypt, sold him to Potiphar, and his wife accused Joseph of trying to sleep with her."

Frederick raised his brows.

"Do you know that part?"

He shook his head. "Tell me."

"Potiphar's wife kept trying to persuade Joseph to sleep with her, but he refused. Then she sent the other servants away so that she and Joseph were alone in the house. She grabbed him and tried to get him to come to bed with her, but he ran away from her, fleeing from the house, leaving his outer garment in her hand." Some of these stories in the Bible were difficult to recount in front of a man. Thankfully, Frederick did not look embarrassed.

"I do not think I've heard this story."

"Then the woman told Potiphar that Joseph tried to force her to sleep with him, so Potiphar had him thrown into prison, where he stayed for many years."

Adela told him the entire story of Joseph's gift of interpreting dreams while in the prison, how he was finally released and then elevated to Pharaoh's right hand. Finally, she recounted the deception Joseph played on his brothers before he revealed himself to them and how he wept loudly at seeing his brothers again.

While Adela talked, they wandered over to the Rathous to stand in an out-of-the-way place under the covered overhang between the building and its arches.

"You are very good at telling stories." Frederick's voice was low as he gazed into her face, leaning toward her as he propped his shoulder against the stone column. "I could see Joseph and all the other people as you were talking."

"And you are good at telling stories with your carvings." As she stood looking up into his eyes, something seemed to shift, and a tenderness welled up inside her. Should she be having these feelings for this man? She enjoyed talking to him and felt safe with him, and she found him very handsome, but he was poor. They could never be more than friends. Whoever married him would only have one or two servants to help with the house and the children. That was not the kind of life Adela had been trained for.

Several moments of silence stretched between them as her mind went to Lord Barthold. How could she ever think about marrying him when this wood-carver was so much more appealing than he was? And he never looked at her like this, with equal parts gentleness and intense attention.

"How did you get that tiny scar there?" He reached out, as if he was about to touch her chin, but just before he did, he let his hand drop.

"How did you even see that?" Her voice was breathless.

"It is very small. What is the story behind it?"

"I was about five years old, I think. My brothers were chasing me—we were playing a game. I was running and looking over my shoulder. I didn't see the tree until it was too late, and I hit it chin first." She laughed at herself. "The healer said I was lucky I didn't lose any teeth."

He looked so concerned, his brows drew together as he gazed down at her. "I hope your brothers were sorry for causing you to run into a tree."

"They tried to warn me, but I didn't hear them. But yes, they did feel bad about it. They carried me all the way back to the—back home." She had almost said, "back to the castle."

"Did you play with your brothers often?"

"Yes, they were my closest siblings. All my sisters were much older than I was. I climbed trees and ran wild with my brothers as much as I could."

"I wish my sisters had been like that. They never wanted to climb trees or play the games I wanted to play. But fortunately, there were neighbor boys for me to play with, and my cousins were about my age."

"That's good that you had friends." She couldn't stop staring at the short stubble on his cheek and the hard line of his jaw and chin. What would it feel like to touch his face? And why did she not have these thoughts when she was with Lord Barthold? He was her suitor, while Frederick never could be.

"Can I buy you something to eat?"

She *was* getting hungry after all the walking they'd done. Would Mother be worried about her? But the sun wasn't straight overhead yet, and she didn't want to leave.

"I saw a woman selling some stuffed rolls."

He smiled at her and turned toward the *Marktplatz*. He waited for her. Should she take his arm, the way Mother took Father's arm when they walked together? She did not want him to feel awkward, so she simply walked beside him.

They approached the vendors and found the woman with the rolls.

"Can I get two for you?" he asked Adela.

"One is enough for me."

Frederick asked the woman for three rolls. She reached into her basket, and Frederick gave her some money—one coin. She smiled and thanked him.

The roll was warm as Frederick placed it in Adela's hand. They were very near the fountain, so they walked over to it and sat on the low wall encircling it while they ate the rolls stuffed with sausage. Frederick ate two in the time it took her to eat one.

"Almost as good as my mother's," Frederick said as he handed her a dipper full of water.

"Mm, your mother must be a very good cook."

"She is. And yours?"

"Mine?"

"Is your mother a good cook?"

Adela couldn't imagine her mother cooking. "My mother is not a very good cook." She tried to think of something else to talk about, quickly, before he asked her anything else about her mother. "So when will you be coming back to town? I can show you the house I know about that is empty. I think you would be able to get it for a good price."

"Though the bishop is paying me well, I cannot afford to buy it. I could only pay monthly to occupy it . . . for maybe six or seven months? I don't know precisely how long the doors will take."

"I think the owner would be happy with that." Though she did not know how she would explain to her father how she knew this wood-carver.

"My sisters are supposed to meet me one hour past noon here in the market. And as it looks to be about noon . . ."

"Then I can show you the house now. Let us go." Adela hurried toward the street, looking over her shoulder at him.

∽❧∾

Frederick caught up with Adela as she hurried to show him the house. Her face was so earnest, so pretty. But she was talking. He should pay attention.

"The house is close to both the *Marktplatz* and the Cathedral, as well as the castle where the healer lives. It is a perfect location."

"You don't have to convince me that I will be pleased with it," Frederick said. "I'm sure it will be sufficient for me, and even for my mother and sisters. We are content with very little."

At least, he and his mother were. He shouldn't say the same for his sisters. But how possible was it that his father would allow his mother and sisters to live in town? Would his mother be willing to leave without his father's permission? His heart sank as he realized how unlikely it was, but he would trust God to make a way.

As they continued to walk, they came to a very wealthy part of town. The houses were three and four stories tall, some of them beautifully decorated with colorful carvings like the ones he hoped to do someday.

Adela stopped. "This is the one." She pointed to a three-story half-timber house. Everything about it looked wonderful. "What do you think?"

"I think it is much bigger and better than anything I can afford."

Her smile disappeared.

"It is a beautiful home," he quickly amended. "It's just so . . . large." At least three times as large as their home.

They stood in silence, staring at the house, its windows perfectly uniform and symmetrical, with real glass panes and window

73

boxes beneath, awaiting some flowering plants. It was set apart from the other houses by its arched red door.

"Do you think you and your mother and sisters could live here?"

"I . . ."

"What is wrong? You don't like it?"

"No! I do like it. It's just that I don't know if I can afford it, and . . . I doubt that my mother and sisters will be able to join me in town. If they don't, it will be too much house for only me."

"Better to have you living here than no one. It's been empty for a long time. And it won't cost you very much. Once I explain to the owner that you need to be close to the Cathedral so that you can carve the new doors for the bishop, he may even allow you to live here for free, as an offering to the Church."

"I couldn't let them give it to me for free. The bishop has already paid me some of my wages, so I can pay. But I only need a small place where I can make a meal and sleep."

"Of course. I understand."

"I hope you aren't upset with me. It is lovely, but it's so much more than I need."

"I'm not upset at all. And I can ask my—ask some other people and perhaps find a smaller place for you."

"Thank you. That would be good."

"I should go now," she said. "I don't want my mother to worry about me."

He had disappointed her. He could tell by the sober look on her face. But what could he say? He wanted to pay his own way. He did not want charity.

"I should go too," he said, wishing he could walk her home first. He did not want to say fare well without knowing he'd see her again. "I will probably come back to town the day after tomorrow.

We could go for a picnic. There are some meadows just outside the town walls."

"That sounds very pleasant." Adela smiled again.

"May I come to your house and walk you to the meadow?"

"Oh, it will be easier for me to come to you. I can meet you at the east gate."

"Are you sure?"

"Oh yes. What time?"

"Noon?"

"Yes. The day after tomorrow. I'll be there."

He wanted to embrace her, to tell her he was happy to have met her, but they were new acquaintances, and though he might not know a lot about what was proper, he knew he shouldn't touch a maiden without her permission. No, embracing a woman he barely knew was not how a chivalrous man behaved.

He wasn't so poor anymore. He was a carver in the service of the bishop. He was skilled and talented. And he would do his best to conduct himself in such a way as to make this young maiden proud to take him home and introduce him to her father and mother.

So even as Adela said, "Fare well," and waved a hand at him, he knew he'd be thinking about her constantly for the next two days and anticipating their picnic.

CHAPTER 8

Frederick was aware of his sisters bickering in the back of the cart all the way home, but he wasn't listening to them. Instead, he was thinking of Adela. He tried to remember everything she had said, the tone of her voice, her mannerisms, the sweetness of her expressions. She seemed so intelligent and refined, even though her clothing indicated that she was poor, like him. He knew she had a lot of brothers and sisters—eight to be exact. But he didn't know anything about her parents or what they did.

He wished she had allowed him to walk with her from her house, but Hagenheim was a rather safe place. The only kidnapping he'd ever heard of had been of the duke's daughter, and since Adela was obviously not wealthy, she should be safe.

Did she not trust him? Was that why she hadn't allowed him to come to her house? Even though he was tall and strong, he thought he was an unintimidating fellow, slow to anger and gentle with women. His mother had taught him that—and so had his father, by being a bad example. He knew after seeing how badly his father behaved with his mother that he'd never want to treat a woman like that. His uncle didn't act that way with women, although their father, Frederick's grandfather, had apparently been cruel to their mother. But the day his uncle had told him that he had always determined to be as unlike his own father as he could be, and Frederick saw how kindly he was with his own wife, Frederick had felt so relieved. He did not have to be like his father. He had determined, just as his uncle had, to be a better man.

And now that he had a pouch full of money from the bishop himself, he felt a surge of power. He could escape his father's cruelty and take his mother with him.

Perhaps he shouldn't have been so quick to refuse Adela's offer of the attractive large house. He would bring his mother to town if she was willing and he could steal her away, and being away from their father might also help his sisters not to be so vapid and quick to hate everyone. Although that seemed unlikely. But a much smaller house would do just fine, even if he had his mother and sisters with him. They were not extravagant people.

They reached home, and Father was standing in the front yard propped against a tree, no doubt waiting for them. Eulaly and Ursula went silent. Even though their father treated them with much partiality, they had seen enough of his anger to be afraid of him.

Frederick drove the horses past his father, who said not a word but stared sullenly at them. Eulaly and Ursula rode the cart to the barn, then jumped down, clutching the few parcels of goods they had purchased in town, and headed toward the house, whispering to each other.

"Out gallivanting like rich nobles," their father said as they hurried past him. He was walking toward Frederick.

"Good day, Father." Frederick unhitched the horses and started taking off their bridles, then rubbing them down, and still Father did not speak; he simply stood nearby, watching him.

"Where have you been?"

"We went to town. I needed to speak to a man about a wood-carving job."

"A wood-carving job," Father repeated.

Frederick continued brushing down the horses. When he was almost done, his father spoke again. "I don't know where you got the high notion that you can leave your work, knowing your family depends on you, and go to town, as if you were some wealthy aristocrat who was at his leisure to do as he pleased."

"Eulaly and Ursula needed an outing. They rarely get to go anywhere." It was beneath him, perhaps, but he used his father's one weakness, his daughters, as an excuse.

Silence reigned behind him, but the hair on the back of his neck tingled in warning of what his father was possibly getting ready to do or say.

He finally finished brushing the animals and led them into the stable, not chancing to glance in his father's direction. But an anger was growing inside. How dare his father behave this way toward him? It was wrong. His father should not treat him with contempt and a complete lack of mercy or kindness. Should he even tell his father that he planned to hire some men to take care of the farm in his place? No, he'd go to his uncle for advice. Uncle Laurentz would help him find suitable men.

When he had finished forking the hay into the horses' stalls, he turned and was just coming out of the stable when something hit him in the head.

Frederick stumbled back a step, then lifted his fists in a defensive stance.

"You left the brush out." Father stood leaning on his walking stick with an evil half grin.

Frederick swayed on his feet, his head pounding and his vision blurring. Something tickled his temple. He reached up and wiped it. His fingers came away with bright red blood.

He looked down to see the grooming brush, with its thick wooden handle, lying on the ground. His head throbbed, but the blurriness was clearing from his eyes. Heat rose from his neck to his head.

"What kind of father are you?" He growled the words.

"I might ask you, what kind of son are you? A son who deserts his family, a son who refuses to help his father who is lame and unable to work? What do you think the Church would say to that? You could be excommunicated for abandoning your family."

It would do no good to try to match words with this man. His father never listened, and no one could reason with him, could ever make him understand anything. He would only badger and confuse with his accusations and denials of the truth.

Frederick could never win, so why try?

Excommunicated, indeed. Frederick walked past his father, his anger so strong that his vision blurred again, this time with a red fog of rage. But he would not be like his violent, unmerciful father. No. He would *never* be like him.

Mother stood in the door of the house, and when she saw him walking toward her, she cried out, a strangled sound. "What happened?"

"Nothing." Frederick wiped at the blood. There was more of it than he'd thought, and it was running into his eyebrow and down his face. He bowed his head and the blood dripped to the ground.

He went into the kitchen and sat on a stool. Mother came to him with a wet cloth and wiped the blood off his face, then dabbed at the cut, which was at his hairline above his left eye.

Tears fell down Mother's face. Frederick's stomach churned at the sight.

"Mother, we don't need to stay here any longer," he said softly.

"I'm getting us a house. Bishop Werner has paid me the money I need to get us out of here and away from him."

Mother didn't speak. She kept dabbing at the blood on his head and wiping her tears with the back of her wrist. Finally, she said in a raspy voice, "I'm sorry. No one should have to endure such treatment, and certainly not you."

"Then leave with me. Come and live with me in town."

"I . . . I will." She bit her lip, probably to keep it from trembling.

His heart lifted at her words. He hadn't believed she'd leave her husband. As terrible as his father was, Frederick knew she felt obligated to be faithful to him. He was her husband, after all, and the Church did not approve of divorce, even in the case of physical mistreatment, and Mother was devoted if she was anything.

"I will go stay with Uncle Laurentz for two nights, and then I will come and get you and the girls. Be prepared to go at dawn, and if the girls aren't ready, we're leaving them." Somehow he'd find them somewhere to stay.

"It's so unfair for a son to have to take care of his mother and sisters this way."

"That's nonsense, Mother. Who else should take care of you? Besides, it makes me happy that I'm able to. Don't deny me that happiness."

Mother laughed, a tiny, short sound, but it raised his spirits.

"Don't worry. Just get ready."

She started preparing a bandage for his head. Frederick touched her hand. "I don't need it. The bleeding's stopped. I have to go take care of the animals."

"I fed the pigs for you."

"Thank you, Mother."

"Stay clear of Father. I don't want anything else to happen. He's furious and he's been drinking."

"I will. Don't worry." He started to head out and then stopped, turned back around, and looked at his mother. "Did he hurt you? What did he do while we were gone?"

"I am well."

He went over to her and stared hard at her face. She was wearing a scarf over her hair, and it covered her neck. He moved the scarf to the side. Blue and dark purple bruises marred her skin. Mother snatched the fabric back over her neck, covering the offending sight.

Frederick's jaw clenched and a red mist descended over his vision so that he could barely see.

"It's nothing." Mother took hold of his arm, still clutching the scarf over her neck.

He fisted his hands. Words bubbled up, but he bit them back. That man was evil, a menace, and if he had to, Frederick would kill him. He would never, ever let that man hurt his mother again.

"You're coming with me to Uncle Laurentz's tonight."

"No, Frederick, please listen. He won't do it again, and he'll only be more enraged if I leave with you now. I shall be well enough for two more nights. Then we'll leave early in the morning before he wakes up, and he won't be able to find us. You shall see."

If his father had been in front of him, he would have punched him in the face. But who would look favorably upon that? A full-grown son striking his father in the face, a father who was shorter and smaller and crippled too? But how much worse to allow that man to hurt his mother?

"What did he do? Did he choke you?"

"No, no, he just . . . just grabbed me too hard. I am well."

"He shouldn't grab you at all." His stomach was sick. He scrubbed a hand down his face. "I will stay here. I won't go to Uncle Laurentz's, but if he so much as touches you, I will defend you, no matter what it takes."

"He won't touch me. He's sorry."

"Sorry." Frederick made a snorting sound. How many times had the man done this? He should die of sorry.

"Go and do your work. I will be well." Mother patted his arm.

Frederick leaned down and kissed his mother's forehead. Then he turned and left to feed the animals and mow the hay. Perhaps the physical labor would drive away some of his fury.

He would be taking his mother and sisters to Hagenheim in two days without a house to go to. But somehow God would provide.

❧

Basina watched her son go back out to finish his chores. Poor Frederick.

Now that no one was around, she could let herself cry. And the tears came. She wondered when she'd be all cried out, when her tears would dry up and she wouldn't have to hide her face from her husband, who would be enraged to see them, or from her son, who would only feel bad for her.

But even though it would embarrass her and bring up a lot of difficult thoughts and feelings, she should tell Frederick the truth about his father.

Her mind went back to the last time she'd seen the man she had loved, the man whose child she had been carrying twenty-two years earlier.

She'd hoped Reichart would take care of her, but when she'd gone to tell him about the baby, he had said he did not have time to talk to her and sent her away before she could tell him the news. She'd been so disappointed that she went outside to cry. It was perhaps the first time, but certainly not the last time, she'd had to hide her tears.

Someone had followed her out. She had occasionally seen the man watching her when she went about her work. He was tall and thin with very dark hair. Something about him made her want to avoid him. She was grateful he had never tried to speak to her. But now as he cornered her behind the kitchen garden, she turned to face him.

"You are one of the servants who cleans the bedchambers, are you not?"

"I am."

"I know about you and the young lord, Reichart."

Her knees started to tremble at his words and the cold, dark look in his small eyes.

"You are with child, yes?" He seemed to look down his sharp nose at her. "Well, Lord Reichart knows, and he does not want you or the child. You would do well to leave before his bride arrives."

The words filled her with fear. And pain. Were the rumors true? Would Reichart have to marry the woman his father wished him to? The pain was too deep for tears, especially in front of this man who obviously felt nothing but contempt and loathing for her.

He went on. "Lord Reichart didn't want to tell you himself, but he wishes you to go. Your service in this household is no longer needed."

"I don't believe you."

"Believe it. The head house servant will not allow you back inside. I have seen to it. And besides"—he paused, licking his lips and taking a step toward her—"you would not want to injure Lord Reichart, would you? Your presence here could only cause him shame and reproach. He needs a proper bride, a woman who will bring him honor and additional wealth, solidifying his power in the region. You could never do that for him."

It was true. It was all true. The kindest, most loving thing she could do for Reichart was to leave. After all, she did not want him to think she had been using him, that she had only wanted to have his child to ensure an easy future for herself. And she knew, had always known, in spite of her dreams to the contrary, that he could never marry her.

And in that moment, her lovely visions of love and a happy future were destroyed forever.

She had raised the child with great love in her heart, but also great pain, as he reminded her so much of Reichart, the man who ultimately had not wanted her. And Frederick had become such a good man. Anyone would be proud to have such a son.

She should tell Frederick who his real father was. She was surprised Stenngle had never told him that he was not his father. No doubt he had some selfish motive for keeping it a secret. Indeed, Stenngle did not know who the father was, as Basina had never told him. At first Stenngle had seldom mentioned the fact that she had been with child when he married her. He'd seemed so understanding and kind and merciful in the beginning. She'd thought him such a good man for accepting her and loving her as she was.

How wrong, how very wrong she had been, thinking that he loved her, that he had pure motives for marrying her. Not long after he married her, his behavior changed. He'd treated her as if she were nothing, deserved nothing. He hadn't loved her at all.

Once she was married, there was no way to undo it. She had dreamed about changing her name and running away to a faraway region, alone with her child. But she'd already run away from one man. She hadn't the heart to do it again, especially with a babe in arms. And then she'd realized she was pregnant again, and this time she'd borne two babies. She certainly could not have survived alone with three small children. Although, if she could have, her children would have been better off than being here with this child beater.

No, she could not indulge these tears or these dark thoughts any longer. She wiped her face and went on with her chores, just as her brave son was going on with his.

CHAPTER 9

"Thank you for agreeing to take a ride with me."

Lord Barthold sounded respectful as they stood together, waiting for the grooms to finish readying their horses.

"May I help you?"

Adela was about to mount her horse. She normally stood on the mounting step, but Lord Barthold was standing between her and the step. She couldn't decide which was more awkward—saying yes, or refusing his offer and walking around him to get to the step.

He must have taken her hesitancy and silence as her acquiescence, because he put his hands around her waist and hoisted her up. Then he mounted his own horse.

At least he didn't make her feel uncomfortable by leering at her or otherwise behaving inappropriately. He seemed like a good person—not lecherous or greedy, not angry or hostile, not cruel or unkind. But that was the problem. She was always defending him in her mind, telling herself that he was not a bad person. If he was the man she should marry, shouldn't she be thinking about all the things he *was*, not what he was *not*? Or was she too shallow to appreciate the important things? After all, her father seemed to like him well enough.

But instead of thinking about Lord Barthold, lately the only person she thought about was Frederick.

She was a little annoyed that Barthold had asked her to go riding with him today, but at least he had not asked her to go tomorrow, when she would be meeting Frederick.

Lord Barthold mounted and was moving his horse forward. Adela followed him as he rode through the castle gate, skirted the edge of town, and left through the east gate.

They rode up the hill where she planned to take Frederick the next day. They kept going until they were traveling down a lane that was overhung with tree branches, making it shady and sheltered. That was when she realized . . .

"There are no guards with us."

"No, but I have my sword. I can protect us." Lord Barthold gave her a slight smile.

"Oh. Of course." But she wondered if Father knew he had taken her out without a guard.

"I wanted to ask you something, Lady Adela. I wanted to ask if you would accept this gift." He held out something that sparkled in the dappled sunlight coming through the leaves overhead.

Adela reached out and touched it without thinking. "It is very beautiful."

The bejeweled necklace winked up at her, but its colored stones seemed cold and lifeless. But that was a strange thought, was it not? She should be appreciating its beauty and worth.

"I have never seen anything like it."

"Let me put it on you."

She couldn't think of what to say, so when he started dismounting, she dismounted too. He took hold of both horses' reins and looped them loosely around a low branch.

She turned her back on him so he could put the necklace on

her. He draped it around her neck and worked on the clasp behind her while the heavy stones settled on her chest.

"There."

She turned to face him. His gaze went from the necklace to her eyes.

She felt acutely uncomfortable. "Barthold, I . . . I don't think I should—"

"I want you to marry me, Adela. I have spoken to your father. He says it's your decision. He is a very permissive father, so I am asking you."

"I don't know, Barthold. I . . . I don't know."

He stared at her. "Shall I send word to the couriers who are bringing the bridal gift for your father, the father of my bride, to turn around and take it back to Grundelsbach?"

"All I can tell you is that I have not decided whether I can accept your offer. I'm sorry. If you wish to send back the bridal gift, then do so. Because I'm not ready to say yes."

He just stared back at her.

She reached behind her neck to unclasp the necklace.

He touched her wrist. "No. Keep it. Until you decide."

She didn't want to keep it. But it seemed easier to acquiesce, and then she could give it back to him when she decided against marrying him.

Was there really no possibility that she might decide she wanted to marry him? Barthold made sense as a suitor, and perhaps she just needed to know him better. Surely he would understand that she didn't just want to marry someone; she wanted to fall in love. And though she was not at all convinced that she would ever be able to fall in love with Barthold, she had not had enough time to be sure.

Instead of going any farther, Barthold turned his horse around and they headed back toward the castle, but on foot, with him holding the horses' reins. He walked quite close to her as he said, "I'm not very good at this. I know about hunting and I know sword fighting and jousting. But I don't know anything about making a beautiful, sweet young woman like you fall in love with me."

It was the most pleasant, most authentic and unassuming thing he'd ever said to her. She looked over at him, and he was gazing at her.

"I'm sorry if I'm not very good at saying the right thing."

"You don't have to say the right thing. You only have to say what is in your heart."

His lips parted and his forehead creased, as if he was puzzling over her words. Finally, he said, "That is . . . good." He smiled and his gaze slipped down to the necklace. But he stared longer at the necklace than he did at her face.

⁂

Frederick hurried to stack the hay onto the hay racks in the field to dry. He had to finish this task before going out to his uncle's house to see if he'd had any luck finding a worker for the farm. He was putting his pitchfork into the barn when he heard someone call out his name, then laugh. He turned and waited for whoever it was to show themselves.

The Eselin brothers, all three of them, came around the side of the barn, their shrewd eyes pinned on him.

Frederick stopped himself from frowning.

"What brings you here?" Frederick went into the barn to finish his task of putting away the hay rake and pitchfork. When he came out, one brother had his arms crossed over his chest, another was chewing a hay straw, and the third was squatting on the ground, but all three were staring at him. Should he tell them? Perhaps they could help him spread the word.

"I'm looking for someone to work the farm. I have money to hire someone if you know of anyone who needs the work."

"You are like an old man, always working," Ditmar said and spit on the ground.

"Or like an old woman." Everwin's words drew guffaws from the other two brothers.

Frederick walked past them. He had no time for their foolishness. He headed down the road to his uncle's house, a short walk away.

"Where are you going?" Everwin said.

"We want to talk to you," Gerhard added.

"Yeah, we have an offer for you," Ditmar called out. "You won't care about this senseless farmwork when you hear what we have planned."

Frederick didn't stop or even turn around. "Stealing from the rich again?"

"Listen, we're still hoping to get that bride money, but we've got an even better idea."

Frederick mentally shook his head. These men were trouble, but they'd only get angry and argue with him if he disagreed or threw water on their fiery ideas.

"Let's hear it." Frederick kept moving.

Ditmar ran up and jumped in front of him. "We've been staking out the castle, and you'll never guess who's been going outside the town, riding alone, without any guards along."

"I can't guess."

"The Duke of Grundelsbach's son and the Duke of Hagenheim's daughter."

Everwin and Gerhard had also caught up with them and were staring at him. He'd never seen them looking so serious.

"Just think of the ransom we could get for those two. Can you imagine?" Ditmar said.

"The four of us could easily take them," Everwin said.

"Nobody would even get hurt." Gerhard looked at him with wide eyes.

How daft were they? He couldn't even pretend to go along with this. "Don't put me in your plans. Pardon me, but I have no wish to get my neck stretched from a scaffold." He pushed past them and kept walking.

They shouted after him, calling him a coward and other names.

Ditmar came running up behind him, getting in front of him again. "Listen, Frederick. Nobody's going to get hanged. I have a plan. We'll send a ransom note through my inside contact. You can write it."

None of the three of them knew how to read or write. But if they were able to pull off an attempt to kidnap these two aristocrats, which was highly unlikely, Frederick certainly did not wish to be caught up in it. He'd hang like the rest of them, high in the town square.

"You aren't vicious enough to want to hurt anyone, are you?" Frederick tried a different tactic.

"We won't have to hurt them. We'll just threaten them."

"And the son of a duke, trained for battle, will just throw down his weapons and let you take him and his bride-to-be captive? I don't think so. He'll fight, and someone will get killed." No doubt it would be one of the Eselin brothers.

Ditmar's eyes turned dark and his cheeks red. "Very well. If you don't wish to help us, you won't get any of the reward."

"We'll find someone else," Everwin said.

"Someone who wants to be rich." Gerhard stalked away.

Ditmar walked beside him for a few moments, then said, "Join with us, Frederick. This is your chance to get away from your father. You know you hate that old farm. You weren't meant to be a farmer. Don't you want to get rich and leave this place?"

The sharp pain that went through his chest at Ditmar's words surprised Frederick. But riches that were attained by such wrongful means were not worth having. Besides, his dreams were already coming true now, with the Bishop of Hagenheim paying him to carve the Cathedral doors.

"Sorry, Ditmar. I'm not interested."

"You know our plans now." Ditmar's voice became hard and menacing. "You had best not tell anyone, no matter what happens. If you keep your mouth shut, we'll still probably share it with you. But you can't tell anyone it was us who held them for ransom."

Frederick wanted to laugh. As if these bumblers could ever get away with such a scheme. But he thought better of the impulse. They may not have been very smart, but they were devious and cruel when someone tweaked their pride by poking fun at them.

"I never asked to know your plans. You shouldn't have told me."

"You'd be more loyal to a duke who never did anything for you than to your friends who grew up beside you? You're no friend of mine, Frederick."

"Good day to you too."

"We'll see how you like it when someone tells the forester that your father shoots the king's deer. When he comes nosing around here, suspicious of your father, he might just say you shot the deer. Eh, Frederick?"

His father was selfish and cruel enough to do it. And even if the accusation did not stick, it might get back to the bishop and make him question his decision to hire Frederick for such a holy job.

Frederick suddenly felt quite weary. He had better things to worry about than the Eselin brothers and their addlepated schemes. And losing their good opinion might be a blessing rather than a curse. He could only pray they were not able to ruin his life.

⊷❦⊶

Adela slipped into the kitchen and found the servants hard at work preparing food. One by one they looked up and stared at her. No doubt they were wondering why the daughter of the duke was in the kitchen.

Adela smiled and greeted them. "Good morning."

The servants were people, like Frederick, like Adela, with feelings and hopes and talents, something Adela suddenly realized she had never acknowledged or thought about before. She felt a pang in her stomach.

"Lady Adela!" Helena, the head cook, called to her from the other side of the large open room and started toward her.

"Frau Helena, may I have two small picnic baskets of food?"

"Of course, my dear. Anything you wish. How many people will be going on this picnic with you?"

"Well, there will be four of us."

"Oh." Frau Helena looked a bit puzzled.

"Yes, some friends and I wish to have a little outing. I'm sorry to make more work for you."

The cook must wonder what friends she could be talking about.

"Oh, that is nothing for you to think about. Do you think I mind making picnic baskets for my own sweet Adela?" She put her hands on her hips, her frown morphing into a smile. "I shall pack roasted and spiced nuts, some little cakes, warm meat pies, and plum and apple pasties—"

"Nothing too fancy, though. Please. Just bread and cheese is fine." Would Frederick see the elaborate foods and become suspicious that she was not who she said she was? Perhaps she could tell him that her mother was in charge of the kitchen at Hagenheim Castle. That wouldn't be a lie. But it would be deceptive, since he'd assume she was a cook—and she'd already told him her mother was a bad cook.

"Just leave it to me." Frau Helena winked.

Adela wasn't sure what that meant, but she hurried back up to her room to change into her servant's clothes. Erma had become so excited about Adela borrowing her clothes, Adela had given her the money to buy more fabric, and Erma's mother, who was a seamstress, had made her a new dress to share with Adela. She had presented it to her that morning.

"Oh, Erma, it's beautiful!"

Erma laughed. "It's not as fine as any of your dresses."

"It's perfect, though. It's a pretty color—my favorite, dark pink— and it looks as if it would fit me perfectly."

"You can wear your lavender underdress with it, and the two colors will look lovely together."

"Oh, that is true." But would her lavender underdress be too fine? Hopefully, being a man, Frederick wouldn't notice. He would only think she looked pretty.

Adela giggled.

"I saw you with Lord Barthold last night in the Great Hall. He doesn't talk much, does he?"

Lord Barthold. She'd tried to get to know him, she truly had, but . . . "That is one problem. He doesn't talk much. And do I want to be married to someone who doesn't know how to talk to me?"

"I understand what you mean. But perhaps it wouldn't be so bad. He is rich, after all. You could continue to live the way you've always lived if you married him. But what about this man you're going to meet?"

Adela's stomach flipped. "What makes you think I'm meeting a man?" She tried to make her face look shocked.

"Why else would you be so excited?" Erma smirked and turned away from her.

Adela stared at her maidservant's back. This was not how Mother's servants spoke to her. Indeed, the servants were more like Adela's friends. Since her sisters got married and left, they were her only friends. But seeing Erma's smirk . . .

"Are you saying that men are the only thing to be excited about? Well, I think there are plenty of other things to be enthusiastic about." Besides that, she wasn't interested in Frederick in *that* way. Was she?

No, certainly not.

Erma did not even turn around to look at her. Adela took in a deep breath, ready to defend herself.

"I can get excited about plenty of things besides men. Being able to look around the market without guards following me, or seeing the colorful carvings on the houses around the streets of town, or going for a picnic in the meadow." Oh yes. She'd almost forgotten her plan for the picnic. After being so defensive, would she have to confess the truth to Erma after all?

"Erma, I'm asking Cook to make a basket of food so that you and a friend can go on a picnic."

"A picnic?"

"Yes. You would like to go on a picnic, would you not? I thought it would be a way for me to thank you for not telling Mother about me going to the *Marktplatz*, and you can invite another person to go with you."

"What will you be doing while my friend and I are on a picnic?"

"I will be on a picnic, too, with a friend I made in the *Marktplatz*, and—"

"Adela! You *are* meeting a man! What are you doing?"

"I'm not doing anything wrong. Is it wrong to spend time with a new friend?" But her stomach churned at the way Erma was looking at her.

"It is if the friend is a man! And you're the duke's daughter and you have to sneak away from your mother and father to do it. This is very bad, Adela. I am afraid for you, afraid of what your parents will say. You should not be doing this."

Tears pricked Adela's eyes. She stared back at Erma.

Erma sighed. "I'm sorry, Adela, but you know it's true."

"I don't want to hurt Mother and Father, but . . . I promised to meet him, and I'm going to. He is a nice young man, a wood-carver who's going to be working for the bishop. He needs a place to stay, and I'm helping him. I've even told Father about him."

"You told your father?" She raised her brows at her. "About this man you met in the *Marktplatz*?"

"I didn't tell him I met him in the *Marktplatz*. I just told him that I'd heard about his need for a place to stay in Hagenheim. Father is allowing him to let my grandfather's house in town for a tiny sum since he's working for the Church. He even gave me the keys to the house."

Erma just stared hard at her.

"I am doing a good deed, see? I'm helping my friend and the Church, in a roundabout way."

"Mm-hmm."

"I told him I'd meet him today, so I will not break my word." Tears pricked her eyes again at the thought that Erma didn't understand, wasn't on her side. Did Erma think she was too much of a child to handle this? Or that she could not be friends with a man and not do something foolish?

"I don't want to get in trouble with your mother and father and lose my place at the castle. So don't tell me anything else about what you're doing. The less I know, the better for me."

Was Adela selfish not to think of how this might affect Erma? If Erma lost her position, her family might actually go hungry, as Erma's father was dead, her mother had several young children, and Erma's wages were their only source of income.

"Forgive me, Erma. I should have thought . . . I won't tell you anything else about it, and I'll . . . I'll tell them everything about how I met Frederick, eventually, especially if we stay friends. I promise."

"So you're going to sneak out again without a guard?"

Her words stung. Adela was not completely without sense or morals. "I am." But perhaps she should swallow her pride for now and placate Erma, as she didn't want her telling Mother what she was doing. "I'm sorry, Erma, but I have to. I promise I will confess everything to Mother soon, and I will be very careful. But please don't tell anyone, Erma. Please."

Erma's expression showed she did not approve of any of this. "It's not a good idea to go without a guard, Adela. But since you are determined to do it . . . I will keep your secret. For now. But you have to tell me everything about him. How do you know he's not just befriending you so he can hold you for ransom?"

"He's not like that! And he doesn't know I'm the daughter of the duke, so there is no reason for him to want to hold me for ransom. And you can judge for yourself. Come with me when I leave today, and you can at least see him before you go on your picnic."

Erma smiled for the first time. "That's an offer I will not refuse."

CHAPTER 10

Adela hurried out of the castle with Erma, each of them carrying a basket. Adela checked the sun. It was directly overhead. She didn't want to be late. They walked toward the castle gate. Adela ducked her head as they passed through. She'd forgotten to wear the servant's kerchief! How could she forget? Had she already become so accustomed to sneaking out? One guard seemed to stare hard and long at her, but he said nothing, and they hurried along.

As they neared the town gate, she caught sight of Frederick and her heart skipped a beat. But he looked so serious, almost worried. Was he all right? Perhaps it was her imagination.

When she was only a few feet away, Frederick turned and saw her. He smiled. This time her heart didn't skip a beat, it stamped like a horse pawing the ground.

She smiled back.

"Oh, Adela," Erma said next to her ear. "I understand now why you keep sneaking out."

Adela felt her face flush.

"Don't do anything foolish, and don't tell him who your father is."

Adela shook her head. She wanted to ask Erma to please be quiet, but she was too afraid Frederick would hear them.

"Erma, this is Frederick. Frederick, this is Erma."

Frederick and Erma exchanged greetings while Adela took the chance to observe Frederick. Just like the last time she saw him, he seemed even handsomer, with even more intensity and gentleness in his expression as he turned to her. She tried to remember what she'd planned to say to him, but her mind was swept clean.

Erma bade them fare well and hurried away, smiling knowingly at Adela—but at least she no longer looked disapproving.

"I'm glad you're here." Even his voice was both gentle and intense, bringing her attention fully back to him.

"And I'm so pleased to see you, as I have some news about the house."

"The house you showed me?"

"Yes. The owner wishes to let the house to you for one guilder per six months."

Frederick stared, then frowned. "One guilder per month is too little for that house, but one per six months is giving it away."

"He wanted to offer it to you, as an alm for the Church, but I told him you would never agree to that. But if you wish to pay one guilder per month, I think he would accept that."

She smiled as charmingly as she could, hoping he would lose that grumpy frown and say yes. But before he could refuse, she said, "Let us go see it now. I have the key. Come."

"I have my sisters and mother with me."

"How wonderful. Bring them too."

He turned and motioned to three women who were standing to the side of the street with a cart loaded with cloth bundles. Adela started toward them.

"Good day. My name is Adela." She never introduced herself in such an informal way, but she smiled inwardly at how enjoyable it was to pretend to be a normal Hagenheim townsperson.

Frederick hurried up beside her. "Adela, this is my mother, Basina, and my sisters, Eulaly and Ursula."

"I am very pleased to meet you. May I show you to your house?"

Perhaps that was a bit presumptuous. But Frederick's mother looked genuinely relieved. Frederick's brow creased as he leaned closer to Adela. "I had not planned to bring them with me today when we made our plans."

"All is well. You can take possession of the house now if you wish."

His brow creased even more, and she had a sudden urge to reach up and smooth it with her fingers. She kept walking, internally shaking herself. Touching his forehead would not have been appropriate at all, even if his family wasn't watching.

Adela and Frederick walked ahead of his mother and sisters as they led the horses and cart behind. Adela had liked the mother, her expression kind like Frederick's, her face still youthful and pretty. But his sisters . . . Their mouths were pinched and their eyes dull. She had thought she'd picked up on a lack of closeness to them in some of the things he said in the few times he'd mentioned them. She could well imagine that he would have a difficult time being close to these two.

They came in sight of the house. Adela pointed. "There it is." She looked over her shoulder at Frederick's mother, who smiled back at her, her eyes wide.

Adela used the key to open the front door and led them inside. It was quite dark, and she and Frederick opened the shutters and the windows, letting in both light and fresh air.

Adela knew the house well. Her grandparents had lived there when Adela was a little girl. Adela called them Grandmother and

Grandfather, though they were actually her mother's foster parents. Her grandmother had died when Adela was five, but her grandfather had only just passed away a year ago, and the house had stood empty ever since.

"The owner says you are welcome to use everything left in the house. Do you like it?" She looked from Frederick to his mother and back again. The sisters had wandered past them and were examining the furniture and decorations, talking in hushed voices to each other.

"It is the home of a wealthy person, I think." Frederick was looking more at her than at the house. "As I said before, it is certainly worth more than one guilder per month."

"I already explained. You are doing a wonderful, sacred, and holy task for the Church, our own Hagenheim Cathedral, and for the Bishop of Hagenheim. You can expect people to do things for you, to bless you as you are blessing our town. Look at it as something that is humbling, a way to bless those who wish to bless you by receiving their gift. You are a conduit for the people to be generous to God."

Was it a bit of an exaggeration? Perhaps, but it was true nonetheless, at least in the case of her father and mother, who were the owners of this house.

Frederick looked unsure. But his mother was smiling, and there were tears in her eyes.

"It is a wonderful home." Basina stepped tentatively toward him. "Perhaps it is God's provision, and to say no would be to let pride prevent God from caring for us."

"That is just what I think." Adela gazed hopefully at Frederick.

"I want to obey God," he said slowly, "and we do need a house."

Adela clasped her hands joyfully, reminding her that she still had their picnic basket on her arm. "Would you like to see the upper floors? I think there are at least three bedrooms." She knew exactly how many bedrooms there were, but she was not ready to explain that to Frederick.

"I don't think we need to see the rest to know that we'd like to take it." Frederick's mother exchanged a look with her son.

Frederick's expression finally changed, his brow relaxing and his eyes losing their troubled look. "I would like to give him six guilders, for the first six months."

"Very well. Here are your keys." Adela handed them to Frederick.

"We packed some food, and I have a basket for you and Frederick as well," Basina said.

"Oh, I have a basket of food. Would you and your daughters like to go to a meadow I know of, just outside town?"

"No, my dear. You and Frederick go. My daughters and I will stay here and explore the house."

"I should unload the heavy things before we leave." Frederick looked into his mother's eyes.

"No, you go on. You can do that when you return." Basina shooed them with her hands. "Go on, go on."

Frederick leaned down and kissed his mother's cheek.

Adela clasped Basina's hand. "Thank you."

His mother smiled. "Thank you, my dear. You are such a lovely gift from God to us." Tears swam in her eyes again.

"It is my pleasure to help."

Frederick brushed against her arm as he took the picnic basket from her, and suddenly she could think of nothing but him and the meadow as they headed out of the house and down the street.

As they neared the gate, she glanced up, and there was Lord Barthold, riding straight toward them. Beside him was her brother Valten.

Adela's heart pounded as she ducked her head and took hold of Frederick's arm.

Frederick took the picnic basket from Adela and carried it as they walked through the street. How pretty she was, so open and sweet-tempered. Truly, she was nothing like his sisters. But he should remember that he hardly knew her.

As they were approaching the town wall gate, some well-dressed men on horseback were coming toward them. Suddenly Adela took his arm and shrank closer to him. She walked very close to his side as they passed through the gate, and he noticed she seemed to be averting her face from the men on horseback. Why would she do that? Was she afraid of those men? He suspected one of them was probably the son of the Duke of Grundelsbach, as he was so well dressed, and the other was probably a son of Duke Wilhelm of Hagenheim, since he was riding beside him and wore the padded leather armor of a knight. A few soldiers rode along behind them.

But the men were soon past them and on their way up the grassy hill. When Adela and Frederick reached the top, Adela sat down under the lone tree, and Frederick joined her.

He watched her as she took the food out of the basket. "Is anything wrong?"

Her smile faltered. "No, everything is good."

He almost pressed her by saying he noticed she hadn't wanted those men to see her, but that might have sounded accusatory. And he might have imagined it anyway. He had liked the way she held on to his arm and walked close to his side. Just thinking about it made his heart expand in his chest.

She handed him a small meat pie he could hold in one hand, and she took one out for herself.

They ate and talked about the wildflowers around them, about the new house he'd be living in, what they thought of Hagenheim, and the doors he would be carving.

"Tell me some more about yourself," he said. "Do you live at home and help your mother? Or do you work somewhere?"

"I help my mother sometimes, at Hagenheim Castle."

"You work at the castle?"

She smiled and shrugged her shoulders. "I don't do much work, except embroider and paint. But my mother does a lot of things there."

"That can't be true. You made all this food, and it's very good."

"No, I don't know how to cook. I'd like you to think that I am a servant at the castle, but the truth is, sometimes I feel so useless." Her eyes looked so sad, he wanted to hug her.

"Why not sell your embroidery and your paintings? Or do embroidery work for Duke Wilhelm's household? I'm sure the duchess or her daughters would have need of your skill."

"Perhaps that is true." She smiled.

"Of course. Women love embroidery on their dresses. My sisters love it, and my mother sometimes does it for them since they don't have the patience." He didn't want to complain about his sisters to Adela, but he could have mentioned a lot more than just lack of patience. Lack of initiative or diligence. Lack of consideration for their mother. But their father had taught them to criticize and scoff at their mother. They'd had no other example of how to treat her other than his.

She asked him about his farmwork, and he told her about the tasks he liked the most. He told her about birthing calves, about his horses, and about how he knew when to plant and harvest. Was he talking too much about things a young woman would never care about?

But she kept her eyes on his face and constantly changed her expression, so she seemed interested.

"When it's nearly time for the sun to set," he said, "I like the way the sun shines on the wheat and the hay. It's very peaceful."

"I like sunsets," she said. "I would imagine this hill is a very good place to see a sunset."

"Would you like to meet back here tonight?" Frederick held his breath. Would she think he was asking for too much?

She smiled and gazed up into his eyes. "I would like that. But I don't think I can get away from home at that hour. I am sorry."

"I understand." He ran his hand through his hair.

"No, I . . ." Her eyes narrowed. She lifted her hand and almost touched his forehead. "Is that a cut? It looks bruised."

He brought his hand up to block her view. How could he have let her see that? He should have made sure his hair covered it. "It's just a little cut and bruise. Nothing at all." He pulled his hair to fall down over his forehead.

"How did you get it? It almost looks like a horse kicked you."

If only that was what had happened. "No, it wasn't a horse." What should he say? He couldn't tell her the truth—that his father was in a rage and threw a grooming brush at him.

She was still staring at him, her eyes wide with concern, waiting for him to explain. He couldn't tell her the truth, but he also couldn't lie to her and say he fell down steps or ran into a wall.

"I will tell you one day, but I would rather talk about pleasant things today."

She gazed back at him with such kindness. "I'm sorry for what happened. I hope you are well."

His heart filled his chest. She had such a look of innocence and gentleness about her, he imagined she'd only ever been treated well and knew nothing of raging fathers who threw grooming brushes with the intent to injure. He wasn't ready to tell her about his own. He didn't want her to think of him as a lowly person from a bad family. And though he was starting to hope she would someday have tender feelings for him, he did not want her to feel sorry for him.

They fell silent, having eaten until they were both full. He searched his mind for something to say, but she spoke first. "Would you like to go horseback riding sometime?"

"I would. Do you have a horse?" he asked.

"I have a horse I can ride."

"Can you meet me tomorrow at the gate at one hour past noon?"

"Yes, I think I can do that."

"I will have to begin my job soon, but I still have five days left before I must return to the Cathedral to begin working."

"And I'm sure you will need to get away, for inspiration, every so often." Her eyes were bright, as if she was happy she had thought of that.

"Of course." The easy, friendly feeling between them was back. "And you will want to get away from your daily tasks on occasion. Would you sometimes come to the Cathedral to keep me company while I work? Perhaps you could paint."

"I would like that very much. I think I could learn some things from you. In fact, I was thinking . . . Do you make your own paint for painting your carvings?"

"I do."

"Could you teach me how to make a brighter red? I am having trouble getting just the right color."

"It would be my pleasure."

Adela glanced over her shoulder. Two young women were walking by them with an identical basket to the one Adela had brought. One was Erma, Adela's friend he had met earlier. She and the other woman were staring at them, smiling. Adela faced forward again, her cheeks turning pink.

"Did you want them to join us?"

"Oh. No." Adela shook her head and her cheeks grew even redder. "They might say something embarrassing."

"They might tell all your secrets?"

She gave a little laugh but kept her eyes turned downward.

He reached out and touched her shoulder, causing her to look up. He longed to tell her that she was safe with him. He wanted her to tell him anything that might be on her mind, and yet . . . he had held back from telling her the truth about his injury and his father. But his desire to keep her safe prompted him to speak.

"You can trust me, Adela. Were you afraid of those men on horseback who passed through the gate with us earlier? Did one of them ever hurt you?"

Her brows drew together. She shook her head. "No. No, nothing like that. My father is very protective and I did not want . . . word to get back to him that I . . . was not with my mother." After a pause, she added, "One of the soldiers was my brother."

Ah, so that was the trouble. "Your father would not approve of you spending time with a strange man."

"I am sure he would like you if he met you. But . . . Forgive me."

"I understand. If I had a beautiful daughter, I would be protective too."

She blushed and smiled, glancing up at him. He was certain he'd never seen a prettier maiden, and yet she blushed at being called beautiful. His heart missed a few beats.

They talked about their creative endeavors—his carvings and her painting and embroidery—and what they hoped to do in the future. She spoke with excitement about his carving the Cathedral doors in a way that made him want to get closer to her, tell her more of his thoughts.

He in turn encouraged her to keep painting what she loved and to ask the duke if she could paint his family.

"I think I need to practice painting other families' portraits first. I have only done a few."

He did wish he could see her paintings. Perhaps someday she would allow him to come to her home and see her work.

When they finally rose and started walking slowly down the hill toward town, Adela let him carry the basket, and then she took his arm. His heart lifted into his throat at her touch, at having her walk beside him. And when they reached the house where he and his family would be living—thanks to her—she turned toward him and put her arms around him.

"Thank you for a lovely picnic," she said softly next to his ear.

He embraced her in return, but he was careful to be gentle and chivalrous. He was a little surprised at how long she held on to him, but he enjoyed every moment of it as he breathed in the flowery smell of her hair. She was quite a bit shorter than he was, but her chin seemed to fit perfectly against his shoulder.

She pulled away without looking him in the eye. "Fare well." And she hurried away.

CHAPTER 11

The next day Adela met Frederick at the gate again. He sat tall in the saddle, and her heart tripped. He looked so powerful and in command on his horse, and yet his hands were skilled enough to carve something beautiful and meaningful, delicate and brilliant.

Adela led her horse by its bridle. She knew none of Father's guards would let her leave the stable with a horse, and they'd never accept a bribe. So she'd sneaked into the stable, saddled her horse herself, and had Erma lure the guard and groom away from the stable on the pretense of helping her find a lost bracelet in the nearby well. Adela had stolen the idea from a story her sister Margaretha had told her, something that happened between her and her now-husband, Colin.

Thankfully, there was only one groom and one guard, and they'd followed Erma to the well. While they were leaned over, staring into the well, Adela had slipped out with her horse.

She and Frederick rode up the hill outside the gate, and she realized Frederick was taking her to the same avenue of trees where she always rode with Barthold. But she said nothing. After all, what were the chances that Barthold would ride through there when she wasn't with him?

As they rode together in companionable quiet, she suddenly imagined Frederick as the son of a duke. If he, instead of Barthold, had presented her with a jeweled necklace and asked her to marry him, would she have had a different reaction? Even though she'd only spent a few hours with him, she might have said yes to Frederick—if he were a duke's son instead of a farmer's son and wood-carver. What a shame that Barthold and he could not trade places in life.

The thought made her heart heavy.

She thrust the sad thought away as they talked about the birds they could hear, about the trees around them, about nothing and everything. Then they sat beside the stream and Adela told him stories about her childhood adventures with her brothers and sisters, careful not to reveal anything that would identify them as the duke's children. Thankfully, Frederick didn't seem too knowledgeable about the Duke of Hagenheim and his family.

Frederick told stories of his own childhood, and she soon gathered that his father was not the kind of father she had been blessed to have.

She asked him questions, drawing him out, until finally he admitted, "My father is not kind to us, especially when he is drinking. My sisters stay away from him when he is in a bad temper, and sometimes I have had to step in and save my mother."

"Even as a child?"

He took a deep breath. "I shouldn't tell you about that. I don't want to make you sad."

She reached out and squeezed his upper arm. Hard and unyielding, the muscles under the linen of his shirt surprised her and sent her heart thumping. She could well imagine him being able to protect his mother.

"I am sorry you endured that. My sister's husband had a cruel father who killed his mother by pushing her down the stairs." She hoped he wouldn't make the connection to her brother-in-law Sir Gerek of Keiterhafen.

Frederick's face grew grimmer. "That is evil. Men like that don't deserve wives."

"I just thought you should know you're not alone. And I know that, like Gerek, you would never hurt anyone."

"I wouldn't, except, perhaps, in defending someone." He looked her in the eye, and she suddenly wanted to hug him again.

"Thank you for telling me about your father. I'm glad you don't mind telling me about yourself, even the sad things."

"I hope you will feel just as open with me." He stared hard at her.

Her stomach churned queasily. How would he feel when he realized she hadn't been open at all about who she was and where she came from? But she couldn't tell him now. It was too soon. She had to make certain that he wouldn't think she was spoiled and rich and only playing a game with him. But what *was* she doing with him?

"You make me want to be open with you, to tell you about myself. And I'm sorry I haven't taken you to my home to meet my family. Perhaps you won't like me when you do meet them."

"That cannot be. I would never judge you by your family. And your family sounds good, almost perfect."

She smiled at him, her heart so torn. Frederick was a good friend. She loved spending time with him and talking to him, but how could they stay friends? Sometimes, by the tender look on his face, she wondered if he was falling in love with her. And sometimes, when she actually deceived herself and thought for a moment that she was a peasant girl, she wondered if she was falling in love with him.

But marrying him was not possible.

His voice became a bit low and gruff when he said, "You are an amazing woman, Adela. Spending time with you makes me happy."

Her heart soared out of her chest. But the next moment tears filled her eyes. Because she was not a peasant girl. She was a duke's daughter. And she was going to hurt this good man. And, very likely, break her own heart too.

But she had to say something, so she said, "Your friendship makes me happy too." But even as she said it, she knew she didn't feel only friendship for Frederick.

He gave her a long, serious look, as if searching her heart through her eyes. *He knows. He knows I am falling in love with him. God, help me.*

Neither of them spoke as they made their way out of the trees and onto a pasture of sheep. Then they began to talk about the mountains in the distance, their favorite wildflowers, and their favorite memories about horses. When they finally turned to go back toward town, she felt so comfortable with him, she kept smiling at him, and he did the same, as if they shared some secret between them.

When they reached the gate, they both dismounted. She embraced him again, but this time they kept their arms around each other even longer than before.

"Thank you, Adela," he said, his voice taking on that hoarse tone again, his breath ruffling her hair by her cheek. "I'm so thankful I met you."

She squeezed him tight, wishing she could stay like this forever, with his arms around her, his voice in her ear, and his warmth surrounding her. But it was wrong. A pang pierced her chest.

She wanted to say, "I'm so happy I met you too, Frederick," but the lump in her throat prevented her from speaking.

She pulled away and her eyes met his. The feelings were so intense, she had to turn away. As she did, her hand trailed along his arm, so reluctant to leave him. Then his hand clasped hers and he squeezed it before letting go.

"Fare well, Adela."

She turned just long enough to say, "Fare well," then hurried back to the stable to return her horse.

❧

Adela's heart was like a heavy boulder in her chest as she left her horse at the stable—to surprised stares from the groomsmen, since they had not seen her take the horse—and headed back toward the castle. Her mind churned with guilty thoughts of Frederick and Barthold and her deception. What would Barthold think if he saw the way she had embraced Frederick today?

And poor Frederick. What if he fell in love with her? He thought she was a peasant girl whose mother worked at the castle.

A guard stood at the door to the castle. He opened it for her. Her head was down as she entered, and she ran right into a man, her feet bumping into his. She reeled back, and his hand grabbed her shoulders, steadying her.

"Oh, forgive me," she said quickly. "I wasn't looking where I was going."

Barthold's face loomed above her. "Lady Adela. Why are you dressed . . . like that?"

His gaze moved up and down her as he held her at arm's length.

Adela felt her cheeks stinging. She stared up at him, hoping he might say something to save her from having to answer, but he only stared back.

"I . . . I went on an outing . . . with a friend. I didn't want anyone to recognize me—it's safer if no one knows who I am—so I borrowed my servant's clothes. Please don't tell anyone."

He raised his brows and didn't speak for a moment. Finally, he said, "I was wondering if you'd be willing to take a ride with me tomorrow."

Thank You, God, that he isn't asking me any questions.

"Yes, of course. I'd be happy to take a ride with you." But immediately her stomach sank. So soon after riding with Frederick, it felt . . . duplicitous. As if she were doing something wrong. But she could not be. After all, she and Frederick were only friends, and he was not her suitor, though she loved spending time with him.

Still, the guilt feelings and tumultuous thoughts that had her so distracted earlier were even stronger now.

❧

Frederick's heart was full as he gathered his notes about his plans for the Cathedral doors and made his way through town toward the *Hagenheimer Dom*, its spire rising above the buildings around it.

He was riding by the gate that led out of town, the same gate through which he and Adela had gone on their picnic. If he weren't going to meet the bishop, he might climb the hill and daydream about Adela, letting his thoughts linger on their conversations, the way her hair fell against her cheek, the way she held him so tight when they embraced. Instead, he kept moving forward.

After his meeting with the bishop, he'd take his horse to the blacksmith for a hoof grooming and new horseshoes.

Two more horses were coming his way. The man and woman would pass just behind him, but something about them caught his eye, making him turn in the saddle to look back.

The man was obviously someone wealthy, a self-important look on his face. He was the man Frederick had assumed was the son of the Duke of Grundelsbach when he'd seen him in the company of a knight and several soldiers. And the woman looked very much like . . . Adela.

But it couldn't be Adela. Adela was poor. Her mother worked in the castle. This young woman was wearing a wealthy woman's riding clothes.

His heart pounded as he recognized the horse—it was the same horse Adela had ridden with him. Everything about her looked like his Adela—same hair, same profile, same tilt of her head and shoulders.

Everyone knew the Duke of Grundelsbach's son was here in Hagenheim to court the Duke of Hagenheim's daughter. Could it be? Was Adela the Duke of Hagenheim's daughter?

A pain shot through his chest, so sharp he lost his breath. Why? Why had she pretended? Why treat him with such familiarity, talking so openly, embracing him so warmly, when she, a duke's daughter, would never think of marrying him? He was much too lowly for her. Why would she even talk to him, befriend him, pretend to like him?

No, it couldn't be her. It couldn't be.

His gaze followed her and her male companion through the gate and up the hill, but even as they passed him, he couldn't be sure if it was really Adela. His heart hurt just the same, thinking she might have duped him. Just as he had started to fall in love with her and to hope that she was falling for him.

He turned his horse and followed after them. They were going riding with no guards accompanying them, just as the Eselin brothers had told him.

Then he spotted Ditmar Eselin fifty feet away, looking sharp and sly as he waited for his brothers to catch up to him. Together they rode through the gate after the nobleman and lady.

Frederick's blood rushed through his limbs and spine.

That beautiful young woman might actually be his Adela, but whether she was or not, Frederick could not allow her to be terrorized by the Eselin brothers, possibly kidnapped and held for ransom.

He stopped at the gate and told the guards there, "The duke's daughter is in danger. Follow me."

Then Frederick urged his horse after the Eselin brothers.

Adela rode beside Lord Barthold, wishing she had already told him that she didn't want to marry him. How could she marry him when she was fairly certain that she would never love him? When she had tenderer thoughts and feelings for a wood-carver than she did for Barthold?

Today was the day she would tell Barthold that she did not want to waste any more of his time. She was certain that she did not want to marry him but wished him very well.

She stared straight ahead as she went over in her mind what she would say. Would Barthold be hurt? Angry? At least no one would be there to witness it, since he had once again dismissed the guards so they could be alone.

Barthold shifted in his saddle as they headed up the hill. Could he actually be nervous about being alone with her? She felt a pang through her middle at the thought of hurting him. He was not a bad person, and she didn't like hurting anyone. But she also couldn't marry someone she wasn't in love with. Better to tell him now, before he became more attached to her.

Their horses were approaching the avenue of trees. It looked darker today. Then she noticed the sky was overcast with fluffy white clouds.

Barthold led the way under the thick canopy of leaves. When they were nearly halfway through it, he stopped and turned toward her. There was a look in his eyes, reminiscent of when he'd given her the necklace. He opened his mouth to speak, then turned his head as if to look behind him.

A hissing sound erupted just before an arrow struck Barthold in the upper arm.

He let out a yelp, then a growl, as they were surrounded by men yelling at them, "Don't move if you want to live!"

A man with scraggly facial hair held a sword point to Barthold's chest.

Barthold's breath was raspy and loud, his face pale. Bright red blood oozed from the arrow shaft in the back of his shoulder.

One of the men grabbed her arm. Adela cried out. Her heart pounded so hard it seemed to drown out the men's voices.

Just as suddenly as he'd grabbed her, the man let go of her arm. He tumbled off his horse to the ground.

In the next instant another man swept Adela off her horse and placed her on his saddle in front of him. They were riding away before she could think.

She was sitting sidesaddle, staring up into Frederick's face. Where had he come from? Why was he in the woods? Had he been following them?

Her mind reeled, her thoughts spinning. "What is happening?"

An arrow hissed by them, just past Frederick's left arm.

Men's angry shouts came from behind them, but Frederick didn't stop or even look back. His arms were on either side of her, holding on to the reins. His body blocked her view—and kept her safe from any arrows.

She shrank against his chest and let him take her away from danger.

More voices sounded behind them, shouted orders, different from the others.

Frederick suddenly slowed and looked over his shoulder. He let go of the reins with one hand, allowing her to peek around him.

"What is happening?" she repeated, her heart still pounding.

Father's guards were holding the men who had attacked them down on the ground on their stomachs. Barthold was still atop his horse, the arrow still embedded in his shoulder. He looked furious, his face now red instead of pale, and she could see his mouth moving, though she couldn't hear what he was saying. Barthold pointed at them as Frederick turned the horse around and set his horse at a slow trot back toward them.

Now that Father's guards seemed to have eliminated the danger, her heart slowed. She looked up into Frederick's stony visage.

What must Frederick think of her? She hadn't meant for him to find out her identity like this. She leaned her back against his chest, and he finally looked down at her.

"Thank you for saving me." Her gaze locked on his mouth, and she suddenly wanted to kiss him. *Irresponsible thought.*

"When were you going to tell me you were the duke's daughter?"

"Soon. I was going to tell you soon." When he stared straight ahead and didn't speak, she said, "I'm sorry I deceived you. I didn't plan it. I just wanted to see the marketplace without the guards following me. I wanted to be a regular townsperson, and I met you and I didn't want you to think differently about me. I wanted you to judge me as you would any other woman."

He still didn't speak, and the guards had nearly reached them.

"Will you forgive me?"

"I forgive you." His expression bespoke pain, but suddenly softened as he gazed down at her. "I'm sorry too."

She searched her mind for what he might be sorry for, but one of Father's guards said, "Lady Adela, are you all right?"

"Yes, I'm perfectly—"

"Unhand her and let her down," the guard commanded Frederick.

"I know this man. His name is Frederick. He saved me." Adela made no move to get down, and Frederick kept the horse walking slowly forward, making no effort to remove her from his saddle.

The guards eyed Frederick suspiciously but said no more as they returned their attention to the ruffians on the ground.

One of the men lying on the ground—there were three of them—looked up, lifting his head as much as he could with the guard's knee in his back.

"Seize him too!" the man said in a strained voice. He was staring right at Frederick.

"What do you mean?" the guard asked.

"He is one of us! He knew all about our plans!"

"Yeah," another one of the captured men said. "His name is Frederick, and he was helping us."

Frederick's face was ashen. "That is a lie. I had no part in this."

The guards were all staring hard at Frederick. Adela's stomach dissolved to her toes and her head began to spin.

Several people were speaking at once. One of Father's guards reached up, and with a hand on either side of her waist, plucked her out of Frederick's saddle and set her feet on the ground.

Guards surrounded Frederick and ordered him to dismount. He slowly complied.

Was it true? Frederick would never hurt anyone. He was a woodcarver, a kind, gentle soul with the heart of an artist. He would never join with rough men like these. And yet . . . how did they know his name?

As the guards pinned his arms behind his back, she caught sight of a line of bright red and a rip in his shirt sleeve at his upper arm.

"Look at his arm! He's injured. If he was helping these men, then why did they shoot him?"

The guards looked doubtful suddenly, and the prisoners on the ground were silent.

"He saved me! He isn't one of them."

Then one of the ruffians said, "He was kidnapping the duke's daughter but then realized he couldn't get away. He's one of us, I tell you."

"I am not!" Frederick's jaw was tight as a muscle twitched in his cheek.

But if Frederick was not part of their scheme, how had they known his name? And more importantly, why else would he have told her, "I'm sorry"?

CHAPTER 12

Frederick's shoulders burned as the duke's guards yanked his hands behind his back. He turned his head so he could see Adela's face.

"I was not part of this scheme. These men are from the same area as me and—"

"You can tell it to the duke!" The leader of the guards spoke in a loud, angry voice, and someone shoved Frederick in the back as they started in the direction of the castle.

The guard's voice was much gentler as he addressed Adela. "My lady, this is no place for you. Go with Lord Barthold back to the castle. We shall take charge of these prisoners."

Adela's eyes were shimmering with tears, and one dripped down her cheek. Her gaze met Frederick's and her lips trembled. But she quickly turned and rode away with Lord Barthold.

His heart ached as if it would burst through his chest. *Dear God, what have I done?* He should have told someone of the Eselin brothers' schemes. If he had, this never would have happened. And yet there was another reason for this pain.

Adela. Why had she deceived him? She was the daughter of the most powerful man in the region. What could she possibly think of him? He was a farmer's son, and now his dream of becoming a wood-carver was seriously in jeopardy. Why had she deceived him, and why would she play with his emotions this way? Whatever the reason, what hurt the most was that his hopes had been destroyed that she could one day be his.

And now he was being herded along with the Eselin brothers to the duke's dungeon.

What would the bishop think when he was told his wood-carver, the man entrusted with carving the doors for the sacred and hallowed Hagenheim Cathedral, had been captured while trying to kidnap the duke's daughter?

Despair gripped him like giant icy fingers around his middle. If only it were just a bad dream. But the angry, disconsolate looks on the Eselin brothers' faces, the bloody scratch from the arrow that grazed him, and the guards roughly pushing him were all too real.

❦

Adela let the tears drip down her cheeks. Horror at Barthold's pain, the ugly arrow shaft protruding from his shoulder, mingled with the hollowed-out feeling in her gut. Had Frederick betrayed her? Was he a kidnapper? Or was he a victim too? And if he was innocent, would he ever forgive her for deceiving her?

She suddenly couldn't bear to think of him in the dungeon. She would go to him and make him explain everything. But for now, with all of Father's guards surrounding them, she had no choice but to obey orders and leave Frederick to his fate.

"Who was that man?" Barthold growled out the words through clenched teeth.

"What man?" But she knew who he was talking about.

"That man who took you on his horse. You went with him willingly. I saw you. You know him."

"I don't like the tone you are using with me. But yes, I have met him. He's the Bishop of Hagenheim's personal wood-carver, and I don't believe he was a part of those evil men's scheme to harm us."

Barthold stared hard at her. Then he faced forward.

"But don't mind that. Now we must get you to the healer and tend your wound. Let us hurry."

His face was scrunched and tense. Was it more because of his pain? Or from his anger that she would dare to defend Frederick?

People gasped, stopped, and stared at Barthold as they passed. He urged his horse into a faster walk until they finally reached the castle. Adela hastily dismounted and showed Barthold the way to the healer's tower chambers.

Accompanying him inside, Adela had never been so happy to see anyone as Frau Lena, who hurried into the room and focused her eyes on Barthold's injured shoulder. She took charge, telling him where to sit and to brace himself.

When Adela realized Frau Lena was about to extricate the arrow, she turned and fled from the room. She had to find Father anyway and tell him about Frederick.

She rushed to his library. Thankfully, he was sitting in his chair, bent over some papers on his desk.

"Father, something has happened."

Before she could say any more, a guard came in behind her. "Your Grace, something has occurred that requires your attention."

Father stood, his eyes calm but attentive. He acknowledged his guard with a quick nod, then looked hard at Adela. "Are both of these 'somethings' the same?"

"Yes, Father. Lord Barthold and I were attacked by three men."

"Are you all right?" Father took a step toward her.

"I am well, but Barthold was shot in the shoulder."

Father put a hand on her arm, then hugged her. How good and

safe was his embrace. But he let go as he turned to the guard who had entered the room. She wished she could bury her face in her father's chest and breathe out all the bad feelings she'd just experienced, but he'd already stepped away.

"Your Grace," the guard went on, "we have apprehended four men we believe were involved."

Adela's stomach knotted all over again.

"Put them all in the dungeon. I will need to speak to Adela and Lord Barthold first."

"Yes, sir." The guard turned on his heel and left.

"Tell me everything that happened." Father's face was rigid, even angry.

Still conflicted about Frederick, Adela told of how she and Barthold had gone riding alone, about the three men attacking them, and about Frederick saving her. She told of the others' accusations that Frederick was in on their scheme.

"But I don't believe he knew anything of it, Father. He would never be involved with people like those evil men who shot Barthold. He saved me from them."

Father's eyes looked sharp and shrewd. "Who is this Frederick? How do you know him?"

"He is the man to whom you are letting Grandfather's old house."

"I see. You told me you knew of this man through the bishop. Was that true?"

"I said I knew of him, but the truth is . . ." Her stomach trembled as she realized her father was about to be disappointed in her. "I met Frederick in the *Marktplatz* a fortnight ago."

"What were you doing in the *Marktplatz*? Who was with you?"

"I was alone. Forgive me, Father, but I just wanted to get away for an hour. I wanted to feel what it was like to be a townsperson, seeing things through other people's eyes, without everyone looking at me like I was different."

"But you are different, Adela."

Father's voice had that hard edge to it, reminding her of how he used to speak to Steffan sometimes, or to his guards when they had displeased him. She'd never heard that tone when he was talking to her. Tears pricked her eyes.

"You are my daughter, and that puts you at risk, as you very well know. Lord Barthold had no right to take you out without the guards, but to think of you wandering around the streets without anyone, even a servant . . ." Father turned away from her, rubbing his hand over his face like he did when he was tired.

A tear slid down her cheek. She wiped it away quickly. She deserved his rebuke. And how selfish and spoiled to cry for herself when Barthold was injured and Frederick was being thrown in the dungeon, wrongfully—probably.

"I'm sorry, Father. But Frederick . . . Please don't leave him in the dungeon if he is innocent."

"And why did the guards think he was guilty? We cannot assume he is innocent because you think he seems a decent fellow. Adela, you've never been out in the world. You don't know how deceitful people can be."

Another tear slipped out. Adela flicked it away and nodded. "I know, Father."

He turned and took a step toward her. He laid his hand on her shoulder. "Don't cry, *Liebling*. I'll examine him and the other men and get to the truth. But we have to talk about this some more, with your mother present."

"Do we have to tell Mother?" Her chin trembled at the thought of Mother's disappointment and the pain it would bring up, thinking of Adela walking alone in the *Marktplatz* after what had happened to Kirstyn, how she had been kidnapped from the street.

"Yes, we have to tell her. I'm sorry, Adela, but this is serious."

She stood with her head down, trying to think of what to say, what to do. "Will you let me talk to Frederick in the dungeon?"

"Absolutely not."

"Then will you talk to him, right away?"

"I will talk with him in due time. I will not rush through this process. If that young man was involved in a scheme to harm you and Lord Barthold, he will be punished, and very severely, as he will deserve."

Her throat ached, but she only nodded. "May I go to my bedchamber?"

"Yes. Shall I send Mother to you?"

Adela nodded and hurried out, praying not to see anyone on her way to her room.

◈

Frederick sat on the stone floor of the dungeon, his wrist and one ankle chained to the wall. His head in his hands, he attempted to pray.

What had led to him sitting on the cold dungeon floor? Listening to the Eselin brothers' schemes? His decision to save Adela from them?

He should have gone to Hagenheim Castle as soon as he heard of the Eselins' first scheme to steal the bride money from the Duke of Grundelsbach. He should have begged an audience with Duke Wilhelm and revealed the facts to him, even if he didn't think them capable of carrying out the scheme, especially after the Eselins told him of their plan to kidnap his daughter. Was he just as complicit for not doing so? Did he deserve to rot in this dungeon?

He had dismissed their request for his help, hadn't he? And the truth was, he hadn't believed the Eselins capable of even a bumbling attempt to follow through with their evil, ambitious plans. If he'd truly believed anyone was in danger from them, he would have told the duke.

But that was not a good enough excuse, and he knew it.

"O God, what have I done?" He'd ruined his life, just when he was about to be happy. And when he thought of his sweet Adela . . . He groaned. He'd truly liked her, very much. He'd even begun to think of asking to meet her father, thinking he might ask to marry her.

But Adela would never be his wife. How absurd even to think of it, now that he knew she was the daughter of the Duke of Hagenheim, a man whose power and name were known throughout the Holy Roman Empire.

He ground the heels of his hands into his eyes. And the Bishop of Hagenheim. Was his opportunity lost forever, an opportunity that had seemed almost too good to be true?

Noisy metal hinges indicated a door opening as footfalls echoed from the stairs. He lifted his head to see if someone was coming to speak to him.

He was all alone in this large open chamber with one torch flickering on the wall. The Eselin brothers had been taken elsewhere—he wasn't sure where—and he could at least be grateful he didn't have to talk to, hear, or see them.

The footsteps drew near. One man was in the lead, and by his dress and age, he was probably the duke, with two guards behind him.

"Frederick? Is that your name?"

"Yes." Frederick's chains clanked and rattled as he stood to his feet. The guards stepped forward and released him from the shackles.

"I wish to ask you some questions."

The guards each took him by an arm, and they followed the man he presumed was Duke Wilhelm.

They went inside a doorway on the same floor of the dungeon. It was a small room with a window very high up, lit by several candles. There were a few stools, but no one sat down.

"For what purpose did you go outside the town gate today?" the duke asked, his voice hard, his expression angry.

"Because I saw the Eselins following Lord Barthold and Adela— Lady Adela—out of the town gate."

Duke Wilhelm's eyes pierced him through. But the eyes did remind him a little bit of Adela, even though hers were always soft and gentle.

"Did you know these Eselin brothers' intention was to harm them?"

"Yes." His chest ached at the confession.

"How did you know?"

Frederick did his best to explain his relationship to the Eselins, that they had grown up near each other, that he'd been privy to their foolish schemes and pranks over the years, but they'd seemed relatively harmless. "I never imagined they could actually accomplish what they were scheming, or that real harm would come to your daughter or Lord Barthold at their hands."

"If that's how you felt, then why did you follow them?"

That was a fair question. Frederick sighed. "I saw the looks on their faces, and I . . ." His heart raced as he remembered seeing Adela, realizing who she was, and seeing the evil looks on the Eselin brothers' faces. "I was afraid they might hurt Adela."

Duke Wilhelm's brows lowered, his eyes narrowing. "So you were in on their scheme, ready to attack, until you realized Lady Adela was the girl you met in town."

"No! That is not true. I was never—I told the Eselins I was not interested in helping them. I never planned to be a part of this or anything else. I told them that they should not attempt it at all. But

I know I was wrong not to come to you, Your Grace, and tell you of their schemes. That is my sin."

"And my daughter? What were your intentions toward her? If you have molested her in any way—"

"Never! I would never behave improperly toward her, and I did not know she was your daughter. She did not tell me, and I had no way of knowing. I . . ." He took a breath as a pain stabbed his heart. "I did not know the girl I met in the *Marktplatz* was your daughter. But I never would have attacked her, or Lord Barthold, or anyone else for that matter. I was on my way to see the bishop. I—"

"You are complicit. You knew of their scheme and said nothing."

"Yes, it is true." Frederick lowered his face to his hands. "O God."

"Those Eselin brothers might have killed Lord Barthold. If they are so incompetent as you say, then how did they manage to injure a fighting man, trained as a knight, and nearly kidnap my daughter?"

Frederick lifted his head. Duke Wilhelm's face had grown darker and more intense as he leaned toward him.

"I am more surprised than anyone, Your Grace. And I am sick at the thought . . ." His voice had grown hoarse and raspy. "If anything had happened to Adela, I never could have forgiven myself."

"*Lady* Adela."

Frederick's stomach sank to the floor. The duke was not giving him any clemency.

"I will have to inform Bishop Werner about this."

Frederick stared straight ahead, doing his best to go numb.

"And I will continue my questioning later." The duke moved toward the doorway and spoke to his guards. "Now I shall question the Eselin brothers and see what their story is."

"Please, sir—Your Grace."

The duke stopped and looked at him.

"Your daughter, Lady Adela . . . She believes me, does she not? She knows I would never—"

"She is not your concern."

The pain in his chest was almost unbearable.

"I suggest you spend your time praying the truth comes out, if you are as innocent as you say."

Frederick was numb as the guards took hold of his arms and led him back to his shackles, fastening him once again to the stone wall.

CHAPTER 13

～

Adela cried for an hour in her mother's room before going back to her own bedchamber. Mother had cried as well when she heard what Adela had done in sneaking away to the *Marktplatz*. But she'd forgiven her and they'd discussed her relationship with Frederick.

"We are only friends," Adela said. "But he's an artist like me. He understands me and understands how I think. He's a good man, and I can't bear to think of him in the dungeon. He rescued me!"

"Father will discover the truth, darling. Don't worry." Mother's expression turned grave. "But are you sure you are only friends? Frederick was getting to know you without knowing who you really are. He may have been falling in love with you. And I'm not so sure you were not falling in love with him as well."

Adela shook her head. It wasn't true, was it? Had they been falling in love? But surely not, not so soon. So why did her breath hitch and her chin start to tremble? Adela pressed her fingers to her lips to still them and took in another breath.

"I know I could not marry a poor man, a man without servants." The thought of her cooking and cleaning and caring for her own children seemed terrifying and . . . not romantic at all.

"Not only that, but you have not known this young man long enough to know his true character."

"I know his character better than I know Barthold's. He's kind-hearted and gentle. He tells me how he feels about things. Barthold never tells me anything about how he feels. I don't even know what he thinks of his brothers and sisters, his mother and father. Frederick is open and honest and—"

"And yet he knew those young men who attacked you and shot Barthold. That does not sound like he's been spending time with people of good character. 'Bad company corrupts good character.'"

Adela had heard that Scripture passage before. "But, Mother, you are condemning him before you know the truth."

"I am only cautioning you to reserve judgment until *you* know the truth."

Perhaps Mother was right. She couldn't know everything about Frederick yet. She'd only seen and talked with him a few times. But was it wrong to trust the way she felt? The way he made her feel when she was with him? Safe and happy and understood?

When Adela was back in her bedchamber, she lay across her bed, remembering how it felt when Frederick held her on the saddle in front of him, his arm like a steel band around her middle, his solid chest pressed against her back. She'd never felt more secure.

She did have feelings that were more than friendship. Even thoughts of screaming children and shelling peas were not enough to make her stop wishing Frederick could hold her again, could reassure her that everything would be all right, that she would see him again, and that he wasn't lost to her forever.

He had rescued her, had snatched her off her horse, out of the hands of those rough bandits, and taken her to safety at great risk to himself. She couldn't stop thinking about it, how strong he was, and the tender way he'd looked at her, even though he was hurt that she had deceived him about who she was.

He must be so aggrieved in the dungeon, feeling deceived by her and punished when he'd done nothing wrong. How could Father leave him there when he knew he was probably innocent? When, instead of trying to kidnap her, he'd only been trying to help her?

She simply couldn't bear it.

She jumped up and took off her dress. She found Erma's dress stuffed into a chest. She put it on, covered her hair with a kerchief, and quickly left the room.

She was careful to avoid notice as she made her way down to the dungeon. How to bribe the guard in charge of the dungeon? That was the problem. But when she got to the top of the dungeon stairs, there was no guard. She heard male voices around the corner, starting to get louder, so she hurried down the steps before they could see her. The stone staircase was so dark she had to keep her hand on the wall to keep from falling.

When she knew she was out of sight of any guards who may have arrived at the top of the stairs, Adela proceeded more slowly, letting her eyes adjust to the dim light.

Her breath shallowed at the thought of seeing Frederick again. And as she reached the bottom of the stairs, she saw someone fastened to the wall in the rather large open room.

She approached him quietly. Whoever he was, he hadn't noticed her. His head was resting on his hands, which were on his knees. He still didn't move. The thick brown hair on the bowed head, the broad shoulders, all revealed this man to be Frederick.

She stopped a few feet away, her heart breaking inside her chest. It was not Frederick who had done something terrible. It was she. She had gotten him arrested because she was the duke's daughter and hadn't told Frederick the truth. If she had, he could have warned her and he would not be here now, chained to a wall.

~❦~

Frederick prayed, obeying the duke as best he could, but his thoughts were so scattered. If only he had told someone, the bishop or the duke or even just one of the duke's guards, about the Eselin brothers.

If only Adela had told him she was the duke's daughter. He would have been sad, disappointed, but he probably would have remembered the Eselins' schemes and he could have warned her.

He moaned and lifted his head, rubbing a hand down his face as he opened his eyes.

Was he dreaming? Or was that Adela standing in front of him?

She dropped to her knees and caught hold of his arm. The torchlight sparkled on a tear as it ran from her eye down her cheek.

"You shouldn't be here." Frederick pulled away, pressing his back against the rock wall and making his chains rattle.

"I'm sorry I didn't tell you who I was." She didn't let go of his arm, even though he moved away from her.

His heart ached. His chance to work on the Cathedral doors was probably gone forever, but he still longed to hold her in his arms and reassure her. Of course, that was foolish. What would the duke do to him if he caught her there? If he saw Frederick touching her? He'd hang Frederick from the highest scaffold.

"You didn't know about those men, did you? That they were scheming to kidnap me?" Her eyes were intense as she stared at him. She leaned even closer, her hands still clasping his arm.

"I . . . I'm sorry, Adela. I never dreamed they would harm anyone, and certainly not you." He could almost feel her soft skin as he imagined brushing the tear from her cheek. "But when I saw them follow after you and Lord Barthold . . . I would have done anything to protect you."

She scooted closer to him, and he stretched out his legs, causing the ankle chain to rattle. Adela laid her head against his upper arm, pressing her cheek against his shirt sleeve.

His heart raced. He reached out with his other hand, making that chain rattle as well. He pulled her closer, and she laid her head on his chest, his arms around her back.

How good it felt to hold her, her body pressed against his, innocently comforting each other. He placed a hand on the back of her head. Her hair was so silky. Did she know how much he cared for her? Even though it was daft and thoughtless, he wanted to tell her.

"I'm so glad you weren't hurt." Thanks be to God, Frederick had been there and seen what was about to happen. His heart expanded at the gratifying memory of pulling her off her horse and onto his. Holding her now felt even better. And it made him think of how his father treated his mother, with contempt and even cruelty. He couldn't imagine how his father could strike the woman who loved him.

"Thank you for saving me." Adela snuggled closer, her arms moving, one hand coming to rest on his side, her other hand resting on his chest. "I'm so sorry," she whispered. "Will you forgive me, Frederick?"

"I forgive you. Will you forgive me? I would never hurt you, Adela. Never."

"I know you wouldn't."

Neither of them moved for a long time. If only he could hold her forever, feel her face pressed to his chest, his arms around her. But she shouldn't even be here.

"Your father doesn't know you're here?"

"No. But it's my fault, my fault that you're in this dungeon." Her voice was muffled against his chest.

"It's not your fault. It's the Eselin brothers' fault."

"If I had told you who I was . . ."

"Why didn't you tell me?" He didn't want to make her feel worse than she already did, but he needed to know.

"I don't know. I just wanted to move about and see the town as anyone else might. I wanted people—you—to see me for who I really was, apart from my position and wealth. I wanted to talk to you as one artist to another, one person to another. If you knew I was the duke's daughter, you would see me as someone who was sheltered, who couldn't see the world the way you saw it, and I couldn't bear it." She looked into his eyes. "I was afraid you would not be open and natural with me if you knew who I was."

She was right about that. He never would have allowed himself to care for her, much less fall in love with her, had he known who she was. And now, if he didn't start seeing her as a duke's daughter, the thing she had feared, he would surely get his heart broken. But how could he push her away? The way she was looking at him made his heart beat double time. Made him wish he could kiss her full on the lips.

A dangerous thought indeed.

"My parents are so angry with me for what I did, for leaving the castle without a guard."

"They won't beat you, will they?"

"Beat me? No." She caressed his cheek with her fingers, so soft, then buried her face in his chest again. "I won't let Father hurt you. I promise. I'll do whatever I have to do to protect you."

He caressed her shoulder. He shouldn't be touching her, but he didn't care what the duke did to him. It would be worth it, this feeling of tenderness, as she leaned into him. He could feel her drawing in a shaky deep breath, then sighing. That sound sent an ache through his chest.

"Don't worry. Somehow I'll get out of this." He hoped.

Her head was just beneath his chin. He bent and kissed her hair, thinking she wouldn't know what he'd done. But then she lifted her head and he found himself staring into her eyes, her face very close to his. She drew herself up, leaned toward him, and pressed her lips to his.

He took her face in his hands and kissed her, one very sweet kiss that turned his heart inside out. He pulled back just enough that their eyes met again. The connection was so strong, as if their souls were meeting in the blue depths of her eyes. Then her eyelids dropped low and she moved forward to kiss him again.

The sound of guards' voices and footsteps broke over his senses. He groaned.

He allowed the briefest kiss, then held her by her arms. He whispered, "You have to go. The guards are coming."

She looked dazed, blinked, then seemed to hear the guards approaching.

He helped her up. She threw her hood over her head and ran toward the steps, but that was where the guards were coming from. He clenched his fists. What would they do when they saw her? If they tried to hurt her . . . She might not tell them she was the duke's daughter. But to protect her, he'd tell them, even if it meant she got in trouble with her father.

If only he wasn't chained up like a dog.

But as she approached the steps, she went underneath them and crouched low, hiding in the shadows.

When the guards reached the bottom, Duke Wilhelm was with them. As they made their way forward to another part of the dungeon, Adela emerged from under the stairs and hurried silently away.

She stopped on the third step and looked at him. He just stared back, wishing he could see her eyes, but it was too dark. Neither of them spoke, and then she continued up the steps and out of sight.

⁓⁂⁓

At the top of the dungeon steps, Adela could see out of the corner of her eye that a guard was looking at her. She quickened her pace.

"Hey, you! Fraulein," he called.

Practically running to the steps that led to her bedchamber, Adela took them two at a time, her heart pounding. She listened for the guard behind her but heard nothing as she reached the top and ran down the corridor to her bedchamber, opening and closing the door as swiftly as she could.

Trying to catch her breath, she stood at the door, listening and waiting. At least a minute passed, her breaths slowing and her heart no longer hurting her chest but continuing to thump erratically, and still no guard.

Adela lay across her bed and closed her eyes, reliving Frederick's kiss. Perhaps it was wrong to kiss him. She really shouldn't have done it, and she felt a pang through her stomach at what her mother would say to her. But obviously she did have tender feelings for Frederick. And she couldn't make herself regret the kiss. It had been innocent enough, and *she* had been the one to kiss *him*.

Her mother had warned her often enough that men might try to take advantage of her, try to kiss her, and more, and she was to be on her guard. But Frederick was not like that. Even when she sat on the floor leaning against his chest, his arms around her, he only tried to comfort her in his sweet, innocent way. And when she lifted her head, he could have kissed her, or done any number of things, and no one would have known. She'd put herself in a position of vulnerability by going into the dungeon, by being alone with him. But he didn't even try to kiss her then.

She had been so close to him, his lips so near—and she couldn't resist. Her stomach did a somersault as she remembered his response. For a moment he seemed to try not to kiss her back, but then . . . he took her face in his hands and . . . his fervency made her stomach do the now-familiar flip just remembering it. Thankfully, he'd heard the guards coming and ended the kiss.

The remembrance of his chains rattling hollowed her out all over again. "O God, please help him," she whispered. "Please don't leave him in the dungeon, and please don't let the bishop take away this opportunity."

A tear slipped from her eye. She wasn't sorry she kissed him. But what now?

She had to convince her father that Frederick hadn't done anything malicious. He hadn't meant for anything bad to happen, had never intended to join with the Eselin brothers at all. And when he saw that something bad might happen, he had intervened. Father would understand and even be grateful to him. Wouldn't he?

But thanks be to God for not allowing her father to see her in the dungeon! A couple of seconds of hesitation—of kissing Frederick—and he would have caught her. Or if he'd turned right instead of going straight at the bottom of the stairs . . . She didn't like to think what he would have said or done. He was a good and kind father. He never would have beaten her, as Frederick had feared, but he would have been angry, and she hated the pain of disappointing him. But worst of all, he might have taken his anger out on Frederick by not listening to her pleas for his release.

She sat up in bed. She had to cease these silly tears and go talk to her father. But what would happen when Frederick was let go? Even if he was cleared of any wrongdoing, her father would probably never allow her to see him again. And could she even live as a wood-carver's wife?

She tried to imagine it, living in a house with Frederick and his mother and two sisters. It would be a typical life for the townspeople of Hagenheim.

Would just being with Frederick be enough? If they married, people would point at her and say, "She used to be the spoiled daughter of the Duke of Hagenheim. Her brother is the Earl of Hamlin, her other brothers are also powerful men, and her sisters are all married to important men of high position. But look at her." Would Frederick's pride be hurt? Would *her* pride be hurt?

Could she be the spoiled child people accused her of being? Whoever married Frederick would be the wife of a wood-carver who had carved the doors of the Hagenheim Cathedral. No doubt his skill would be in high demand after such an important job. Any woman would be proud of a husband like that—any woman whose sisters weren't married to knights and lords and wealthy aristocratic men. But Adela would be proud of him, and she would dare anyone to look down on her.

She closed her eyes and remembered his gentleness, the goodness that always shone out of his eyes, the tender way he held her in his arms.

If she was indeed falling in love with Frederick, and if he loved her, and if he was cleared of wrongdoing, could she stop caring what everyone said? Could she resign herself to a life without privilege? Would she be safe from evil men wanting to hold her for ransom without her father's guards to protect her?

Perhaps she should not have kissed Frederick. She didn't want to hurt him.

Her heart felt heavier than ever.

❧

"I don't trust that Frederick," Lord Barthold growled.

Duke Wilhelm stood in Frau Lena's chambers watching as the healer finished up her treatment of Lord Barthold's wounds. He'd live, but he was in a lot of pain, and he was angry. Rightfully so. No doubt his father, the Duke of Grundelsbach, would also be quite angry that his son had been thusly treated under Wilhelm's very nose.

But as Barthold admitted, he had taken Adela out without a single guard accompanying them. Foolish, even if he was hoping to speak with Adela about marrying him. With all the guards at Barthold's disposal, he could hardly blame Wilhelm for this breach and the subsequent consequences. Still, it was hard not to feel a little responsible, as the incident occurred on Hagenheim soil.

A high-pitched voice could be heard outside the chamber door. "Where is he? Where is Lord Barthold?"

Barthold's father's adviser, Lord Conrat, who had accompanied Barthold to Hagenheim, burst through the door. His eyes went to Barthold, and he sucked in a loud, dramatic breath. "What has happened? This is outrageous." He started asking Barthold questions. "An arrow? Who did this? Are you able to move your arm?"

"I am well," Barthold said gruffly. "Don't fuss over me like . . ." He let his voice trail off. "I don't know what happened. Some men came out of nowhere, and one shot me through the shoulder."

Everything was relatively clear, except for Frederick's role. Wilhelm explained it briefly for Conrat, but Barthold spoke up. "I think this man Frederick was in with them. He had no other reason for knowing about their scheme."

"The bishop says Frederick is an upright young man, very spiritual and conscientious. He doesn't believe he would have anything to do with harming you or Adela."

"I don't trust that man," Barthold reiterated. "He looked so sly when he was holding Adela on his horse. He is one of them, I tell you. He should not be set free."

Barthold was sweating, no doubt from the pain in his shoulder. And his opinion of Frederick was probably due more to jealousy than anything else. Wilhelm had seen the way his daughter spoke of the young wood-carver, the expression on her face. The young man did have a look of goodness and innocence, and he could imagine that a woman might find him handsome. But he was a peasant. Nothing good could come of their friendship. Nevertheless, Wilhelm had no wish to face his Maker and be told he had punished an innocent man.

Wilhelm assured both Lord Barthold and Lord Conrat he'd find out the truth, and he headed back to the dungeon. He wanted to question the three Eselin brothers. He had examined Frederick first, making the Eselins wait. Perhaps they'd be more prone to see the error of their ways after stewing in the dungeon for a few hours and be more apt to tell the truth about the wood-carver's role in the business.

Wilhelm's guards were waiting for him in the dungeon. They went down to the oldest Eselin brother's cell. He was still surly and angry but less so than when Wilhelm had observed him briefly when they'd first brought him in. Wilhelm stared hard at him. He could tell a lot about a man just by staring him down. He saw immaturity and fear in his eyes and in the way he fidgeted. Anyone who would waylay a man and woman and shoot a man from behind was no man, but a small, shriveled-up excuse for one.

"Who is Frederick to you?"

Ditmar Eselin snorted. He didn't speak for so long, Wilhelm nodded at his guard. The guard used the flat of his hand to slap the back of Ditmar's head.

"He's nobody. A peasant. His father's a drunk." He sneered, showing brown-stained teeth.

"Did he have anything to do with your plan to kidnap my daughter?"

Ditmar Eselin's eyes widened a bit. Perhaps he didn't realize he was the duke. His throat bobbed as he swallowed, but then his eyelids lowered and his jaw hardened. "Frederick knew all about it. But he betrayed us. He was supposed to take the lady to a safe location, but he lost his nerve at the last minute and decided to pretend to help her instead."

Wilhelm studied his face. No doubt this man was very well practiced in lying. But he could be telling the truth. And if he was, Wilhelm would never let Frederick near Adela again.

CHAPTER 14

Adela changed back into her own clothes and went down to her father's desk in the library. He wasn't there. When she asked his guards, they looked askance at her, and one finally told her, "He's questioning some prisoners. But it's nothing for you to worry about." He gave her a patronizing smile.

Adela turned away from them, then over her shoulder said, "If you see him, tell him I wish to speak with him in the library."

And there she waited. She tried to read a book. Even her favorites didn't hold her attention for more than a minute.

The sun was going down when Father entered the room. He had dark circles under his eyes. Adela stood and hurried toward him.

"Are you all right, *Liebling*? A guard told me you were waiting for me."

"Yes, Father, but I wanted to talk to you about Frederick."

Was that a frown on Father's face? But his expression quickly went blank. She rushed into what she'd been planning to say before he could speak. "I know it seems bad that he already knew these men and that they had told him of their plan, but he never dreamed they could hurt anyone, that they were actually capable—"

"How do you know this?"

"Oh, well . . ." Her heart stopped beating for a moment, then raced ahead. "He told me." She just wouldn't tell him when and where he'd told her.

"He told me that himself," her father replied. "But I have to decide what is the true story. A man condemned to die will say anything to save himself."

"What do you mean, 'condemned to die'?" The breath rushed out of her, and her face tingled as if the blood were draining from her head.

"Sit down before you end up on the floor." Father gently took her arm until she sat back down in the chair. "I've just been questioning the Eselin brothers. The older two say Frederick was helping them, but the youngest says he wasn't, that he refused to help them when they asked him."

"Oh, I'm sure he's the one who's telling the truth. The older two are the meanest. They are lying out of spite. They—"

"Very well." Father held up his hand. "I am inclined to believe the youngest one myself. But none of this concerns you, *Liebling*." His voice was kind and low, but the words cut her nonetheless.

"It does concern me." Her eyes filled with tears, and she blinked them back with much effort. "Frederick is my friend and I . . . like him very much."

Father straightened his shoulders, then relaxed again. "*Liebling*, you have not known this young man long enough to know his character."

"It doesn't matter how long I've known him. I know him, and we understand each other. We are both artists, and he is a good man."

Father raised one eyebrow as he gazed down at her.

"He is very like you, Father. Kind and tenderhearted, humble and spiritual. You would love him if you only knew him."

His expression was kind and pitying, making her eyes sting with tears again.

"He is a good man, and I . . . I'm not the spoiled child everyone thinks I am."

"I don't think you're a spoiled child."

"Some people do. And maybe I have been, at times."

"Adela, your mother and I don't think you're spoiled, but you must look at this rationally and not just with your emotions. This man is a peasant."

"He is the son of a farmer who owns his own land."

"Adela, he is not even a burgher. He lives far away from town."

"Not anymore. Now Frederick is a wood-carver and lives in town."

Father's face hardened. Was he remembering that she had deceived him about who was going to be renting her grandparents' house?

"I don't like this obsession you have with this man."

"It's not an obsession. You've met him, and you are usually very discerning. Is he not a good man?"

Father frowned again. "I don't know him. I've only talked to him twice now. It takes time to truly know a man, time and shared experiences, and it helps to know his family."

"Did you not fall in love with Mother before you'd had very much time and shared experiences?" She knew he couldn't argue with that.

"Mother and I did fall in love rather quickly, but . . . you are not in love with him, are you?"

"No, we are only friends. So how can you disapprove?"

Father frowned on one side of his mouth. He didn't speak for a few moments, then said, "You're my daughter and I don't want you to be hurt. I thought you were beginning to have feelings for Lord Barthold."

"I was going to tell Lord Barthold that I have decided I don't want to marry him. Father, I never had feelings for him. He is a cold fish and Frederick is . . ." *Open, warm, and wonderful.* "He's an artist like me. I can talk to him. I can't talk to Barthold."

Father raised his brows and looked as if he didn't know what to say. She noticed again the dark circles under his eyes.

"I know you're only thinking of what is best for me, Father, but I believe Frederick is innocent. He didn't do anything wrong, and I beg you, Father, please believe him. He never intended any harm to anyone. Please release him, Father. Please."

He stared at her. "I am not sure that is the wise thing to do."

"Why not? You know he is innocent."

"I do not know that. I believe he is, but . . . the wise thing is to wait and see if any more witnesses come forward, to talk to other people who may have been privy to the truth."

"The truth is exactly what Frederick said, which was corroborated by the youngest Eselin brother. I've heard you say yourself that if two witnesses who have not communicated tell the same story, then that is invariably the true story."

"I don't think I said 'invariably.' And Frederick doesn't count as a witness."

Adela clasped her hands. "Please, Father. Don't leave an innocent man in that horrible dungeon chained up, a man the bishop believes in and needs to carve the doors to the sacred Cathedral."

Father took a deep breath, then blew it out. He ran a hand through his hair. "Very well. I will release him for your sake." He patted her on the shoulder.

"Oh, thank you, Father."

"But he will not be allowed to leave town, and he must go to the Cathedral every day to work on the doors. He's not allowed to go anywhere else. I shall release him, even though Lord Barthold is very much against it."

"Why should he be against it? He knows nothing of Frederick."

"He was shot, Adela."

"I know that, Father."

"He thinks Frederick was part of the plot to harm him."

"He is only jealous of Frederick." She crossed her arms over her chest.

"Should he be jealous?"

"No, because even if I didn't know Frederick, I wouldn't want to marry Barthold."

Father didn't blink. "Should I tell Barthold this, or shall you?"

Her stomach flipped as she imagined how Barthold would feel. He was already physically wounded. She hated to wound his heart, but she could not let him waste any more time waiting on her.

"I suppose I should tell him."

"Better sooner than later." Father patted her shoulder again. "I wouldn't worry too much about Lord Barthold. He is the son of a duke. He will have a lot of other prospects for marriage."

That was certainly true. "Is he still in Frau Lena's chamber?"

"I think he's probably in his room by now. Would you like me—"

"No, I can do this myself. Thank you, Father. But you did say you would release Frederick. When?"

Father's eyes narrowed just a bit. "I have not decided that yet."

She wanted to run down to the dungeon and tell Frederick that he would be released soon. But she could not let Father know she was thinking of such a thing. And she could find Frederick at his house once he was out of the dungeon, now that he was living in town, to talk to him. But when would she ever be able to leave the castle again without a guard? Probably never. No doubt Father had already told the guards to keep a sharp eye out for her leaving the castle. Well, she'd simply have to take a guard with her if there was no other way to see Frederick.

But was it wise to spend time with him now that she had kissed him? She'd have to ponder that later.

Adela took her leave from Father and headed to Lord Barthold's room. She knocked on the door.

"Who is it?" The voice was gruff and angry.

"It's Adela."

There was a short pause, and when he spoke again, his voice had lost its hard edge. "Come in."

Adela opened the door. Barthold was getting up from where he was sitting on the side of the bed. He walked toward her.

"How are you feeling? I'm sorry if I woke you."

"I feel like someone who's been shot through with an arrow."

She almost laughed, but since he didn't even smile, she stifled the nervous impulse. "I'm very sorry. I hope Frau Lena took good care of you."

"She did. And I was not asleep."

Adela's stomach tightened as she stood facing Barthold. But better to get this over and done. "Barthold, I am sorry, but I cannot marry you. You are a good man, but I think someone else will be better for you."

As she finished speaking, Barthold's adviser, Lord Conrat stepped out of the corner of the room, startling Adela. Had he been there the whole time?

A muscle in Barthold's cheek twitched, while his eyes were locked on her face.

"This is about that peasant, Frederick, is it not? Do you realize what you're doing, Adela? A man like that? It is shameful that you, the daughter of Duke Wilhelm of Hagenheim, would associate with such a man."

"Why? Because he is poor? He is a kind, honest man."

Barthold frowned and raised his brows at the same time, as if he couldn't decide if he was more disgusted or amused. Meanwhile, Lord Conrat stood without moving, but she could feel his eyes on her.

"You may think what you wish, but Frederick meant you no harm and was not scheming with those men." She frustrated herself by trying to explain to Barthold, who obviously thought less and less of her and Frederick the more she spoke.

"He will desert you as soon as he realizes your father won't allow him to marry you."

Adela's heart pounded at what he was saying, at the ugly little smile stretching Barthold's lips.

"You know nothing about him, or about what my father will or won't allow."

"Come, come, Adela. Your father is the powerful Duke of Hagenheim. He would never—"

"Frederick did not even know I was the duke's daughter."

"He will disappear from your life when there is nothing for him to gain."

"Fare well, Lord Barthold, and I hope your shoulder heals quickly." She turned and was out the door before the last word was out of her mouth.

❧

Frederick was released from the dungeon the next day. He went straight to Hagenheim Cathedral to speak to the bishop. Indeed, he had been ordered to go only to the Cathedral every day to work, then straight home afterward.

Frederick found the bishop in his study chamber and begged to be allowed to speak to him.

"Of course, my son."

Frederick explained everything that had happened. "I hope you will not consider me unfit to do the work on the Cathedral doors."

"No. I believe what you say, and the fact that Duke Wilhelm set you free tells me that he is confident you are innocent of any serious wrongdoing."

Frederick thanked him and promised to return the next day to work on the doors. As he walked home, Frederick's thoughts were tangled up with Adela.

Her father would never allow him to court her, or marry her. But how could he give her up? And yet, if he cared about her, he *would* give her up. He would see the heartache that was inevitable, the pain if he were to pursue her against her father's wishes. How could it end well?

He shouldn't have let her kiss him. But the kiss was so sweet, his chest ached just thinking about it.

But perhaps God would make a way for them. There must be a reason they met. Of all the people Adela might have met in the *Marktplatz* that day, she had met him, he who was so rarely there before that day. And what about the day he'd come to get help for his neighbor's baby? She just happened to be in the healer's chamber on that very day, the moment when he arrived. God must have a purpose, must have a plan. At least he hoped so.

He was grateful he'd been there to stop the Eselin brothers from harming Adela. So many things could have gone wrong. Again, he thanked God that he had been in the right place at the right time, even though it hurt to see her with Lord Barthold and to realize she had deceived him and was not the peasant girl he thought she was.

He couldn't think about his pain. More pressing matters were afoot. The two older Eselin brothers were persisting in their lies about Frederick. If somehow Duke Wilhelm changed his mind and decided that Frederick had been helping the Eselins, if the youngest brother suddenly changed his story and said Frederick did help them, he might be seized again and taken back to the dungeon.

Even if that happened, God must have a plan. But in the meantime, he could not let Adela contest her father's will. Nothing good could come of defying the Duke of Hagenheim. But how could he force himself to stop seeing her? His heart ached for her, and he'd never felt this way about anyone before. It reminded him of how he felt when he was too busy to do any carving for several days in a row. When he couldn't carve and create something from wood, he was restless, longing, frustrated. And the thought of not being able to talk to Adela evoked the same restless, longing, frustrated feelings.

He'd better get used to them. She was the daughter of the Duke of Hagenheim, and he was just a peasant with an impossible dream.

CHAPTER 15

Two days later Frederick was sitting down to dinner with his mother and sisters when Eulaly said, "A note came for you, Frederick. A boy from the castle brought it."

Frederick looked at her expectantly. "Where is it?"

"Over there." She swept her hand in an indeterminate manner.

Frederick jumped up.

"It's here." Mother handed him the small rolled-up piece of paper tied with a string.

Frederick opened it quickly and read it to himself.

Frederick,

Please meet me at the Cathedral in the southwest corner of the nave tomorrow at noon. I need to talk to you.

Adela

"When did this come?"

"This morning," Mother said.

"You're sure? It was this morning? Today?"

"Yes, son. Is anything wrong?"

"No, Mother. All is well." He sat back down to eat his supper.

Of course he wanted her to come. Would he be able to tell Adela what he had determined to tell her? That they couldn't see each other anymore unless her father approved? His stomach felt sick thinking about it. Would Adela be hurt? He wasn't sure he could bear it if she cried. He'd surely take it all back if she cried. But perhaps they could just be friends. No more kissing. He would at least tell her that. Even though the thought of being with her and not kissing her seemed impossible.

"Is something wrong, Frederick?" his mother asked.

He shook his head. "No." Just that he'd fallen in love with the most wonderful woman in the world, and she could never be his.

❦

Conrat made his way down the dungeon steps, following behind his most trusted guard. Most of the prisoners would be asleep, since it was the middle of the night. He followed his guard the rest of the way to Ditmar Eselin's cell. His guard unlocked it, and they went inside.

Ditmar Eselin rolled over from where he lay on the stone floor and blinked up at them.

"Good evening. I am Conrat of Grundelsbach. I wish to speak with you. You are Ditmar Eselin, are you not?"

"I am." Ditmar sat up and propped his back against the stone wall.

"I can help you if you will help me."

"The only way you can help me is by getting me out of this dungeon."

"I am willing to free you from the dungeon if you—"

"Me and my brothers?"

"Yes, you and your brothers, and give you a sum of money to help you get far away from here if you will give me some information."

"Information?"

"That is all I require."

The surly man stared up at him, as if waiting.

"I wish to know about this Frederick the wood-carver."

"What do you want to know?"

"Everything you know about him."

"I know that his father is a drunk who beats his mother."

"Does his father know that Frederick and his mother and sisters are here in Hagenheim?"

He took a moment to process this information. "I would imagine not. If he did, he'd come to town and take his wife home, dragging her by her hair, I'd wager."

Very interesting. And if the father took the mother back home to their miserable farm, might he not also coerce Frederick to go home as well?

"Tell me more about Frederick and his family. Where does his father live? How do I get there?"

"Are you going to set me free tonight?"

"I will need a little time to plan. But if you tell me everything you know about this Frederick, I will make sure you are freed by this time next week."

Ditmar Eselin gave him a shrewd look—as shrewd a look as he could muster, since he was obviously not very clever. Then he began to talk, saying mostly things that Conrat could not use and did not care about. But he let him talk on, as a plan began to formulate in his mind.

❧

The next morning Frederick dressed more carefully than usual, thinking of Adela's small hand curled against his chest and then touching his face when they were in the dungeon. His heart raced, more and more unsure of what he would say to her today. He made sure his hair looked presentable before leaving to go to the Cathedral.

He went to work in his little workshop at the back of the church. He was carving the section that depicted Joseph being put into chains in the prison. He'd never imagined he would be able to relate to Joseph so much. But now he vividly remembered how it felt to be chained to a wall.

Frederick was thinking less about that and more about Adela. Why did she want to meet him? What would she say? The time seemed to drag by.

Finally, it was nearly noon. He left his workroom and walked the short way to a back door and went inside. He made his way to the front of the nave, to the southwest corner as Adela had instructed. Someone was already kneeling there on the floor, hands clasped and head bowed, and one of the duke's guards was standing near the figure, between her and the front doors.

Frederick approached slowly, his breath shallow. The guard saw him and shifted his feet, suddenly more alert, his hand resting on his sword hilt.

When he was only a few feet from her, Adela lifted her head and looked him in the eye. She didn't speak, but when the guard moved toward them, she turned and said, "It is well. He is with me."

The guard's expression remained tense as he stayed where he was and stared hard at Frederick.

Adela stood and sat on a bench positioned against the wall. She waved Frederick toward her and patted the bench beside her, and he sat.

He couldn't take his eyes off her. So fair of face. And she'd kissed *him*.

"Are you well?" she asked, leaning toward him.

"Very well. And you?"

"You are not angry with me, are you?" Her voice was soft and low. "I can't bear to think you are angry with me for deceiving you."

"I am not angry with you. I understand why you did it. But does your father know you are here with me now? That you came here to see me?"

"No, but I brought a guard with me, so I am not doing anything wrong."

"But he disapproves of you seeing me, does he not?"

Adela pursed her lips, then sighed, staring past his shoulder. "He does not understand, but that doesn't mean he won't ever understand."

"Does not understand what?" He swallowed the lump that came into his throat.

"That I . . . that we are friends." She bowed her head. Was that a tear that dripped from her face? She rubbed it into the fabric of her dress.

His heart constricted with a sharp ache. Before he could stop himself, he reached out and brushed her hand with the back of his own.

He'd be in the dungeon again yet.

⁓❧⁓

Adela's heart expanded inside her chest at the touch of Frederick's hand, so gentle. She turned her hand over, and he clasped it in his own.

"Why are you crying?" His voice was gruff but kind.

"I—" She almost said, "I'm not crying," but that was only because his hand holding hers made the tears dry up. "I missed you and I worried about you. I wondered if you wanted to see me."

"Of course I wanted to see you." His thumb brushed her hand in a way that sent shivers up her arm, then stilled. "But I do not believe we should evoke your father's wrath by meeting secretly."

She bowed her head again. She'd felt so torn. One minute she told herself she should be very distant with him, pretending only to care for him as a friend. The next she just wanted to forget that he was poor and kiss him again. Even now she could hardly untangle her thoughts enough to know what she would do or say from one moment to the next.

"I don't want to cause your father to lock you in your room and force you to marry someone you don't want because of your secret visits to a poor peasant like me. And I believe the best course of action is for me to try to earn your father's favor so that we don't have to sneak around, against his wishes, to see each other."

"But if you don't see me, you will forget me."

"That is not possible." He lifted her hand to his lips and closed his eyes, kissing the back of her fingers.

Her heart tripped over itself at the feel of his warm lips touching her hand. The guard was behind Frederick and so was blocked from view. Would he even know if she leaned forward and kissed him?

"You should probably go." Frederick was looking into her eyes.

"Why? I don't want to leave. Can you stay a little longer?"

"Of course." His eyes held a look almost of pain.

She held tight to his hand. "I hope the bishop did not treat you badly because of what happened. If he did, I will tell him it was my fault."

"He was very understanding. Do not worry." He squeezed her hand.

"You said you don't want us to meet secretly. But . . . how will we meet?"

"I will write a letter to your father. I will get his permission, if possible. We will have to have a guard with us, but at least we can talk and see each other. If he allows it."

"And if he doesn't allow it?" She could feel her lip start to tremble, so she bit down on it.

"Then I will keep writing to him. I will find out what I need to do to gain his favor."

But what if Frederick never gained Father's favor? She rubbed her finger over the rough callouses on his palm. Who would ever want a man with no callouses on his hands? A man who didn't work hard with his hands to make beautiful scenes out of wood? She never would.

Again, she gazed at his lips and wished she could kiss him.

"I won't give up," he whispered. "As long as you want me to, I'll keep trying."

"I will always want you to." Her throat closed up, choking off her words. She bent over his hand and kissed it.

His other hand was suddenly caressing her cheek, brushing her hair back from her temple. Her breath shallowed as he leaned forward and kissed the spot.

The guard cleared his throat behind Frederick's back.

"You should go," Frederick said.

He stood up, but Adela clung to his hand and stood up with him. "Fare well, Frederick." Her voice sounded as breathless as she felt.

He was staring down at her, his gaze dipping to her mouth. Still holding his hand with both of hers, she leaned forward. When she did, he bent and kissed her lips.

It was the briefest of kisses, but it made her heart beat like birds' wings.

When she opened her eyes, he was starting to walk away. Their eyes met for a moment before he strode across the nave.

"Lady Adela? Are you ready to go?" The guard's expression was dour.

She watched Frederick's back until he was gone, then let the guard escort her out of the Cathedral.

❧

Lord Conrat watched from the shadows, hiding behind a pillar, as Adela had her intimate conversation with Frederick. That peasant. What right did he have even to speak to Lady Adela? And what did she see in him? How could she choose a man with nothing, a nobody, over Barthold, a man who would one day be the Duke of Grundelsbach?

And still they sat there talking. Why didn't the guard do something? Stop that man from talking to Adela and touching her hand? Would Conrat have to intervene himself?

Finally, they were standing up. Conrat stayed in his hiding place, but his hand squeezed the hilt of his sword as he watched the way Lady Adela was clinging to the peasant's hand. And then the man bent his head and kissed her on the mouth.

Heat shot up Conrat's neck and into his forehead. How dare he? But the kiss was over in a moment and the oaf was walking away.

This had to end. Conrat would end it. And he knew just how he would do it.

❧

Frederick went to work the next morning, obeying the duke's order to go straight to the Cathedral every day to work and directly home after working. As far as he knew, the Eselin brothers were still locked in the castle dungeon and Lord Barthold was still staying at the castle, no doubt hoping Adela would marry him.

Was Frederick wrong to hope she didn't marry Barthold?

He reached the workshop and took out his tools and the panel he had been working on. Each of the two massive Cathedral doors would be made up of six panels that were to be fitted together when he was finished carving them.

"Good morning," said a soft voice behind him.

Frederick turned to find Adela standing at the open entrance to his workshop. "Good morning. Come in."

Such a beautiful sight she was. She came farther into the room, and a guard followed her.

His heart sank a bit at seeing the guard, but his presence was good. The guard would keep them from getting in trouble with her father. He had not had time to write the letter he'd promised to send to the duke.

"I know you're probably surprised to see me, but—"

"It's a good surprise. I'm very glad you're here."

"But I wanted to see your doors, to see which stories you decided to use."

He smiled, his heart filling up at the thought that she was so interested. "I also promised to tell you what I know about making paints."

"Yes, that is true." She smiled back at him.

The guard, on the other hand, wore a scowl as he stood against the wall, watching them.

Adela came close to peer at his panel that was propped against the wall. He explained which stories he would carve in which section.

"Bishop Werner told me a story about the man who was swallowed by a giant fish."

"Jonah?"

"Yes, Jonah. So I am carving that one here." He pointed to one of the panels. "And he suggested I put Jesus outside of the tomb after the resurrection beside it, here. That is a good idea, do you not think?"

"I do think it is a good idea."

The way she was smiling at him made him want to put his arm around her and pull her close. Instead, he smiled back.

"But I don't want to distract you. I'll sit over here." She motioned to a stool a few feet away from his working area. "I'm interested to see you work. I've never seen anyone carve wood before."

"It's not very exciting. But if you talk to me, it will make the day much more enjoyable."

Adela began to talk about painting. She told him about a portrait she had started of her mother.

"I'm not as good at painting portraits, but I cannot improve if I don't practice."

"You should bring your paints and your canvas and brushes and paint while I work."

"Perhaps I will."

They were both ignoring the guard, who, thankfully, was silent and unmoving.

Frederick spoke quietly as he asked, "Does your father not mind you coming here to talk to me? Or does he not know?"

"He knows. I remembered what you said yesterday, so I asked his permission to come here. He said it was all right as long as I took a guard with me, and as long as the bishop did not disapprove."

"Did you speak to the bishop?"

"I did. He said he did not mind. But he has always liked me, I think."

"I can't imagine anyone who would not like you." Frederick glanced up at her. She was staring at him while he worked, using a chisel to scrape away at the wood panel, which was laid on top of a trestle table. What was she thinking? It must be so strange for her, as a duke's daughter, to watch a man carve out wood.

"So let me tell you how I make my paints." While he worked he explained how he made some paints from berries he picked in the woods and others from soil and flowers and fruits. She made comments and asked questions. Soon they were talking of more personal things. It was as if they had known each other for a long time instead of only a couple of weeks.

When he started to work on the face of Isaac on the panel where he was depicting Abraham sacrificing his son, duplicating the medallion the bishop had bought, Adela got up from the stool and came close to watch him.

"Does it not feel as if you know the people you carve?" Adela asked. "When I paint people, I feel as if I can read their thoughts. Does that sound daft?"

"No. I feel the same way. As artists, we feel things more deeply, perhaps."

"Yes, exactly."

She was so near that they spoke just above a whisper. He was so close he could see her eyelashes, could see the tiny flecks of green in her blue eyes. He longed to touch her skin, to kiss her, but his hands were covered in wood dust.

The guard cleared his throat. Adela moved away half a step.

She said, "Do you ever feel like no one in the world understands you, understands how you think and feel?"

"Yes. I know that feeling." The longing to kiss her was like an ache in his chest, while his arms ached to hold her.

He thought he would enjoy her being with him while he worked, and while he did enjoy it, to be so near her and not be able to touch her was difficult. But it was worth the ache to be with her.

Around noon, as Frederick was cleaning off his hands to take

163

a rest, Adela said, "I should go home. I've distracted you from your work long enough."

"I wish you could come and distract me every day." He moved closer to her, and she did the same, until they were standing very close.

Out of the corner of his eye, Frederick saw the guard cross his arms over his chest.

"Perhaps I'll come back tomorrow," she said.

"I would like that."

Adela closed the gap and put her arms around him, embracing him and pressing her cheek to his chest. He put his arms around her too. He wanted to kiss her, but she let go and turned away without looking into his face. She wouldn't want to kiss him in front of the guard, who would undoubtedly tell her father.

"Fare well," Adela said over her shoulder.

"Fare well, Adela."

He watched her walk away, the guard following her.

❦

The sun was about to set when Conrat saw Frederick leave Hagenheim Cathedral. He followed him home, surprised to see how large and comfortable the house was where he and his family were living. But he'd inquired and knew that Duke Wilhelm had practically given him the house.

He wasn't sure what he would gain from watching the house, but he always liked to know as much as possible about his adversaries. All was quiet except for the sounds of servants serving supper. Or in Frederick's case, instead of servants, it was probably his mother and sisters cooking and serving.

A man was coming down the street toward the house on a

donkey. He looked inebriated, his nose red and his shoulders slumping forward. He rode up to the neighboring house and dismounted by swinging one leg over the pommel and sliding off the saddle on his stomach. It took him a few moments to steady his feet under him, then he pushed off the donkey and stumbled toward the neighbor's door.

He knocked, or rather, pounded on the wood door. Someone answered it, and Conrat heard a man say, "What do you want?"

The inebriated man swayed slightly as he said, "I am looking for my wife."

"I don't know anything about your wife."

"Basina! Her name is Basina."

"I don't know any Basina."

"Isn't there a Basina who moved in next door?" a woman's voice said from inside the house.

"Check the house next door," the man said and closed the door in the drunk man's face.

He stumbled over to the house Frederick had gone into. He didn't even knock, just pushed open the door and went inside.

Conrat went to a window on the side of the back of the house, down the narrow alley. It was open, and he could see the entire family—the mother, Frederick, and two sisters. He watched and listened intently as the family still was unaware that the drunk man had entered the house.

Conrat's being there on this night could prove to be very fortuitous.

Suddenly he recognized the woman. He stared hard, trying to remember how he knew her. And slowly it came to him.

This was a fortuitous night indeed.

Frederick and his family were eating supper around the table at the back of the house when he thought he heard a noise at the front door.

"Did you hear something?"

Mother, Ursula, and Eulaly shook their heads.

Frederick sat and listened. Perhaps he was imagining things. Mother and the girls continued to eat and talk. But then he thought he heard another sound, like shuffling feet.

He stood. "I'm going to go see—"

Father came walking in, bracing himself against the doorway with one hand. He swayed, obviously drunk.

Frederick's whole body tensed. At least he was closest to his father, so he'd have to go through Frederick to get to his mother.

Mother and his sisters stood up, too, and stared at Father.

"You're coming home with me—all of you!" Father took a step into the room, swayed, and knocked a pottery bowl off the shelf against the wall, sending it crashing to the floor.

Mother shook her head and said, "No."

Father roared, yelling at the top of his voice.

Ursula started crying, and Eulaly edged closer to the door.

Father lunged at Mother and grabbed her. Frederick stood between them and pried his father's fingers from her arm.

"She's coming home with me!" the older man shouted.

"Go get the guard at the gate." Frederick pointed at Eulaly. She ran through the doorway and out of the room. Ursula followed her sister, though more tentatively, out the door.

"Send for the guard!" Father shouted. "Go ahead, send for him! Because you're not man enough . . . man enough . . . to stop me." He stumbled backward even as he stumbled over his words.

Frederick kept his body between his father and mother.

"You need to leave. Now," Frederick said in a low voice.

"You don't give orders to me."

"Just go. Mother, Eulaly, and Ursula live here now."

"No, she doesn't! Your mother lives with me."

"You need to go. Let her choose where to live."

"Let her choose," he mimicked. "She chose already! She chose me. She didn't choose your father. She chose me!"

Frederick's blood froze in his veins.

"Ask your mother," he said. "Go on. Ask her who your father is. Because you're not my child. She was carrying you when I married her."

He glanced at Mother. Her face was crestfallen as she stared at Frederick. "I should have told you. I'm sorry."

"That's right," Father said, "so you stay here, but don't interfere with me taking my family back home. To *my* home."

He lunged toward Mother again, bumping into Frederick's chest as his hand reached for her. She snatched her arm out of his grasp.

Frederick blocked him, using his body to push him back.

He should have known. He was at least five inches taller, and he looked nothing like this man.

"Get out of my way! She's my wife."

The sound of heavy footsteps came from the direction of the front door, and soon two of Duke Wilhelm's guards appeared.

"Is there trouble here?" the guard said.

"This man is drunk and has invaded our home," Frederick said.

Frederick looked at his "father" and motioned toward the door. "Just go." The older man's face grew so red, Frederick wondered if he'd have an apoplectic fit and die right there.

"You'll regret this." He pointed his finger in Frederick's face, only inches from his nose. "You'll both regret it."

The guards put their hands on his shoulders to guide him out of the house.

Frederick stood staring after the man whom he had lived with, who had beaten him and abused his mother, and he suddenly felt free for the first time.

"Forgive me for not telling you."

He turned to his mother and pulled her into his arms. "All is well. I forgive you."

"I didn't want you to think badly of me."

He could tell by her voice that she was crying.

"I'm so sorry I never told you that Stenngle was only your step-father. And I'm so sorry I did not know of his evil character when I married him."

"Don't torture yourself anymore, Mother. All is well now. All is well."

⁓✦⁓

Conrat hurried around to the front of the house. The guards were standing watch as the drunk man struggled to mount his donkey. After a full minute of failing to hoist himself into the saddle, he gave up and led the animal by its bridle.

Conrat's mind had chipped away at the wall that blocked where he'd seen that woman before. It must have been a long time ago, so he had pictured what she would have looked like as a very young woman. And then he remembered who she was and where he'd seen her.

His heart actually trembled inside him at what was being revealed. How dangerous this situation was now. So much more dangerous than Barthold losing the lucrative marriage he had hoped for.

Conrat had to make certain he took action, and quickly.

He hurried to follow the drunk man a short way, then came up beside him and asked, "Can I buy you some wine?"

CHAPTER 16

Mother pulled away and dried her face on her apron, then sank down on the bench at the table.

"I should have told you sooner. I'm surprised Stenngle didn't tell you a long time ago."

"Does he know who my father is?"

"No. I've never told anyone." Her voice was low and solemn.

"And is my father still alive?"

"Yes." She sighed. "I will tell you everything. Especially now that you might be falling in love with the Duke of Hagenheim's daughter."

What could that have to do with it?

"I was a servant in the castle in Grundelsbach. I served the duke and his family. Lord Barthold's father had just taken over the title from his father. He was not married, but his father had pledged him, years earlier, to the daughter of a count from Bohemia. And I foolishly . . . fell in love with him." Mother stared sadly at the floor.

"He must have been much older than you were."

"Only a few years."

"You were his servant. He took advantage of you."

"I suppose you could say that. But I was . . . just as much to blame as he was. The day I realized I was with child, his new bride arrived in Grundelsbach. I came to Hagenheim, where my aunt and uncle lived, and I married the first man who showed any interest in me—Stenngle. It was a mistake, but I just wanted to keep you safe and raise you well. Then your sisters came along. But Stenngle . . . He was a cruel man, and I'm so sorry for the way he has treated you. I did not know what he was until after I married him."

"The Duke of Grundelsbach." Frederick rubbed his hand down his face. "Lord Barthold is my . . ."

"Half brother? Yes. Barthold looks so much like his father. And I can see a resemblance between you and Lord Barthold. I'm surprised he didn't see himself in you."

"Mother, please. That man hates me."

"Because the girl he wants to marry is in love with you."

"She has never said she was in love with me."

"But she must be, or she would have married Lord Barthold, do you not think?"

He did like to think she was falling in love with him. But . . . half brother? To Lord Barthold?

"Does the Duke of Grundelsbach know . . . about me?" Frederick swallowed, hardly believing those words were coming out of his mouth.

"I was told that he knew, but I never told him. He couldn't marry me, and I . . ." She shook her head, her lips pursed.

"Did you tell him where you were going? Anything?"

She shook her head. "There was a man, your father's close adviser and cousin, who told me your father knew about the baby. He wanted me to go, to be rid of me and the child. I think if I had not left when I did, that man might have had me killed, just to keep you from inheriting anything from your father, the duke."

Frederick reached out and squeezed her hand. "I hate that you went through that, and that you married someone like Father." And the truth was, though he was shocked, he was also relieved that the man he'd always thought was his father, wasn't.

"I'm sorry I married someone who mistreated us both as he has. But I won't go back to live with him." Her lips trembled and she pressed her hand to her mouth. "Being away from him these past two weeks has been . . . very good."

Frederick enveloped her in a hug. "I'm sorry, Mother."

"You have nothing to be sorry for. I should be apologizing to you, for what I did to you. I took you away from Grundelsbach when the duke might have at least given me money and made sure we didn't starve. Perhaps I could have found a good man to help raise you. But no, I had to go my own way and marry a man who would abuse you." A sob escaped her as she buried her face in her hand.

"You did the best you could, what you thought was best. It does no good to torture yourself."

"A mother should protect her child."

He let her cry. What else could he do? But he was heartened by her declaration never to live with Stenngle again. Thank God, Frederick could protect her and give her a home. God had provided a way.

Mother pulled away and wiped her face with her hands.

"Sit down. You haven't had your supper."

Already Mother had pasted on a smile, putting her sadness aside, as she always did. Eulaly and Ursula came quietly back into the room and sat down.

After eating, even though he was tired, Frederick didn't want to put off writing the letter to Duke Wilhelm. So he sat down and scribbled some notes on a scrap piece of wood. He'd get up early the next morning to write the letter properly, on parchment, before going to work.

Should he mention to the Duke of Hagenheim that his father was actually the Duke of Grundelsbach? Even if he had the proof, which he did not, he shrank from the thought of using a father who didn't even know he existed to gain favor with Adela's father. No, if he was able to win Adela, it wouldn't be because he was the illegitimate son of some wealthy, powerful man. Because, as far as anyone knew, he wasn't. And perhaps now he could understand, just a bit more, why Adela had not wanted him to know her as a duke's daughter but, rather, as just an ordinary girl.

He got up and headed for bed. What a day. Being with Adela all morning, then finding out the man he'd always known as his father was not in fact his father, and that his father was a duke. That his poor mother had left Grundelsbach alone and pregnant. With him.

He rubbed his eyes to get it all out of his mind. He needed sleep, so he'd wait and think about it in the morning. Troubles and circumstances were always clearer after a night's sleep.

❦

Conrat looked in disgust at the man sleeping off his drunken state in the small anteroom beside his bedchamber. But Frederick's step-father was the perfect person to help him pull off his plan to rid Lady Adela of her peasant suitor—and Barthold's rival—once and for all.

He glanced out the window, and a young man caught his eye. It was Frederick, striding across the castle yard from the gate toward the front doors of the castle. In his hand he held what appeared to be a rolled-up missive.

Conrat ran from the room, hurried down the corridor, down the steps, and out the door, just in time to find Frederick handing the letter off to a guard.

"I'll see that the duke gets it," the guard said.

Conrat attempted to look inconspicuous as he stood by the door trying to catch his breath, not looking directly at Frederick. Out of the corner of his eye, he saw Frederick staring curiously at him before turning and walking away.

The guard was opening the door to go inside. Conrat followed him in.

"Would that happen to be a letter to Duke Wilhelm?" Conrat went on quickly before the guard could answer. "Because I am just on my way to see the duke and can take the letter for you."

"That is not necess—"

"It will keep you from having to leave your post. I insist." Lord Conrat gave him his best smile while holding out his hand.

The guard stared at him for a moment, then handed over the letter.

Conrat gave him a curt nod, then headed back to the stairs.

Making sure he wasn't followed, Conrat stepped back into his bedchamber and closed the door. He slipped the string off and unrolled the paper.

"Presumptuous peasant." Conrat read through the letter that explained how Frederick and the duke's daughter had met and formed an attachment to each other. Did Frederick think the duke would be moved by his entreaties to allow him to continue to see his daughter? She didn't belong with a poor man. She belonged with Barthold, and only Barthold would have her, as the Duke of Hagenheim was the wealthiest and most powerful duke in the German regions. No one should marry her except Barthold. The only thing this peasant had to recommend himself was his skill at wood carving. As if wood carving would make him a fortune or gain him favor with the king and emperor of the Holy Roman Empire!

Perhaps he should give the letter to Duke Wilhelm. The duke might even be angered by the confessions and hopes of such a lowly man who had the audacity to try to court his daughter. But the more he pondered it, the more he was convinced Adela learning from her father that her peasant suitor had lied about writing him a letter was much better.

He crumpled the paper in his fist. It was time to wake up the drunken sot in the next room and set the plan in motion.

✻

Adela arrived at Frederick's workshop around midmorning. The smile that spread across Frederick's face when he saw her made her heart expand. But they were just friends, she had assured her mother.

She'd asked her mother the night before if she could go and visit Frederick the following morning.

"Again? Did you not visit him today?"

"Yes, but . . . we enjoy talking to each other. We are both artists, so we have a lot to talk about. We are friends, Mother."

"The guard said the two of you embraced when you left."

"Yes. Friends embrace each other."

Mother looked at her with gentle eyes. "Since you are just friends, you won't mind if I bring a basket of food and take you both on a picnic."

"I would like that very much." Adela's heart lightened at the thought of her mother getting to know Frederick.

"Good. Because I would like to meet this young man for myself." Mother smiled.

So as Adela stood looking into Frederick's blue eyes, she said, "I don't know what you will think of this, but . . ."

"What?" Frederick stared even more intently into her eyes.

"My mother is taking us on a picnic in about an hour."

Frederick's brows rose. "That is very good. I would like to meet your mother."

Adela let out the breath she was holding. Frederick looked genuinely pleased. Her heart thumped and a lump threatened to close up her throat. She'd had so many conflicting thoughts the night before. One minute she had told herself she could not ever be more than friends with Frederick, as she could not possibly marry a wood-carver. The next minute she was remembering how it felt to talk to him, how he seemed to be the only person she'd ever met who really understood her. And his kisses, his arms holding her . . . Of course she could marry him. She could learn to keep house, cook, whatever she needed to do, in exchange for the kind of love Frederick gave her.

But then the reality of what her life would be like with Frederick would hit her and she'd be crying, whispering to God, "No, I can't! I am not used to that life. I just can't." Frederick would wonder why he'd ever married a spoiled duke's daughter. He'd resent her, and she couldn't bear to be married to someone who saw her as spoiled and incompetent.

But she was getting ahead of herself. She wasn't ready to get married. She wanted to be an artist, to travel and accomplish great things. How could she do that if she was married?

No, she and Frederick were just friends. Only friends. She could refrain from kissing him. Of course she could, especially when there would always be a guard around watching them.

And now her mother.

But standing here with Frederick, watching him work, seeing his smile, talking with him as if they had always known each other, she felt those feelings stirring inside her again, remembered his kisses, his arms around her . . . No. She had to stop this. She could and she would.

Noon seemed to come very quickly, as they never ran out of things to say, and her mother arrived with a basket and yet another guard to loom silently in the background. Frederick stopped working, quickly wiping his hands on a cloth, and greeted Mother with a smile.

Mother smiled as well. "I am so pleased to meet the man who helped save my daughter from ruffians. I want to thank you."

Was Frederick blushing? His face looked a little red.

"I am thankful to God that nothing terrible happened to Adel—Lady Adela."

"Yes, God was watching over both of you. May I see your carvings?" Mother stepped closer.

"I am sorry for the mess." Frederick looked down at all the wood shavings and dust on the floor.

"Do not worry." Mother came close and complimented him.

"It does not look like anything at the moment. I have a lot more work to do. I promise the doors will look much better when I am finished."

"Oh, of course. You are only beginning. I am anxious to see what they will look like. I know you will make them beautiful and edifying. Adela has told me a lot about your plans and your beautiful artistry."

"Both Adela and you are very kind."

Soon they were all walking up the little hill to picnic under a tree.

"Have I told you the story," Mother said as she took the food out of the basket, "of when your father caught me climbing this tree? That was when he didn't know me very well."

"No." Adela laughed. "You must tell me!"

"I was climbing this tree, and your father came riding up on his horse. He startled me and I fell flat on my back." Mother laughed.

"I cannot believe it! Were you hurt?"

Mother shook her head.

Frederick's eyes were wide, and he had a slight smile on his face.

"There, Frederick. Had you ever imagined a duchess climbing a tree?"

"Or falling out of one?" Adela laughed again.

Frederick only shook his head. "I would like to hear more about this. Was that how you met the duke?"

"No, we had already met. I was the healer's apprentice, and I had sewn up a gash in his leg. When I fell out of the tree, he made sure I was not hurt, and then he played his lute for me, right here where we are."

"That sounds romantic." Adela stared at her mother, hoping she would tell them more.

"Yes, it was. But I want to hear about Frederick. When did you start carving wood?"

Mother asked him several questions, and he talked freely, even confessing about his father, who drank too much and was violent to his mother and even to him sometimes. It made Adela's heart ache to think of him being so mistreated. She was so glad that he and his mother and sisters had been able to escape the man.

Their talk turned back to more pleasant subjects, but soon it was time for Frederick to go back to work.

"Good day, Lady Rose."

Mother clasped his hand in both of hers. "It was an honor to meet the creator of the Cathedral doors."

"Thank you. I am humbled by your kindness." Frederick bowed to her.

As they walked back down the hill, Adela said, "I'll walk with

Frederick back to his workshop. I left a shawl there. I'll be home shortly after you."

Was that a smirk on Mother's face? "Very well, dear. I'll see you soon."

They went their separate ways, one of the guards following Mother and the other walking just behind Adela as she fell in beside Frederick.

Of course, the real reason she wanted to go with Frederick back to the woodworking shop was so she could embrace Frederick without her mother seeing them. And the way Frederick was looking at her, he knew why she was walking back with him as well.

Her heart thumped wildly. To try to appear nonchalant, she asked, "Did you like my mother?"

"Of course I liked her. She is a lovely woman." He shook his head. "I can hardly believe she would want to talk to me, but she was very gracious and warm. You are very blessed."

"I know. She is a wonderful mother."

As they stepped into the small shop, Adela saw her shawl lying on the stool. "I suppose I should take my shawl and go."

Frederick stood facing her. Was he also wishing they could kiss? But they shouldn't, even if the guard had not been there.

Frederick was looking over her head. He whispered, "The guard just stepped outside."

Adela glanced over her shoulder. He was right. The guard was gone.

When she turned back around, Frederick was standing quite close. Her heart beat erratically again. But she had planned to embrace him, had she not? She placed her hands on his shoulders, then slipped them around his neck. The next thing she knew, she was kissing him.

She shouldn't kiss him. But she wanted to, and she could no longer remember why she shouldn't.

She pulled away. He gazed into her eyes, as if willing her to read his thoughts and feel his emotion. She touched his jawline, such an intimate moment. She hoped she'd never forget this feeling of gazing into his eyes.

Someone cleared his throat behind her, and she turned away from Frederick and hurried toward the doorway, where the guard was standing. But then she scurried back and snatched her shawl off the stool.

"Fare well, Frederick."

"Fare well, Adela." His smile was so gentle. She had the strangest feeling that she might not see that smile again for a long time. She did her best to carve it into her memory as she rushed away.

❧

Frederick walked home after dark with the same thing on his mind that he'd been thinking about all day—whether or not Duke Wilhelm had read his letter. If he had, what did he think? Would he continue to allow Adela to see him? Honestly, Frederick wasn't sure he was above seeing Adela in secret. He'd told her he wouldn't, that he wanted her father's approval, but the thought of not seeing her was torture. Especially when she was so close, only a short walk through town from the Cathedral, or from his rented house, to her home at Hagenheim Castle.

He rubbed his eyes as he arrived home. He hadn't slept very well the night before, thinking about his letter, and then he had risen early to write it.

Mother smiled at him as he entered the dining room, with its fireplace and trestle table and benches.

"How was your day? Did you do a lot of carving?"

"It was good. I got more done today than most days." Thinking of Adela and of seeing her always inspired him.

Should he tell her about meeting Lady Rose today? No, he was so tired, he'd tell her about it later.

"You haven't seen any more of Father, have you?"

"No." She shook her head, the smile disappearing from her face.

"I asked the guards at the gate to keep an eye on the house and on you and the girls when I'm not here during the day."

"Thank you."

Mother served the food, with Eulaly and Ursula helping. Then they all sat and ate. His sisters told of their adventures at the market. Frederick was barely listening as he ate his food.

"Frederick, can we have some money? You said you would give us money for new dresses." Eulaly's voice was pleading, but her expression was confident.

"I will give you a little, but spend it wisely." He was surprised she hadn't asked him sooner.

"Is it spending wisely if we use it to buy ribbons and material for more dresses?" Ursula looked at her sister and giggled behind her hand.

Frederick smiled and shook his head. Truly, since they'd left his father's influence, his sisters weren't so bad. A little foolish and flighty, but they hadn't said or done anything unkind to him in at least two days.

He finished his food and went to retrieve the pouch of money the bishop had given him. He went on the other side of his bed, knelt, lifted the loose board between the bed and the wall, and pulled out the small leather bag. He took out what he had intended to give his sisters and put the rest back, covering it up with the board, fitting it into place.

He went to find Eulaly and gave her the coins.

"Oh, thank you. You're the best brother, Frederick." She hugged him, throwing her arms around his middle.

"You never thought I was the best brother before."

"You have money now." She smirked up at him, then ran off to find Ursula.

He shook his head but smiled as he went back up to his room. He took off his shirt and was just starting to wash himself in preparation for bed when he heard heavy footsteps downstairs, then men's voices.

He threw his shirt back over his head as he strode across the room and flung open his door. Heavy boots were coming up the stairs, and as he stepped out and looked down, he saw guards, but they weren't wearing Duke Wilhelm's colors. They were the Duke of Grundelsbach's men.

Then he heard his father's voice downstairs, yelling.

"What is this?" Frederick did not like the looks on the guards' faces. And he counted at least three of them as they crowded the top of the stairs.

"Come peaceably with us or we shall take you by force."

"Take me where? By whose authority?" Frederick took a step back. He had no weapon, and these soldiers were armed with swords. Could he push past them and escape?

Where were Mother and the girls? Just then his mother cried out, "No!"

His father's raised voice was harsh and familiar.

"What do you want?" Frederick demanded, longing to get past them and save his mother.

Two of the soldiers came at him and seized him by the arms, pinning them behind his back. Another soldier shoved a cloth in his mouth. Frederick threw himself backward and broke free, but the soldiers pounced on him. They pulled him to his knees, then shoved him to the floor on his stomach. They pinned his wrists against his back. He couldn't move.

His vision started going dark. The cloth kept him from breathing through his mouth.

They yanked him to his feet, having secured his hands, then pulled him roughly to the top step.

Frederick searched the floor below for his mother and sisters. They were standing together in a huddle as the man he'd called Father shouted at them.

"Get your things together. You're going home with me."

His sisters were visibly shaking and starting to cry.

An older man walked in the door, and Mother gasped. She took a step back and whispered, "You."

As Frederick descended the steps, everyone was focused on the man with the smirk on his long, thin face.

"I see you remember me." The man moved toward Mother and said with a nod, "Conrat Volker, adviser to the Duke of Grundelsbach."

"What are you doing here?" Mother's voice was breathy and strained.

"It took me a few minutes." The man, Lord Conrat, was dressed in a deep red color, which matched his strangely red, shiny lips. "But I remembered you as the fortune-seeking serving maid who got yourself with child at Grundelsbach Castle. And this must be the child you claimed belonged to the Duke of Grundelsbach." He directed their attention to Frederick with a wave of his hand.

"What have you done to Frederick?" Mother's expression changed when she saw him, and she ran toward the stairs. "Let him go! He hasn't done anything wrong."

Frederick's chest ached, and he tried again to free his arms, but the bonds did not even loosen a fraction. He continued to work at them, nonetheless, and to use his tongue to push at the cloth in his mouth.

"Of course he has done something wrong," Conrat said. "He has attempted to kill his half brother, Lord Barthold, in order to steal his birthright as the heir of the Duke of Grundelsbach."

"That is a lie." Mother's face went pale and she swayed on her feet. "He did not even know he was the duke's son until I told him yesterday."

Lord Conrat's expression did not change. "No one will believe that. Now, go with your husband. You must submit to your husband, you know." He looked pointedly at Stenngle, who took her by the arm.

"No, I won't go with him!"

"Yes, you will." Lord Conrat waved at a guard, and he took her arms and forced her toward the door. Two more guards moved toward Eulaly and Ursula, whose mouths hung open, staring in horror, but they obeyed the implied order to move forward and follow Mother.

"Frederick! Where are you taking him?" Mother clawed at Father's hand on her arm.

"Stay here," Lord Conrat said, pointing at the guards holding Frederick. He turned toward Mother. "If you do not cooperate, he will be killed. If you leave your husband's home, he will be killed. If you say anything to anyone about me or about Frederick being the duke's son, he will be killed. But if you do as you are told and say nothing, he will not be hurt. Do you understand?" Lord Conrat spoke quietly but coldly.

Mother was staring up at Frederick. He couldn't speak, could hardly move. Mother's eyes were full of fear. But she clenched her jaw and said to Conrat, "I understand. Just do not hurt him."

The guards pushed her toward the door.

Eulaly glanced back at him as she followed. Ursula covered her face with her hands and sobbed.

As soon as they were out the door, Frederick shook his head and finally managed to spit out the cloth in his mouth. He stared at the thin man who seemed to be behind all this.

"Why would you risk the wrath of the Bishop and the Duke of Hagenheim? Am I such a threat to you? To Lord Barthold?"

"You are no threat to us. You are nothing." Lord Conrat stayed near the door. "But I will not allow you to steal what rightfully belongs to Lord Barthold. He is my responsibility, and I will fulfill my duty to him."

"And what would that duty be?"

"To see that he marries the daughter of the Duke of Hagenheim, and apparently that entails making sure that you . . . disappear."

"So you will kill me, then." He went numb all over. Even his thoughts seemed to go numb. But he would not show fear.

"I have found that killing is much messier than some other means of making people disappear."

"The way you made my mother disappear when she found herself with child by the Duke of Grundel—"

"Shut your mouth." Glancing at the guard beside him, he ordered, "Shut him up."

"The Duke of Grundelsbach," Frederick said quickly as the guard pulled out a strip of cloth. "Is the duke the kind of man who takes advantage of young girls in his service? Then sends them away with noth—"

The guard wrapped the cloth around Frederick's head, stuffing it in his mouth and tying it behind him.

Lord Conrat stepped closer to Frederick. "Your mother was nothing. Who really knows if you belong to the duke or some other man? If the duke had acknowledged an illegitimate child, his new bride might not have married him, and it was his father's wish that he marry her, and it was what was best for Grundelsbach. I protect what belongs to the duke, and I do what is best for Grundelsbach."

What a coward you are. Frederick stared into his cold black eyes.

"I am not planning to kill you. I want you to disappear, not become a martyr the duke's daughter can blame Lord Barthold for killing. Though he knows nothing of these plans. I can protect him better if he doesn't know. Besides that, he might not approve. He is not as cunning as a man in his position ought to be. But that is why he has me."

Lord Conrat smiled, obviously pleased with himself. He held up a hand to the guards. "Let me see if they've left." Conrat stepped outside the door.

Had the guards relaxed their hold on him? Frederick lunged forward, breaking free, and turned and kicked the sword out of the one guard's hand. Then he stumbled toward the door, knocking over a table and candlestick in the process. But hands grabbed him from behind and slammed him on the floor, flat on his back, knocking the breath out of him.

He seemed to choke for the longest moment before he was able to draw in a breath. He twisted his body to the side, but the guards were on top of him. A fist connected with his mouth. For a moment he couldn't see, his consciousness leaving him, but when he sucked in a breath through his nose, he started coughing, tasting blood as they pushed his face into the wooden floor.

Lord Conrat's voice was harsh and raspy as he came back in. "Somebody get some water!"

Yellow-orange flames shone at the edge of Frederick's vision. The candle he knocked over must have set something on fire. Lord Conrat and one of the guards beat it out with a rug.

Frederick's face ached from where the guard had punched him, and the blood from his lip and the inside of his cheek was soaking the gag in his mouth.

Lord Conrat bent over beside him. "The dungeon of Grundelsbach Castle will take the fight out of you soon enough." He straightened. "Get him up and be off with you. And I don't want anyone seeing him, you understand?"

"Yes, Lord Conrat."

Frederick's vision spun in a circle, and he stumbled forward, struggling to stay upright. The men shoved him down on a wooden cart, then covered him with a rough linen cloth.

How would he ever get out of this? *God, if I ever needed You, I need You now.* No one knew where he was going, not even Mother or his sisters. And they would be held against their will out in the country. Who would care or listen to them, even if they tried to tell someone that he was in trouble, that this Lord Conrat, adviser to the Duke of Grundelsbach, had taken him away?

Worst of all, what would Adela think? Would she take his disappearance as proof he didn't care about her?

His head ached sharply now, and the blood was pooling in his mouth. But he could not give up. No, he somehow had to get free and go to the bishop. The bishop could help him. He couldn't bear to think of either the bishop or Adela and her family believing he would leave his work and his relationships without a word.

But unless God gave him a miracle, he might very well never see Adela's lovely face, or feel her lips on his, ever again.

CHAPTER 17

Adela did not go to see Frederick at his workshop the next day. Visiting him too often didn't seem wise. But the day after that, she did go, only to discover he was not there. She found the bishop and asked him where Frederick was, but the bishop had not heard from him.

"I am becoming worried about him," the bishop said. "Will you let your father know that he has not been here for the second day in a row?"

"Of course." Adela's heart was in her throat as she hurried away down the street toward the castle. Now that she thought of it, her father hadn't mentioned receiving a letter from Frederick, and he should have sent it by now.

She found Father and asked him, "Has Frederick sent you a letter?"

"No, darling. I haven't gotten anything from him."

Had Frederick changed his mind? Had he decided not to try to curry Father's favor in order to visit with her?

"Father, he has not shown up to work at the Cathedral today or yesterday. The bishop said he was worried about him. You must send out guards to look for him."

"That is strange." Father's forehead creased and his eyebrows drew together. He opened his mouth as if to say something, then shut it, his expression changing.

"What? What is it, Father? Tell me."

"It is only that the Eselin brothers somehow escaped from the dungeon two days ago."

"Oh, Father! Could they have done something bad to Frederick?" Adela suddenly couldn't breathe. The air seemed to fly away before it reached her lungs.

"Now, don't assume anything terrible has happened. I'm sure all is well."

"All is not well. Something has happened to Frederick. He would be at the Cathedral if all were well." Again, her breath left her and she couldn't talk. Her vision started to blur.

"Sit down." Father led her to a chair in his library. "I will go and talk with the bishop."

She wanted to say, "The bishop can't do anything. I was just there." She wanted to scream, "Go find Frederick! Go search for him. He must be in danger!" But she couldn't even speak, could only concentrate on breathing and not fainting.

Her father kissed the top of her head and left.

Adela could not sit here doing nothing while something terrible could be happening to Frederick. The Eselin brothers, at this moment, could be harassing him, torturing him, could have taken him somewhere against his will. But she would do something about it.

Her vision had cleared, and she was breathing normally again. She made up her mind. She rushed out to the stable and asked a groom to saddle her horse and asked a guard to accompany her to Frederick's house.

❦

Adela and the guard arrived a few minutes later at Frederick's house. She knocked on the door, listening. She knocked again, louder this time. She turned the door handle, but it was locked and didn't open. Moving to the window, she stared in, but could see very little through the gnarled glass.

"Seitbart, please break through the door."

"Are you sure, Lady Adela?"

"Yes, I'm very sure." She kept her voice hard and cold.

Seitbart used his booted foot to stomp into the doorknob. On the third kick, it gave way and opened. The guard stepped forward. "Allow me to go in first, my lady."

Adela let him go in but was on his heels, peeking around his side.

The house smelled of smoke. Soot—evidence of a fire—covered an area on the floor and up one wall near the door. There was a small broken table and a candle lying there.

"Frederick!" Adela called. "Frau Basina?" But no one answered.

Adela looked around, her hands starting to shake. There seemed to be very few personal items in the ground-floor rooms, mostly just the furniture that was there when her grandparents lived there. She went up to the upper floors of the house. She searched through the bedrooms. Again, personal items such as clothing were mostly missing, except for a few stray articles, as if whoever had taken the items had left in a hurry and had taken their things rather haphazardly, with a ribbon lying on the floor here, a set of hose there, and an apron tossed over the stair railing.

Seitbart stayed near her as she explored each room more quickly than the last.

"Where are they? What happened here?"

"It looks as if they took their things and left, my lady."

"But why?"

Seitbart gave a tiny shrug of his shoulders. "It does seem strange about the fire. Perhaps someone forced them to leave."

Adela's heart thumped harder. She didn't know where Frederick's farm was. Had they gone back there? If so, why? Tears stung her eyes. What if she never saw him again?

"Something is wrong. Something is very wrong."

"If something bad happened to these people," Seitbart said, "perhaps the neighbors heard or saw something."

"Yes. Yes, that is a good thought." The air rushed back into her lungs.

They descended the stairs to the bottom floor and went outside. They went first to the neighbors to the left. Adela knew them slightly. She knocked on the door, and a woman answered.

"Frau Blume, is it?"

"*Ja.*"

"It's Adela."

"Oh, Lady Adela." The woman bowed at the waist two quick times. "Won't you come inside?"

"Thank you, but no, I just need to ask you some questions. May I, please?"

"Of course. I will help you if I can."

"The people next door. Did you know them?"

"In your grandparents' house? Yes, a little."

"Did you see them leave?"

"No, but it was very strange. They were there one day, and the next day they were gone."

"Did you hear anything? Anything out of the ordinary?"

"Two nights ago we heard some shouts and loud noises."

"Can you describe them?" Adela's heart pounded against her chest. She glanced behind her to make sure Seitbart was listening. His eyes were on Frau Blume.

"We heard a few loud crashes and then a woman cry out, and a man's voice shouting. My husband looked out the window, but it was dark and he didn't see anything, and we were already in bed. I'm so sorry, Lady Adela. The noises stopped after that, so we assumed everyone was fine."

"No, no, it's all right." Adela's body was numb, and when she brought her hand to her face to push back her hair, her fingers were shaking.

"If you think of anything else you heard or saw, anything unusual," Seitbart said, "please send a message to Lady Adela or Duke Wilhelm at the castle."

"I will. But wait. There was something that happened the night before that."

"What?"

"A man came and knocked on the door. My husband opened it and asked him what he wanted. My husband told me later that the man was obviously drunk. He said he wanted his wife."

"He wanted his wife?"

"Yes. He said, 'I want my wife, and her name is Basina.' I didn't know any better, so I told him Basina lived next door. He went away, and we didn't think much of it."

Frederick's mother's name was Basina. A drunk man looking for his wife? It must have been Frederick's father.

"I hope the people who were there are all right."

Adela nodded. "Thank you."

She turned to the neighbors on the other side of the house. "Can you tell me what happened two nights ago at my grandparents' old house?" she asked. "Did you see or hear anything?"

"Yes," the young man said. "I had not yet gone to bed and was standing outside taking in the night air, as I like to do, when I saw some men go into the house."

"Some men? What kind of men?"

"It was dark, and I couldn't see them very well. I heard one of them talking about his duties in Grundelsbach. I wondered if he might be a soldier from there."

She pointed at Seitbart. "Were they dressed like Duke Wilhelm's guards?"

"I don't know. But when they went inside, I thought I heard a woman cry out. There were some other noises, like someone falling down or something heavy getting thrown down."

"And did you see anyone come outside?"

"I did see a group of people come out, but I didn't want to intrude, so I went inside. I didn't hear any other loud noises. Then I went to bed."

Her heart sank to the pit of her stomach as she said, "Thank you," and turned to leave. She and Seitbart asked at the houses across the street, but none of them had seen or heard anything.

As they walked back toward the castle, she pressed a hand to her forehead. This had not been very helpful. Frederick's father was the drunk man who had come looking for Frederick and his mother three nights ago. Then two nights ago, some men, possibly soldiers, had come and taken the women away.

Tears pricked her eyes as pain and pressure built inside her chest.

Father would know what to do. He always knew what to do.

She hurried to the castle, doing her best to stay calm, and searched for Father in every room, asking all the servants if they'd seen him. Then Seitbart found her.

"He's talking with the captain and said for you to wait for him here."

Adela's heart started beating almost normally again. Yes, Father would be here soon. He would take care of things. She waited in the open doorway until she saw him walking toward her.

"Do you have news of Frederick, Father?"

"No, daughter." His brow was furrowed. "Come inside." He closed the door of the library behind him, something he rarely did, and they sat down.

"What is it? Tell me quickly."

"I don't know anything. The bishop is worried about Frederick. He wants my guards to search for him, and he wants me to question Barthold."

"Barthold! Yes, Father, perhaps Barthold did something to Frederick. He was jealous of him and—"

"Now, let us not be quick to falsely accuse anyone. It could also have something to do with the Eselin brothers escaping from the dungeon."

"Something has happened to Frederick. Please, you must find out what happened. He must be in danger."

"Do you know where he lived before he came here?"

"No, but surely you can ask, can find someone who knows. I don't know his surname, but someone must know it."

"There is something else I need to show you." Father pulled out a letter from the small pouch on his belt.

"What is it?"

"It is a letter from Frederick. I found it on my desk this morning."

"What does it say?"

"You can read it for yourself."

Adela took the letter, and it fluttered in her hand, which shook at the way her father was looking at her—with kindness and pity.

Dear Lady Adela,

    I am sorry to tell you that I have decided to go back to the farm with my family. I realized the Cathedral doors were too difficult for me, and so I am giving that up as well. I've never carved anything that large before, and the scope of it was too much for me. Please don't try to find me. It is for the best. You are a duke's daughter and I am just a peasant.

Fare well, Lady Adela.

Your father's loyal subject,

Frederick

Adela shoved the letter at her father. "Frederick did not write that. It doesn't sound like him at all."

"How do you know? Perhaps he did write it. You have to at least consider the possibility."

"No, Father. He would not have said those things. And Frederick would not have gone back to the farm. His father was cruel, and he wanted his mother and sisters away from that man. And Frederick was very excited about carving those doors. He had drawn up detailed plans. If you don't believe me, ask the bishop."

"I have asked him and shown him the letter. The bishop seemed very surprised, and yet he did not think it was impossible that he wrote it. Besides, who would want to lie about Frederick in such a way? It seems farfetched that anyone, including Barthold, would have harmed him."

"Not nearly as farfetched as Frederick writing such a letter. Being too afraid to carve those doors? That's nonsense. And wanting to go back to that farm, where he had to work from sunrise to past sunset? His father was a cruel man, someone who drank constantly and beat him and his mother. Perhaps his father did something terrible to him and his mother and sisters."

Father's brows drew together. "We should find his father and question him."

"Yes, Father, we should."

"Very well." Father still had that look of pity in his eyes as he stared at her.

"I don't understand why you aren't taking this more seriously." Adela felt tears sting her eyes. "He has been missing for two days. Anything could have happened to him." She bit her lip as the tears filled her eyes and blurred her sight.

"I will send my men to try and find Frederick's home and his father."

"And in the meantime you should question Barthold. I think he may have wanted to get rid of Frederick."

"Darling, there is also the suspicious coincidence of the Eselins escaping from the dungeon the same night Frederick went missing. Perhaps Frederick had something to do with helping them get away."

Adela blew out a loud breath. "Of course he would not have had anything to do with that! Frederick would never—and the Eselins hate him. And Barthold hates Frederick, too, and thinks he tried to harm me. You should speak to him, please, Father."

"I shall go and speak with him now."

"I want to know everything he says."

Father drew in a long, slow breath and then let it out. "I shall report back to you what I learn." He reached out and caressed her shoulder. "I promise. Now, go and speak with your mother. You know she always makes you feel better."

"I don't need to feel better. I need to find out—" *what happened to Frederick.* The lump in her throat choked off the rest of her words.

"My men and I will do our very best."

But she saw the look in his eyes, as if he was afraid. He wasn't promising that they would find him. Was he remembering how her sister had gone missing and it had taken so many months to find her? Her father and his men had searched and searched to no avail. Would the same thing happen now with Frederick?

CHAPTER 18

⁓

Duke Wilhelm went in search of Lord Barthold and found him talking with one of the guards from Grundelsbach. As the duke's young son listened to the guard, his brows drew together, forming a crease between his eyes.

"Is anything amiss?"

Lord Barthold looked up and saw him. "Oh. No, nothing is wrong."

But there was something in the way he hesitated. Wilhelm stared at him.

"It's just that some of the guards went back to Grundelsbach two days ago. It's strange that no one told me." He shook his head and looked away.

"Some guards went back to Grundelsbach? And you said that was two days ago?"

"They were needed at home to help Father."

"Who said they were needed at home?"

Barthold stared back at Wilhelm as if he didn't understand his question.

"Who told you they were gone?"

"The soldier I was just speaking with. He told me when I asked about one of the other guards. He and five other guards went back to Grundelsbach."

"Did your father send for them?"

"It seems as if he did. Is something wrong, Duke Wilhelm?"

"Forgive me for all the questions, but . . ." He noticed Lord Conrat walking across the castle yard toward them. Something about his narrowed eyes made Wilhelm ask, "Can we go to my library and speak in private?"

"Of course."

He led Barthold inside to his library and closed the door. He turned around to face Barthold, studying his reaction as he said, "Did you know that Frederick the wood-carver is missing?"

"No."

Barthold's expression gave no indication of either feigned surprise or shrewdness.

"Frederick has not been seen for two days."

"I suppose the coward ran away." His eyes opened wider. "This proves he was involved in shooting me and trying to seize Lady Adela."

"Perhaps." Wilhelm was inclined to think that Barthold had nothing to do with Frederick's disappearance. But the disappearance of his guards on the same day . . .

"If you hear anything about what happened to Frederick, would you let me know?"

"If you wish my guards and me to track him down and throw him in your dungeon, I would be pleased to do that." An eager look sharpened his eyes.

"I would not be against you searching for him. I am very curious to know what has happened to him—although I must tell you, the Eselins escaped my dungeon two nights ago."

"Escaped?" Barthold's eyes grew bigger and his chest rose and fell. "All three of them?"

"I'm afraid so. No one seems to have seen anything."

"I will hunt them down."

"I have guards searching for them. How is your shoulder?"

Barthold rolled his shoulder. "It is mending well. I shall be fully healed in a few weeks, says Frau Lena."

"I am glad."

"I'm going to take my men and search for those miscreants."

Wilhelm nodded. "I will continue the search as well, but first I need to speak to someone."

Wilhelm needed to figure out how to question Lord Conrat without making him suspicious.

❧

Frederick lay bruised and aching on the cold stone floor of the dungeon. It had taken three days and nights to get to Grundelsbach, and the guards had availed themselves of several opportunities to kick him awake, which was why it hurt to take a good breath. And the one time he'd tried to escape, they'd beaten his face until his lip was swollen and crusted over and his eyes were nearly swollen shut.

Since he'd arrived the night before, he'd been sleeping and listening, trying to discern if the dungeon guards were as brutal as the guards who had brought him here, trying to determine how he might escape. Trying to determine how he could overcome the crushing sense of being abandoned by God.

His cheek lay against the cold, damp stone, against the grit of unknown dirt and grime. But it was better than being jostled by the horse-drawn cart they'd brought him here in, his hands tied behind him, his head covered by a hemp sack that had him wondering if he'd suffocate before they arrived.

But he hadn't suffocated, and perhaps the only reason he was glad he had not was because he didn't want Adela, or his mother, to be tormented wondering what had happened to him. He had to stay alive, and he had to escape so that he could get back to them.

He must have fallen asleep, because he suddenly heard footsteps near his head.

He jerked himself upright, his chains rattling. A man stood over him, staring hard at him in the dim light.

"Are you all right? Your face . . ."

"Who are you?"

"Name's Heinryk. Here's some food." Heinryk held out a handful of something.

Frederick reached out without thinking and took what was offered. It felt like bread.

"Am I in Grundelsbach?" Frederick asked. "Is this the dungeon?"

Heinryk's face registered sadness in the downturn of his mouth and eyes. Then he nodded.

"I've done nothing wrong, and the man who had me brought here knows I've done nothing wrong. I need to send a message back to Hagenheim, to let someone know I'm here." He spoke quickly, fearing any moment he might be silenced.

"That is impossible." Heinryk shook his balding head as he turned away.

"Why? Who's in charge of this prison?"

"You are one of Lord Conrat's prisoners, so I cannot grant you any privileges, and no one is supposed to know you're here."

"Not even the duke?"

The man again shook his head.

"Are you in charge?"

"Me? I am only a prison guard. But you don't want to meet the man in charge. He hates all the prisoners. But I'm not supposed to be talking to you. I have to go." Heinryk shuffled quickly away.

Frederick looked down for the first time at what was in his hand. It was a thick slice of bread and nothing more.

His head was throbbing, so he lay back down. Heinryk came around with a cup of water, which he silently handed to Frederick, then waited. Frederick drank it, draining the cup, and gave it back. Heinryk shuffled away again.

Frederick ate the dry bread. Then he moved the chain from underneath his shoulder and arranged his arm into a pillow. He stared up at the tiny window above him through the slits of his swollen eyes. Somehow he had to escape.

He knew from listening that there were many other men around him. He'd heard their chains clanging and their voices and moans. He'd also heard Heinryk walking around and handing out food. But Frederick could see no one, as he was blocked in on three sides by stone-and-plaster walls. The fourth side of his cell was open. There was no need for a locked door when he was held by these chains.

But he had to escape. He had to. The alternative was unthinkable.

He pushed himself toward the wall so he could lean back, then occupied his thoughts with memories of Adela, of her sweet smile, kind words, and soft lips. And he quietly prayed, "God, please don't forget about me."

❧

Adela found her father the next day in his library.

"Father, what have you learned about Frederick? Did you talk to Barthold?"

"I did talk to Barthold, but he knows nothing about Frederick's disappearance."

"You mean, he *says* he knows nothing about it. That doesn't mean he doesn't know."

"Darling, it is a serious thing to accuse someone falsely, and from what I've observed of him, I believe Barthold is telling the truth. But I am suspicious that someone from Grundelsbach may be responsible for him disappearing. And yet, the fact that the Eselin brothers escaped the dungeon the same night that Frederick seems to have disappeared, the same night several of the duke's guards left for Grundelsbach . . . That is a lot of strange things to happen in one night."

Adela's heart beat faster.

"I have someone I'm planning to speak to about it, but I need you not to say anything to anyone about my suspicions."

"Yes, Father. But can I be present when you question this person?"

"Absolutely not. That would not be wise."

"But, Father, I am mature enough. I can—"

"That is not why you must not be present. I don't want this person to know I am suspicious of him. Besides, he may not know anything of Frederick's whereabouts. And I don't need him telling the Duke of Grundelsbach that I believed him capable of something dastardly."

Father did have a heavy burden on him to keep the other nobles on friendly terms with him.

"Will you at least tell me what you discover?"

"When I believe I've uncovered the truth, I will tell you. Even if that truth is painful." He gave her that pitying look of his.

Her stomach sank, but she swallowed and nodded. "Yes, Father."

Wilhelm tried to draw out Lord Conrat that morning when they went on a hunt with Barthold, but they ended up being too busy chasing and killing a wild boar that had been terrorizing people near the town wall. He knew from his own experience how much damage a wild boar could do with its tusks.

After the hunt, while Barthold went to rest his sore shoulder, Wilhelm invited Conrat to sit with him in his library with the pretense of discussing a canal system the Duke of Grundelsbach had been considering.

After some minutes discussing the canal, Wilhelm said, "I noticed some of your guards left a few days ago. Is anything amiss in Grundelsbach that the duke needed them?"

Lord Conrat's eyes darted to the side, staring at the wall behind Wilhelm's head, then flitted in the other direction. "No, nothing was amiss. The duke wanted to send a detachment to escort a prisoner who was captured . . . in Lüneburg, I believe."

"I see. Speaking of capturing prisoners, did you hear that the young wood-carver has vanished?" Wilhelm studied Conrat's reaction.

Conrat stared right back into Wilhelm's eyes. His whole body was completely still.

"I had heard something about that. You were searching for him, I believe. But I'm sure he has fled. As Barthold and I both warned you, he is not to be trusted. He pursued your daughter in secret and then joined with nefarious men bent on harming her, and—they shot Barthold. A despicable and cowardly act. They would have held your daughter for ransom. I know you believed in his innocence, but his running away has proven his guilt."

"Perhaps, but I'm not so sure he did run away." Wilhelm continued to study Lord Conrat. He did not seem to be lying, although he'd been taken by surprise when Wilhelm asked him about the guards leaving abruptly. But Wilhelm had questioned many guilty men, and in his opinion, either Lord Conrat was telling the truth or he was a very practiced liar.

"We also made note that his family had left Hagenheim. You wouldn't happen to know where they went?"

Lord Conrat stiffened his back and shoulders. "Why would I know the whereabouts of a peasant family?"

"I only ask because you are the adviser to the Duke of Grundelsbach. I'm sure you are very adept at knowing what is happening around you, anything that affects the duke or his family members, especially Lord Barthold, the heir."

"Yes."

The shrewd, narrow-eyed look on Conrat's face told Wilhelm he'd perhaps gone too far.

"I only wondered."

"Do you not also think it suspicious that the Eselin brothers have escaped the dungeon and run away? It seems obvious that this Frederick fellow ran away with them. If you find one, you find them all."

"You are probably right. Frederick must have been guilty, and instead of risking getting thrown in the dungeon again, he left town, either with the Eselins or with his family." Wilhelm turned toward the door, signaling he was ready to move away from the discussion.

"It is the only reasonable explanation."

When Wilhelm turned back toward Conrat, his eyes were on Wilhelm's face, and there was a dark shallowness in those eyes. If he'd been asked what color Lord Conrat's eyes were, he'd have had to say they were black. His lips looked pinched, even when they morphed into a small smile.

Wilhelm made an excuse for leaving Conrat's company. As he

was turning to go, Conrat said, "The duke is sending some fresh guards who should arrive tomorrow."

"And you will not need to return to Grundelsbach?"

Lord Conrat lowered his brows. "The duke has entrusted me to stay by his son's side. Since his beloved wife died a year ago, he has started many new projects, such as the canal system, to keep him busy. He values my assistance, of course, but he felt it was more important for me to stay with his son and advise him at this time."

"And you and Lord Barthold are remaining here in Hagenheim for the full six months that was agreed upon?"

"Yes, if that is well with you, Your Grace."

"Of course. I enjoy Lord Barthold's company."

But Wilhelm still had no more answers than he'd had before. Perhaps Frederick had been taken somewhere by the Grundelsbach guards, or perhaps not. Perhaps Lord Conrat knew more than he was telling, or not. But Adela might need to accept that Frederick may truly have not felt equal to the task of carving the Cathedral doors, had realized he was only breaking his and Adela's hearts by pursuing her, and he simply left and returned to his home and his land. But it was all suspicious enough that Wilhelm would continue sending his guards out to search for the young wood-carver and his family, and continue looking for answers.

❧

Frederick had been in the Grundelsbach dungeon for seven days. The swelling in his eyes and face had gone down and his ribs were less sore, but his heart hurt worse than ever. What must everyone in Hagenheim be thinking about him? Lord Conrat had surely made certain that there was no trace of him, no way to know where he'd been taken. It probably looked as if he'd simply left.

Mother must be so worried about him, but as she and his sisters were back with Father, what could she do? No doubt Stenngle would threaten her with dire consequences if she left him again. But he hated to think she was worried about him, in addition to being trapped with that man who treated her so badly. If only he could get a message to her telling her he was safe.

Safe. He was hardly safe, but at least he could say he was alive.

Voices came from the other side of the left wall of his cell. Frederick had seen no one except Heinryk since he'd been here. But now he heard Heinryk's voice and someone else's.

"Who is in this cell?" the stranger's voice said.

"One of Lord Conrat's prisoners," Heinryk answered. His voice sounded as sad as the expression he always wore.

After some words too low for Frederick to hear, the two men appeared in his open doorway. Frederick rose to his feet amid much clanking of his irons and chains.

The stranger was older, with gray hair and rounded, open eyes that were fastened on Frederick. He asked, "What's your name?"

"I am Frederick, a wood-carver from Hagenheim." He was also the illegitimate son of the Duke of Grundelsbach, but he decided not to mention that. They would think he had gone mad. "I was taken from my home by Lord Conrat, I have done nothing wrong, and I've had no trial. No one has questioned me about my supposed crime."

"Yes, yes," the man said, motioning with his hand as if to tamp down a smoking coal. He fastened hard eyes on Frederick's face. "I am Mertin, and I'm in charge here. What does Lord Conrat say you did?"

"Mertin, sir, Conrat knows I've done nothing wrong." How much should he tell this man? He certainly didn't know if he could trust him, and the truth sounded too farfetched. "He was jealous of the favor I was gaining with the Duke of Hagenheim and the Bishop of Hagenheim."

"You are friends with the duke and the bishop, eh?"

"The bishop hired me to carve the new doors for the Cathedral. Please. If you would give me a bit of paper and a pen, I could write a note for the bishop and he could at least know where I am."

"You can read and write, then?"

"Yes."

The man crossed his arms over his chest. He seemed to be chewing his lip as he continued to stare at Frederick.

"Or if you would allow me to send word to Duke Wilhelm in Hagenheim—"

"Lord Conrat would have my head if I allowed you any such privilege."

Frederick's stomach sank. "But he would never know."

The man raised his brows, then sighed. "Frederick the wood-carver, eh? How well do you write?"

"I write well enough."

"How many occasions does a wood-carver have to write?"

"I write verse, stories, and rhymes, for many years now."

The man slowly nodded. Suddenly he uncrossed his arms and began to move away. "Carry on."

"Sir, please." Frederick's heart leapt inside him. "I can be your scribe, write anything you need. I just need to get a message back to Hagenheim."

The man stopped and looked at Frederick again. "I cannot grant such a privilege to one of Lord Conrat's prisoners. It isn't as if I don't wish to. I simply can't." He smiled as if trying to cheer him up, as if he were denying him a small favor rather than dooming him to rot in prison.

"I am innocent." Frederick moved as far as his chains would

allow. "I need an audience with the Duke of Grundelsbach. If you will take me to him I will explain—"

The man looked as if he might laugh, raising his brows higher than ever. "Impossible. You will never be allowed to speak to the duke." He started walking away.

Heinryk's mouth twisted as if in pain, and he followed the cruel man as they disappeared around the side of the wall of his cell.

The ache in Frederick's wrist and ankle reminded him of the irons that were fastened around them. Already the heavy metal was wearing away the skin.

He dragged his leg chains back toward the wall and sat down, feeling a trickle of blood ooze down his ankle. If he didn't die of the damp—many of his fellow prisoners coughed incessantly—he'd die of a putridness from the wounds inflicted by the leg and wrist irons.

He put his head in his hands, but he knew he must not sink into despair. He had to find a way out of here. And if the *gaolers* could not be reasoned with, their humanity appealed to, then he'd just have to escape by force. He was a strong man. He'd plowed many a field, wrestled with cows giving birth, done all manner of physical labor. He could surely break himself free from this dungeon.

He had studied the chains before, but he did so again. He could find no weak links, but surely if he pulled on them hard enough . . . He examined where the chains fastened to the wall. His wrist iron was fastened in one place, his leg iron in another.

He took hold of the chain attached to his wrist iron and, wrapping the chain around his hand, tugged with all his might. Nothing happened. He pulled again, this time throwing his weight backward, but the chain held. He did the same with his leg-iron chains, and with the same result.

He ran his fingers around the bolt holding each chain to the wall. They were somehow embedded into the rock. But surely if he pulled at it often enough, he could work it loose. What else did he have to do?

He set about working at the bolt and ring that attached his leg iron to the wall. He pulled and pushed at it with all the strength in his hands and fingers. After a long time of this, what seemed like hours, his hands trembled with exhaustion. But the bolt had not moved, not the slightest bit.

He looked around the small cell, crawling on his hands and knees in search of a rock, anything he could use to scrape at the bolt, to loosen the mortar around it. But someone must have swept it clean.

Still, he couldn't let himself get discouraged. He would keep trying, keep himself strong the best he could. Evil could never defeat good. Though evil could lie and steal and destroy for a time, it was only for a time; God always had the final say.

CHAPTER 19

A dela sat in the rose garden on a bench. The roses were beautiful, even though it was hardly the season for them. They bloomed nearly all year in this garden, as their gardener was so clever with roses. He knew how to nurture and attend to them to keep them full and healthy.

One red bush was so near to her bench, she could reach out and touch one of the blooms. It was soft and tender as she held it in her hand, caressing its petals with her thumb. If she pressed too hard with her thumbnail . . . She stabbed the petal and broke it off in the middle.

She had not beheld Frederick's face in two weeks. Where had he gone? What had happened to him? Father and his guards had searched for Frederick, but no one seemed to know where he came from or his family name, and she did not even know which general direction his farm was from Hagenheim. She remembered him saying his mother was from Grundelsbach, so perhaps she had family there, but where was his father's family from? No one seemed to know.

She wiped at the tears that streamed down her face. They did not help anything.

"Lady Adela?" Lord Barthold's voice came from behind her.

Her stomach sank. She didn't want anyone to see her like this. Certainly not Lord Barthold. She dried her wet fingers on her skirt and then wiped at the tears still on her face. But he came around in front of her before she had finished.

"What is amiss, my lady?" Barthold sank to his knees in front of her.

She drew in a breath at his sudden attention and close proximity. The last time she'd spoken with him, he'd been angry because she'd told him she couldn't marry him.

She shook her head. "I am well. It is nothing."

"Something is wrong." He continued kneeling, patiently watching her face.

"I do not wish to speak of it. It is . . ." She couldn't honestly say it was nothing. She cared for Frederick, and she was terrified for him. Something terrible must have happened to him.

"Is someone unwell, someone in your family?" His voice was gentle, and the look on his face was kind, but she wished he would go away and let her cry in peace.

"No one is unwell. No one in my family, that is."

"Someone is unwell. Is it a favorite servant? Your horse?"

"No, no." She shook her head, and the thought of Frederick—so much dearer to her than any horse—made the tears return too suddenly to blink them back. She turned her head, but he was too close to miss her flicking away the tears that escaped her eyes.

He didn't move, and when she peeked at him, he was still staring at her with a look of concern in his eyes.

"Won't you please tell me what is wrong, so that I can fix it?"

She took deep breaths, willing away the tears, calming herself. She had already told Barthold that she couldn't marry him. Should she tell him again? Her mother always told her, "The truth is kinder than a lie."

"Frederick has been missing for a long time, and I'm afraid something terrible has happened to him. Forgive me. I know you don't like him, but . . . he is my friend and I . . . care for him very much."

She watched Barthold's expression change as his jaw hardened, then flexed. His throat bobbed as he swallowed.

"I have heard about this from your father. I also heard about the letter he wrote explaining that he was abandoning the wood-carving project for the bishop and leaving Hagenheim."

"I don't believe he wrote that letter."

Barthold spoke slowly, as if coming to a decision. "My men and I helped searched for him for three days, but I would like to continue to help because it will give you peace if we can discover what happened to him."

She blinked. Could he really want to help? Perhaps he did care for her, more than she realized.

"That is very kind of you."

She wasn't sure if he could help, since Father was doing everything he could, and Barthold wasn't from Hagenheim. But the more people searching for Frederick, the better.

A pain went through her chest. The poor man. If he did care for her, as he seemed to, then this must hurt him very much, knowing she had feelings for Frederick.

He took her hand before she had time to react. "I will do my best to find him, and when I do, you shall be the first to know. Are you sure you want to know—no matter what I discover?"

Her stomach sank at the thought of what he was suggesting. The worst thing he might discover was that Frederick was dead. Although he probably thought Frederick had just run away and that that was the worst thing, knowing he had left her like a coward. But she was certain that was not what had happened. It simply wasn't possible.

"I am sure I want to know," she said.

Barthold released her hand and arose from his kneeling position. "I shall begin right away. Good day, Lady Adela."

"I thank you, Lord Barthold."

He met her eye and nodded, then strode away.

Perhaps she had misjudged Barthold a bit. He had seemed genuinely concerned about her and seemed sincere in his desire to find out what had happened to Frederick, even after she admitted she cared very much for this other man. She only hoped Barthold would not be too disappointed when she chose Frederick over him. She was certain Frederick was still alive. She had prayed so many times, and each time she felt an assurance, almost as if God was telling her that Frederick was alive.

If only she could do something to help find Frederick.

An idea suddenly came to her, and her heart lifted. She would paint a picture of Frederick!

She could remember every detail of his face, and once she had painted it, she could take the painting to the countryside and show it to people, asking if anyone had seen Frederick. She would eventually find someone who knew him and knew where he lived.

She hurried to her room to start painting.

❧

"Where are you going?"

Barthold stopped and turned around as Lord Conrat addressed him.

"I'm going to see if I can find the man Frederick. He is missing." Barthold didn't particularly wish to involve Lord Conrat in this. He had a way of trying to take control of things that were not his responsibility. But Conrat also would never leave him alone until he answered his question.

Conrat's face did not register surprise. He had that dead-eyed look he sometimes got.

"Frederick? Why would you wish to find him? Is he not the man who tried to woo Lady Adela and was involved with the men who tried to kill you?"

"I do not know if . . ." He did not wish to argue any of those points with Lord Conrat. "Yes, that's the man. Lady Adela needs to know his whereabouts." He dared Conrat to criticize him for caring about Lady Adela's peace of mind.

"But he wrote a missive saying he was not equal to the task the bishop had given him and he was leaving Hagenheim. Surely Lady Adela read the letter."

"She does not accept that he wrote that missive."

"I see." Lord Conrat was strangely silent. Then he added, "Of course."

Barthold wondered if Lord Conrat was talking to him or to himself.

"Allow me to help as well," Conrat said, suddenly looking quite interested. "After all, what concerns you, as the future Duke of Grundelsbach, concerns me." He smiled.

Barthold wasn't sure he trusted Conrat. What were his true motives for wanting to help?

"Allow me one guard, and he and I will do our best to find this Frederick for Lady Adela, so that she can see once and for all what a coward he is. And then . . ." Lord Conrat smiled again. "Then perhaps she will finally see what is right in front of her eyes, eh, Lord Barthold?"

Yes, that might make up for how she had preferred that wood-carver over him, if she were to repent of her high opinion of the peasant and finally realize that he, Barthold, was exactly the hus-band for her. Who could be better suited than the two of them?

213

"Very well."

Barthold and Lord Conrat went downstairs together, discussing what was known of this Frederick. Somehow they would find him, and Adela would see that the man was not worthy of her. Barthold could comfort Adela, and then she would cease to think of that peasant and would think of him instead.

◈

Adela had worked on her painting of Frederick for two days, from sunup until sundown, until she was satisfied that anyone who knew Frederick would recognize him in the painting. Then she took two guards with her—Father would not allow her to leave the town gate with only one guard—and went half an hour's ride to the north of town to begin searching for Frederick. She showed her painting to everyone she saw, but no one knew who he was. No one had seen him.

She went home tired but hopeful she would find him tomorrow. It felt good to take action, to be doing something.

The next day she went into the stable to talk to the grooms who were preparing her horse. She'd decided to ride west. But when she came out of the stable, a man was watching her. It was Barthold's adviser, Lord Conrat. Something about the way he looked at her made a shiver go down her spine. But he had always been friendly enough toward her. So when he approached her as she prepared to mount her horse, she turned and greeted him.

"Lady Adela. I am curious where you are going. You appear to have a lot of supplies."

"I am doing what Lord Barthold has been doing. I am searching for the man who has gone missing."

"So you do not believe he has left of his own will?"

"No, I do not."

"He has a very good friend in you. If I should disappear, I should hope to have a friend like you to search for me."

Adela nodded at the compliment.

"How do you propose to find the man?" he asked. "Do you have a strategy?"

"I have a picture of him that I painted myself, and I am showing it around to try and find someone who has seen him or perhaps knows him and his family."

A strange look flickered over Lord Conrat's face. "That is very clever of you. Where are you going today?"

"To the west."

"Ah, I see. And how far will you go?"

"My guards and I will ride hard for a little more than half an hour, then stop and make our way slowly back to Hagenheim. I believe I will find someone, eventually, who has seen him."

There was a hard glint in his eye as he stared back at her. After a moment, he said, "I am sure you will find him."

Adela's guards were ready and waiting for her, so she mounted her horse and started after them. But as she rode out of the castle yard, she noticed Lord Conrat waving two of the Grundelsbach guards over to him, as if he had something urgent to say to them. Which gave her an uneasy feeling.

❧

Adela showed her painting of Frederick to some people in a small village, but no one recognized him.

They'd been out for at least three hours when they came upon a young man on a rather lonely stretch of road with trees on both sides.

Adela drew out the painting, which was becoming quite worn around the edges. She approached the young man, who looked as though he hadn't had a bath in a very long time. And by the way he smelled, she was more certain of it.

"Have you seen this man?" she asked.

The man looked quite carefully at the picture, his eyes going wide.

"His name is Frederick," she said eagerly, "and he's quite tall."

"I have seen him, a while ago. Yes, I remember him going through the woods in that direction." He pointed through the trees. "And a few minutes later I thought I heard wolves howling."

Adela felt sick. But the man was probably lying. He did not look like the most trustworthy person.

"When was this?" Adela asked.

"Two weeks ago, I think."

The guards were staring at her, no doubt waiting for her instructions. But her mind was spinning.

"Should we go look?" one of the guards finally said.

"I'll show you which way I saw him go," the young man said, and he started off the road at a trot through the trees.

Adela and her guards guided their horses after him. They followed the young man until he suddenly stopped at a small ravine and pointed down.

"I think I see something," he said, then started down the ravine.

Adela's guards dismounted, so she did as well. As she stepped to the edge of the ravine, she saw something pale blue on the ground farther down.

The skin on her arms began to tickle unpleasantly and her stomach churned. She kept moving but allowed the men to go before her. When they reached the blue object, Adela was still several feet away, but she could see that it was a shirt.

A shirt that was ripped and torn and covered in what looked like dried blood.

The guards were kneeling beside it, gazing up at her. Their expressions were anxious and tense.

"I don't think you should look, Lady Adela," one said.

"Best not to," the other agreed.

Adela had to examine the shirt to assure herself it wasn't Frederick's. So she kept moving down the steep embankment until she reached it. But the closer she came, the more it looked like . . . but she wouldn't believe it. Couldn't believe it.

Torn and dirty, on the sleeve was a blue patch that had been sewn on the shirt with gray thread. There was no mistaking the patch. This was Frederick's shirt.

She picked up the shirt from the ground and clutched it in her fists. The laces at the neck, the knots tied in the ends . . . How familiar they were. She held the shirt to her nose and smelled lilac and lavender, the dried herbs Frederick's mother used on his laundry.

Her fists unclenched and her hands shook. *No. No, no, no. It couldn't be true.*

Her vision started going dark. She was sinking.

Strong hands held her up as voices faded in and out.

She blinked, finding herself sitting on the ground with her guards staring down at her.

"Are you all right, Lady Adela?"

"Go look for him," she said, then had to blink the dark away again. "He might be nearby. He might be hurt."

"You stay with Lady Adela," one guard said. "I'll go look around."

Frederick couldn't be dead. He couldn't be. She would know if he were dead. She would surely feel it.

But she couldn't tear her eyes off the shirt, which lay across her lap.

No one could survive losing that much blood or being torn by a wolf's teeth and claws as badly as this shirt was torn. The men weren't looking for Frederick so much as they were looking for his mangled body.

She was losing her senses again. She leaned forward, trying not to fall over.

Horses' hooves sounded on the road behind them. Adela blinked. Lord Conrat and two Grundelsbach guards appeared above them. The way the young man who'd led them there looked at Lord Conrat was strange, almost as if he knew him.

"What is going on here?" Lord Conrat asked.

One of her guards explained about the boy recognizing her picture of Frederick and their finding the shirt.

"What are you doing with poor Lady Adela? Can you not see she is overcome? Take her back to Hagenheim, and my men and I will find what we can of the man's body."

Adela nearly retched at the picture his words conjured up. But her father's two guards came along either side of her, holding on to her arms and helping her up the side of the ravine.

Don't think. Don't think. Don't think. But her mind kept going to the shirt, to Conrat and his guards moving down into the ravine to see . . . what else . . . was left.

⁕

The ride back to Hagenheim was a blur. Frederick's precious face haunted her, along with his perfect, strong body. Whenever she imagined the wolves attacking him, she whispered, "Don't think. Don't think," and squeezed her eyes shut.

One of the guards must have ridden ahead, because her father and mother were there waiting for her when she came into the stable yard.

"Darling, let me take you to your room." Father helped her down off her horse. She must have fainted, because she didn't remember anything until she was on the stairs and her father and Lord Barthold were half carrying her up, her feet barely touching the steps.

When they reached her room, her mother was waiting for her. They sat her on her bed, and she clung to her mother's arm and shoulder.

"He's not dead, Mother. He can't be." So why were tears running down her face?

"I'm so sorry, darling." Mother put her arms around her.

She tried to shake her head. "It was his shirt, but he can't be dead."

She wasn't sure how long she sat there with her mother holding her. She felt cold and numb, but she was not crying anymore. When she pulled away, she saw her father and her little brother, Toby, standing in the room.

"Did you see the body, Father?"

"I did not."

"Will you come and tell me as soon as they find him?"

"Yes, darling. I'll go now and see if Lord Conrat and his men have returned."

He couldn't be dead. Frederick could not die.

"I'll go track down those wolves for you, Adela," Toby declared, his brows drawn down and his jawline set. "I'll find them and kill them."

Mother gave Toby a tiny shake of her head and said softly, "Not now, darling."

"Let me get you some water." Mother stood and poured her a cup of water from the pitcher on the table.

Adela heard a commotion outside in the bailey and went to the window. Several guards were riding in, and she picked out Lord Conrat among them. She was too far away to see his expression, but he dismounted rather quickly and turned toward the castle.

She stood frozen. Had Conrat found something more? Her knees shook, but she could not wait. She hurried out of the room. Mother called after her, but she continued through the corridor and down the steps. She met Barthold halfway down.

"Lady Adela." His eyes were sober and he stopped.

She could hardly breathe as she watched Barthold's face.

"Come, my dear. We will tell you all. Let us go back up the stairs to your room."

"Adela?" Mother was calling to her from the top of the stairs.

"Go back up to your mother."

Her heart thudded in her chest, then seemed to beat in her throat, almost choking her. "Just tell me. Please."

But she could see the look in Barthold's eyes as he stood still, holding out his hand to her. He would not tell her until she complied. So she put her shaking hand in his and let him lead her back up the stone steps.

She would not believe them if they said Frederick was dead.

When they were back in her room, her mother tried to get her to sit, but she couldn't. Instead, she stood, her mother beside her holding her hand.

Conrat appeared in her doorway. Something about his face made her focus instead on Barthold, on his kinder, gentler features. Strange that she should think Barthold gentle. He was not as gentle as Frederick, nor as handsome, but she trusted him not to hurt her intentionally.

Her mind was numb as Father entered her room behind Conrat. "Frederick is not dead," she insisted.

"Darling." Father reached out to her.

"No! Tell me what you found."

"I am sorry to inform you, Lady Adela," Conrat's grating voice said, "but my guard and I found . . . him . . . in the ravine. He had been mauled by a wild animal."

"I don't believe it." But her stomach sank to her toes. What if it was true? But if she protested, if she showed them she did not believe, then perhaps it wouldn't be true. "It could not have been Frederick. It was someone else."

"My men are there now, burying what was left of his body," Conrat went on, "but I brought back the shirt that was found nearby." He lifted a leather bag he'd been carrying and pulled out the torn and bloodied shirt she'd seen before.

"But you do not know Frederick." She turned to Barthold. "Did you see the body?"

"No, my lady," he said gently.

"Only my men and I saw the body," Lord Conrat said, "but it was him. His face was still intact, and I did know him—had seen the young man. It was him. But I don't think you'd want to see it yourself."

"That's enough." Father and Barthold were both glaring at Lord Conrat. "You may go."

An image of Frederick's lifeless body pierced her thoughts, of his limbs and torso bloodied and mangled. Her vision started to go black.

Mother held her up until Father's arm went around her on one side and Barthold's on the other. They drew her to her bed and laid her down.

She squeezed her eyes closed and pushed the horrible picture from her mind. But then an image of her sister's childhood friend, Aladdin, flashed before her eyes. She had been very young, but she could remember when he was mauled by a bear while protecting Kirstyn. She had caught a glimpse of his leg when Frau Lena had changed his bandage, the flesh mangled and torn. She shuddered.

Why was she not crying? She was not thinking correctly, aware of a cloud of pain hovering over her. Frederick. Poor, sweet Frederick. It just couldn't be true. It couldn't be.

Someone placed a hand on her shoulder. "Adela?" It was Mother's voice. "Do you need some water? I can send for a cup of wine for you."

"I . . ." She shook her head. "I don't believe it." But even as she said the words, tears began to stream down her face. She hadn't realized they were coming, and she couldn't stop them.

Mother pulled her into her arms. But Adela didn't want this, didn't want comfort or to hear Father and Barthold speaking in hushed tones by the door. She didn't want Frederick to be gone.

"It must be someone else, Mother." But then a sob shook her chest, and another one. And she realized she was holding on to Frederick's bloody shirt. She turned her head so her cheek was resting against her mother's shoulder and whispered, "Please make them leave."

Mother must have motioned with her hand, because she ceased hearing her father's and Barthold's voices. There was no sound in the room except Adela's own sobs. She lay on her side on the bed, and finding a spot on the shirt that wasn't stiff with blood, she brought it to her nose. It smelled like Frederick.

Memories of him holding her in his arms in the dungeon flooded her senses, of him kissing her in the Cathedral nave, of him embracing her.

Her heart ached, burning as if on fire. She surely loved him, must have been spoiled and foolish to think she wouldn't want to marry him just because she wouldn't have servants to cook and clean for her.

She would never see him again, never be able to tell him she loved him.

CHAPTER 20

⁓

Frederick stared down at his hands, bloody and bruised from pulling on his chains and working at the bolt that fastened them to the wall. His tally marks on the wall showed that he had been here for twenty-one days, the longest, most miserable twenty-one days of his life. His one consolation was his daily visit from Heinryk.

Truthfully, it wasn't a visit. It constituted Heinryk giving him his daily ration of food and avoiding looking him in the eye or engaging in conversation. At first Frederick didn't try very hard to talk to Heinryk. His soul was bitter and desperate to escape from this place. But the loneliness of never seeing another face, of never talking to another person, began to consume him.

So when he heard a voice talking and Heinryk answering back, his spirit rose inside of him. How strange that his disposition could be so tied to such a simple thing as seeing another human face, of the chance to interact with another person, a person completely unconnected with him, at that.

The other prisoners often asked Heinryk for things, protested their innocence to him, and even hurled curses at him. But Frederick had decided on a different tact. After all, their fates had not been brought about by poor Heinryk. He was only a prison attendant.

Finally, after fending off the other men's requests and even curses and angry words, Heinryk appeared in the opening of Frederick's cell.

"Good morning, Heinryk. Did you sleep well?"

Heinryk's face registered surprise. "I . . . Tolerably well." He tried to hand Frederick his bread, but Frederick looked away, as if he didn't see it.

"Do you have a wife and children, Heinryk?"

"I do. If you will take your bread, I have something for you."

Frederick was too curious not to comply. He stepped forward and let Heinryk place the bread and small bit of cheese into his hand. Then Heinryk reached into the bag that was strapped to his belt and pulled out something furry.

"I brought you some lamb's wool to wrap around your wrist and ankle. It will help with the chafing."

"Heinryk, you are indeed a kind soul. I thank you." Frederick took the lamb's wool. "May I ask why you always look so sad?"

Heinryk's eyes met his for a moment, but then he shrugged and looked away. "I have nothing to complain about." He started moving away.

"I will pray for you not to be so sad today."

Heinryk glanced back at him but said nothing, disappearing around the bend.

The next day Frederick was again waiting for Heinryk's appearance with a friendly greeting. "Good morning, Heinryk. Did you sleep better last night?"

"Better, yes." He handed Frederick his bread and a handful of nuts and dried fruit.

"You said you have a wife and children. How many?"

"Only one wife." A ghost of a smile lifted Heinryk's lips. "And five children."

"Only one wife? That is amusing, Heinryk. You are funny. I hadn't guessed that."

"I am capable of laughing, like most people." Heinryk again smiled, briefly, and nodded his head.

"And five children? How old are they?"

"Ten, eight, six, three, and one year old."

"That is a blessing, five children."

"Yes." Heinryk gave a real smile this time as he paused and stared past Frederick's head, as if thinking of his children and not Frederick at all.

"It is good to see you smile, Heinryk. You never told me why you look so sad most days."

Heinryk looked into Frederick's face. "My troubles are nothing compared to yours." He pointed at Frederick, then gestured around him. "Compared to everyone's here."

"But you do have troubles. I would help you if I could. I can listen and give advice, if that would help."

Again, Heinryk paused to look into Frederick's face. "You've never cursed me or asked for anything after that first day. And now you are asking to help me? Why?"

"You always seem so sad. I was curious why, and you seem a good sort of fellow. I would like to help you if I can. It makes me happy to help people."

"And if you can help me, I might help you as well, I suppose?"

Frederick shrugged. He never lied, and now that he so desperately needed God's favor, he wasn't going to start. "Yes, I admit, I hope you might."

"Well, I can't help you. There is nothing I can do to help anyone here. I am just a worker, a paid slave with no power or skill or . . . I'm sorry."

He turned and hurried away before Frederick could think of what to say.

☙❧

Was there anyone's shoulder in Hagenheim Castle that Adela had not cried on?

She at least had not dissolved in front of anyone in the last full day and night. That was a victory. But it was too hard to imagine going for long without crying in the privacy of her own room.

Today she was restless. Frederick had been gone for over a month. That was a long time not to see his face. There had been many times she was sure she couldn't possibly have any more tears left, only to discover she seemed to have an inexhaustible supply.

She wandered down to the bailey, walking across the flower garden toward the apple orchard, and noticed Lord Barthold riding down the hill just on the other side of the town wall. He seemed to see her at the same moment and waved a hand at her, then made his horse go faster.

Adela waited for him. It would be impolite not to, since he was obviously going around to the gate and coming to speak to her. Her heart fluttered a bit. He'd been nothing but kind and gentle, his manner compassionate. She was beginning to understand why her father seemed to favor him as a suitor for her. But of course, her heart was still devoted to Frederick, even if he was lost to her forever.

Soon Barthold's horse came into view as he skirted around the rose garden and came toward her. When he was close, he dismounted and walked the rest of the way.

"Lady Adela. It is good to see you. A good day for a walk. Were you going to the apple orchard?"

"I was headed in that direction. Were you going anyplace in particular?"

"Just riding to exercise my horse." After a short pause, he said, "May I walk with you?"

"Of course."

They walked side by side, with his horse next to him, down the slope from the castle to the apple orchard. Lord Barthold wasn't much of a talker, so Adela tried to think of some story she could tell to fill the silence.

"My sister Margaretha is the one who discovered that Lord Claybrook was plotting to take over Hagenheim Castle. Do you know how she did it?"

"How?"

"She had climbed one of these trees when he came here to meet with one of his guards. While they were talking, she was overhead, listening."

He raised his brows and smiled. "I remember when that happened. I was very glad your father was able to defeat Lord Claybrook. But that was clever of your sister."

"Yes, and brave. She had to stay quiet so they wouldn't look up and see her. But now she is happily married and lives in England. I rarely see her." Normally such a statement would not cause her eyes to fill with tears or her throat to clog or her to suddenly long to hug her sister. But tears always seemed close to the surface now. *Oh Frederick, Frederick.*

"I am so sorry your sister is far away and you don't get to see her very often. I believe I understand that feeling of missing someone you love, since my mother died."

She'd rarely heard Barthold speak of his mother's death. She had forgotten about it, to be honest, and felt a pang of guilt that she'd been so thoughtless of Lord Barthold and what he had suffered.

"I'm so sorry for the loss of your mother. It must still be very painful."

"It is, sometimes. At first I did as my father did and kept very busy. And then I came to Hagenheim, which also helped take my mind off of it, as there were not as many things or places here to remind me of her."

"But it's not bad to remember and to grieve. There is a scripture, words of Jesus, that says, 'Blessed are those who mourn, for they will be comforted.'"

He looked thoughtful as he stared off into the trees, then nodded. "I would never argue with Jesus." He gave a slight smile.

Adela almost laughed, whether because what he said was so unexpected or because it reminded her of something one of her brothers would say.

She gazed up into Barthold's face. Was she imagining things, or were his eyes similar to Frederick's? Even the shape of his jawline and chin reminded her of Frederick.

Perhaps she was going daft.

Her heart felt raw and sore, like when she'd twisted her ankle stepping in a hole, or like a burn that had not healed, but this pain was so much worse because the ache enveloped her whole being. It was good to be with someone who did not talk very much, who seemed to understand that she needed slow movements and soft words. After all, he'd had to mourn for his mother and had witnessed his father's grief. And even though she was grieving for a man Barthold probably considered his rival for her affections, he did not show even a hint of resentment or peevishness. Much to his credit.

Oddly, she liked him better now than she ever had before.

❧

Frederick made another tally mark on the wall. Forty days he had been in this cell. His hands were calloused, bruised, and sore, but the chain still was stuck fast in the rock wall, not the least bit loosened.

God, it rained on Noah for forty days and forty nights. How long will You let it rain on me? But of course, he had no right to complain to God. God had not put him in this dungeon, and God had never promised to give him a happy or easy life with no troubles.

He heard the familiar sounds of Heinryk coming around with their morning meal. Frederick stood and was waiting for him when he arrived.

"How is little Jorgen? Did his fever break?"

"Yes, this morning before the sun rose." Heinryk smiled. "Thank you for the suggestion of the feverfew and ginger root. And the steaming water mixed with mint leaves helped his breathing."

"It's the healer in Hagenheim's remedy, Frau Lena."

"We need a healer like that in Grundelsbach. But yes, little Jorgen seems much better now, thank you. I brought you something my wife made for you." He lifted a bundle out of his pouch—an egg and a roll. "The roll is stuffed with cabbage and sausage."

Frederick took the bundle, a lump forming in his throat. "Thank you. And tell your wife thank you."

"I wish I could do more. There is just so little . . . but there's no use talking about it. I hate seeing you wrongfully imprisoned, and I even hate seeing the ones who are rightfully imprisoned. It pulls at my soul, as if I'll suffocate if I have to see the suffering for one more day." Heinryk turned his head away so that Frederick couldn't see his face, then raised a hand and wiped at his eyes.

"Come to Hagenheim with me," Frederick said in a low but urgent voice. "You can bring your family. You all would like it there."

Heinryk was already shaking his head.

"Why not? No one will know you helped me escape. You can wait a few days and disappear."

"You don't know how attached my wife is to her mother. She'd never leave her."

"Bring her with you. I have a large house, big enough for both our families. And I am sure you could get a job in Hagenheim. Vendors always need people to help them. Hagenheim Castle needs gardeners and servants. Would those jobs not be better than this? Could you be happy with those?"

"Of course. Yes. But it's just not . . . People do not just pick up their things and go to a new region."

"Why not? When your child is crying because he is sad, do you not pick him up and see what is the matter? Try and fix what is making him cry? Yes? So why do nothing to change your sad state?"

But Frederick remembered the years of working on his step-father's land, of how trapped he felt. He worked so hard for little reward, wishing all the time that he could escape and take his mother with him, away from the mistreatment, and do what he loved, which was carving wood. Yes, he knew very well how it felt to be trapped in a situation he hated.

Heinryk was silent as he twisted his mouth, as if thinking. "That is sound reasoning, I suppose."

"Of course it is. And I know the bishop. He will help me prove that Lord Conrat wrongfully imprisoned me, and the Duke of Hagenheim would not refrain from speaking out to the Duke of Grundelsbach. They—either the bishop or the duke—would help you find work, I am sure of it."

"It is a risk." But there was a hopeful lift to Heinryk's lips.

"But a risk worth taking, do you not think? I know it seems as if I am only telling you this for my own benefit, but what I say is true. If you are miserable in your work, if you never see the sun, if you hate every moment of your day, would it not be worth trying something new to change your situation?"

Heinryk smiled. "You are very persuasive, my friend."

"Just think how persuasive I could be if I were out of these chains. *Ja?* I could then persuade the Duke of Hagenheim to help save all of Lord Conrat's innocent prisoners—and persuade him to help the man who saved me."

"My family's lives are at stake, Frederick. Do you understand that? What that means to a man?"

"I can imagine. I need to get out of here so I can protect my mother and sisters. But if all works out well, think how much better all your lives would be."

Heinryk's face grew quite sober, almost troubled. "I just . . . I don't think it would be worth the risk. A guard could catch us before we were even out of the castle. I'm sorry, Frederick. You know I would help you if I could." His face was sadder than ever as he walked away. And Frederick's heart sank to the floor.

❧

Basina knelt beside her bed, her lips moving in prayer.

She prayed every day, all day, for her son to be safe. What had happened to Frederick? What had Lord Conrat done to him? The thought tortured her constantly.

God, please let Frederick still be alive. Please show me.

She had tried to leave her husband, but he'd found the small bag she had packed with her things that she'd hidden under the bed. He slapped her across the face, yelling, "What kind of wife and mother are you? Would you leave your husband and daughters? Selfish. That's what you are."

When had she ever done anything for herself?

She averted her thoughts from the beating of words as well as the blows from her husband's fists and went back to her prayer.

"God, only You know where Frederick is," she whispered, emptying her mind of all thoughts except God and the words she was saying. "Only You know how I can escape. And You can show me what to do, and if You are willing, I pray that You will. Show me."

Grundelsbach. Go to Grundelsbach.

The words came into her mind, quiet and fleeting. Basina latched onto them and repeated them silently, *Grundelsbach. Go to Grundelsbach.*

A peace came over her. She looked around and saw the bag where her husband had thrown it into the corner. Her things were still inside. If she waited until Stenngle was asleep—until he'd drunk himself into a deep slumber—why couldn't she simply take the bag, and take Eulaly and Ursula, and start on her way to Grundelsbach? If Stenngle found them, he'd beat her, but what if he didn't find them? Besides, she had that voice, those words in her mind telling her to go to Grundelsbach. It had to mean that God had made a way for her to get there.

The sun was beginning to go down, but as she peeked into the next room, Stenngle was sitting on a stool staring into the fire. Why wasn't he drinking? He was always half-drunk by now. Why was today different?

She went back into her room and sat on the bed. Perhaps she had heard God wrong. Perhaps the words had been conjured up by her own mind and her own desires. After all, the only time she'd been truly joyful had been in Grundelsbach. And if Lord Conrat had been truthful, that is where he had taken Frederick.

Eulaly and Ursula were standing in her doorway.

"What is it, loves?"

"Mother," Eulaly whispered, coming into the room and sitting beside her, Ursula just behind her. "We don't want to stay here with Father. If you leave, take us with you."

"Yes, please take us with you," Ursula said.

Basina stared back at them. Did they understand just how little she owned, how precarious their situation would be if they left and struck out across the region to Grundelsbach? But their situation was already precarious, without Frederick to take care of the farm, and with a man as angry and violent as their father.

Basina looked them in the eye, each in turn. "I have no way of protecting you or providing for you. Your father would kill us if we took the household money."

"But Frederick had money, and he kept it hidden somewhere in his room at the house in town," Eulaly said.

"We might be able to find it if we look," Ursula added.

"But your father will never let us leave."

"We can sneak away while he is asleep." Eulaly's eyes were wide and shining.

They'd had a taste of life without their father, and they wanted more of that, something better than being subject to his whims of cruelty and anger. She could not blame them. She wanted that too, for herself and for her children. And if there was a way she could find Frederick and help him, she would.

Her daughters were staring at her with pleading faces when a loud bang sounded from just outside her door. They all jumped and turned around.

Stenngle was standing there, a terrifying look on his face. His eyes were black and his face a strange shade of purple.

CHAPTER 21

Sneak away while I'm asleep." Stenngle's voice was raspy and low. "Get out of here. Go on. Leave. I want you all to starve in a ditch somewhere, to fall in a river and drown. May the devil take the three of you."

The girls were trembling and shrinking away from the door, which he was standing in and blocking.

Basina held her breath, waiting for what he would do next. No doubt he would beat her, and though he'd never beaten the girls, she feared he would beat them, too, this time.

He lifted his walking stick high in the air. "Go on. What are you waiting for? I'll be glad to be rid of all of you. The sight of you makes me sick."

He stepped back, as if making room for them to pass out of the room. Eulaly and Ursula didn't move.

Basina's stomach churned as she tried to muster the courage to walk past him. But what choice did she have? And why should she continue to cower before him? She had a responsibility to her daughters to defend and provide for them, and a responsibility to find Frederick and help him. She was his mother and he needed her.

Love welled up inside her, and she stood to her feet. Her knees weren't even wobbly. She picked up the bag she had packed, straightened, and held her head up, meeting his eye. She put one foot in front of the other and walked straight to him. Her insides trembled, but she would make certain that he did not see her looking afraid.

Just as she passed through the doorway, out of the corner of her eye she saw his arm move. A loud crack coincided with a stinging pain across her back and shoulders as he brought the walking stick down on her. She stumbled, bending forward, but did not stop or even slow her walk as she kept going.

The sting turned into a sharp ache, but she ignored it. Would he come after her? When she heard the thump of his walking stick on the floor behind her, she realized he was following her. Good. At least he had moved out of the doorway so Eulaly and Ursula could escape.

She kept walking. If she had to run to get away from him, though, she was not too proud to do that. She'd done it before.

"Where are you going?" he said behind her. "Will you go back to your lover, the one who got you pregnant with Frederick and then abandoned you?"

Now that the secret was out, Stenngle seemed to relish mentioning it every time he got angry.

"He wouldn't have you, and why would he? You're a faithless wretch." He continued to berate her and call her names, but she just kept moving, passing out of the house and into the yard.

She could hear him moving faster, getting closer. She quickened her speed.

"I forbid you to leave," he shouted.

She wasn't sure where she was going. She had hoped she might take Frederick's horse, but in the time it would take her to saddle him and get him ready to ride, Stenngle could have beaten her to death. So she walked in the direction of the road. Somehow she would come back and get the girls away from this awful man.

Her thoughts condemned her for letting Stenngle hear her and her daughters talking, condemned her for not making a well-thought-out plan and following it instead of having to run away from him like this, in haste and without direction. Her thoughts even condemned her for leaving her husband. But wasn't she saving him from future sins by leaving? The longer she stayed, the more he would harm her and do things that were contrary to the ways the Holy Scriptures taught a man to treat his wife.

She was nearing the well, which stood between the house and the road. She could hear his limping footsteps behind her, moving faster than she'd ever known him to move. She spun around just as he seemed to leap at her.

As if moving in a strange, slow dream, he came at her, his eyes crazed, his lips pulled back to expose his teeth. His hands were outstretched to grab her neck.

Basina screamed and stepped aside. His fingernails caught the side of her neck as he missed her and slammed into the low wall of the well. His eyes flew wide as his feet were swept off the ground by his momentum, and he tumbled headfirst into the well.

A loud but hollow splash followed.

Eulaly and Ursula screamed from where they stood in front of the house.

Basina looked over the side of the well. The late-day sun had been blotted out by dark rain clouds, and she couldn't see to the bottom of the well. She saw only darkness below.

"Stenngle!" Basina listened, but there was no sound, not even the slight sound of someone thrashing in the water below.

"Father!" Eulaly screamed as she reached the well, out of breath. She peered over the side, and her face turned as white as new snow.

"Run and fetch the neighbor!" Basina told Ursula, who seemed rooted to the spot, her mouth open. "Run!"

Ursula lifted her skirts and ran to the road and turned toward their nearest neighbor's house.

Basina hung the bucket on the windlass and turned the handle as fast as she could, sending the bucket splashing to the bottom. But in her heart she knew. He was dead.

❧

Adela lay on her bed. She heard someone come into her room. She sat up and stared.

Frederick stood in her doorway. Chains dragged on the floor, hanging from his wrists and ankles, just like when he was in the dungeon.

She jumped out of bed and hurried to him. She flung herself against his chest. He wrapped his arms around her and held her tight. She could actually feel the hard surface of his chest against her cheek, the softness of his linen shirt against her skin. She clutched him tighter, but he was fading away, slipping through her hands.

"Don't go!" Her voice choked off, and she opened her eyes.

She was lying in bed, clutching at the air.

A sob escaped her. It had felt so real. She could still feel his chest against her face. How could that be? It had only been a dream.

Her heart beat fast as tears leaked from her eyes. If only it had been real. But something about that dream . . . It did not feel like a normal dream. What if it was trying to tell her that he was alive? It was possible, was it not?

Adela had fallen asleep wondering when it would get easier, this pain of not seeing him, of knowing she'd never be held in his arms again. That must have been why she dreamed that dream. Her heart couldn't accept that he was never coming back.

How long would her heart be heavy? How long would she cry?

The sun was already up, so Adela got up and dressed herself without waiting for the servant. So many days she had lain in bed crying until nearly noon, but that did not bring Frederick back.

Tears filled her eyes again, but she set her teeth and refused to let the tears fall.

Crying never did any good at all. It just made her look like the spoiled duke's daughter whom everyone always thought she was, pining for something she could never have.

She went down the stairs and found her mother coming out of the library.

"You're up early. How are you feeling today?"

"I am well. I just want something to do, somewhere to go."

"You can go and visit the orphanage with me." Mother smiled, looking pleased. "The children love your stories about your sisters, and they especially love that rhyme that—" She caught herself before saying Frederick's name.

"The rhyme that Frederick wrote? Yes, I know." Even if no one remembered Frederick a hundred years from now, they might remember his rhyme.

Her heart seemed weighed down with many stones, but she would not let it show. She would not let this defeat her. She was stronger than that.

Her sisters had always been brave, and she would be too. She might not have to prevent an evil man from taking over Hagenheim Castle, or escape from an evil woman who kidnapped her, or overcome the effects of being held captive against her will for many long months, but she would fight against this pain and grief of losing Frederick, and she would win.

"Come with me." Mother patted her cheek with the back of her hand, and Adela embraced her. She could be strong and still get comfort from her mother.

After getting the basket of supplies from the kitchen, the women found a guard to accompany them, and they set out toward the orphans' home.

"I was talking to your father just now about Lord Barthold. His stay is almost over here. We had planned to have a ball at the end of his visit, and the ball is set for ten days from now."

"Oh. I had forgotten."

"I know you are not feeling much like a ball, but you will attend, will you not?"

"I . . ." She remembered her vow to be brave and strong. "Yes. Of course."

"Lord Barthold has made a favorable impression on you in the last few weeks, I think. I know you were not planning to marry him, but . . ." Mother faltered, in both her step and her speech. She turned and looked Adela in the eye. "Lord Barthold still wants you for his wife, but if you do not wish to hear his marriage proposal, Father can tell him so you won't have to. But I know it is his plan to ask you to marry him again at the ball."

Did she wish Barthold to ask her to marry him? Would she wish it ten days from now?

"I don't know what I want." Tears filled her eyes yet again. But that wasn't entirely true. She wanted Frederick. But that was never to be. "Barthold has been very gentle and kind to me, much more so than most men would have been, I am sure, given the circumstances. And it's strange, but . . . he almost reminds me of Frederick." She smiled as tears blurred her vision, but she managed to blink them back.

Mother placed an arm around her shoulder. "You don't have to decide today, but . . . I sense you do wish to give Barthold another chance. Your father thinks he is a good man, and he is a good judge of character."

Adela nodded, not trusting herself to speak. She took a deep breath as they walked on.

❧

Basina sat at the kitchen table with her two daughters. The girls had sometimes followed their father's example and been cruel to their older brother, knowing he would never fight back or lash out at them. They had been peevish and behaved badly, but when forced to choose between right and wrong, when called out and made accountable, they usually did the right thing.

But at that moment even Basina was not sure what was the right thing to do.

Ursula's eyes were red from crying. Eulaly's lips were pursed and her jaw set.

"I know your father has only been dead for three days, but the funeral is over, and I will be going to Grundelsbach tomorrow to look for Frederick."

"Are you not afraid that Lord Conrat fellow will hurt Frederick if you go and look for him?" Eulaly asked, her voice hushed.

"How will he know? Besides, I'm weary of living in fear. Fear has not served me well." She said this last statement more to herself than to her daughters.

Since the neighbors had pulled Stenngle's lifeless body up out of the well, Basina had felt a profound sense of relief, as if a heavy boulder had been removed from her back. Pangs of guilt assailed her for her relief. She had moments of sadness and confusion, of pain and loss, but it was more the pain of what she had lost by marrying an abusive man who respected neither God's laws nor man's.

Mostly she just felt relief.

"We can't stay here," Ursula said, biting her bottom lip.

"You can either go with me to Grundelsbach . . ."

"Or we could go to Hagenheim and live in the house there," Eulaly said. "Frederick paid for six months."

"Yes, but you'll be unprotected and will have no money."

"We could find work," Eulaly said.

"But Mother will be alone if we don't go with her," Ursula said, sniffing.

"I can trade our horse in order to get one of the neighbors to go with me."

"Or you could go to Hagenheim Castle." Eulaly's eyes widened at the new thought. "I would imagine that Lady Adela would persuade her father to send one of his guards with you if she knew there was a chance of finding Frederick."

"She liked him very much," Ursula said.

"But Lord Conrat is still at the castle, is he not?" Eulaly's face fell. "It's too great a risk. If he thought you were looking for Frederick . . ."

"He would kill you, Mother." Ursula's eyes welled with tears again. "No, we will go with you to Grundelsbach."

"I agree with Ursula." Eulaly folded her arms across her chest. "We're going with you."

"You can take the horse, Mother, and we'll take the donkeys." Ursula actually smiled.

"I suppose the three of us can protect each other against most threats." Basina could feel the lift in her spirit, as if a holy breeze had wafted into the room.

"We can take our kitchen knives and Father's walking stick."

They glanced at each other, hope in their eyes.

"A good night's sleep and we're off at dawn?" Basina asked.

"Yes." Ursula grinned.

"Absolutely." Eulaly nodded.

❧

Frederick's heart sank when he heard Mertin's voice and realized he wouldn't get to speak to Heinryk alone. But he greeted Heinryk and Mertin, the man who was in charge of the dungeon and its prisoners, as cheerfully as he could.

It had been a week since he'd first spoken with Heinryk about going with him to Hagenheim, but every day he seemed a bit more open to the idea.

"You are looking as healthy as when you came in here," Mertin said, looking Frederick up and down. "Has Heinryk been feeding you food from the duke's table?" He looked askance at Heinryk and then laughed so loudly the sound echoed through the underground prison.

Heinryk just gave the prison officer a half smile and carefully avoided looking at Frederick. Frederick folded his arms and smiled, as if it were a good joke. He had lost quite a bit of weight since entering the dungeon. He hoped Adela wouldn't think him too skinny now.

"Give him his portion, Heinryk, and let us—"

A guard came toward Mertin and began talking next to his ear in a low voice, something about one of the prisoners.

While Mertin spoke with the soldier, Heinryk moved closer to Frederick and said quietly, "I'll come back tonight."

Frederick's heart leapt in his chest.

Mertin said something quick and decisive to the guard and suddenly turned back toward them. Frederick stopped smiling and tried to look as if nothing had been said as he took the bread from Heinryk's hand.

"Let us go, Heinryk." And they walked away.

CHAPTER 22

Frederick couldn't sleep for thinking about whether Heinryk would actually come and help him escape. If he did, Frederick could be back in Hagenheim in a matter of days. But he spent a lot of his time praying he truly could help Heinryk find work in Hagenheim, that he hadn't led Heinryk to believe something that wasn't true. He did believe he could help Heinryk, but he couldn't promise him anything. He should have told him that, and he would, even if it prevented Heinryk from helping him.

He adjusted the lamb's wool around his wrist and ankle. The woolen strips were dirty, encrusted with blood. How did the other prisoners survive this year after year? How many people had died in here?

It seemed as if it must be past midnight. Frederick lay down to conserve his energy, though he still wasn't sleepy. When he heard a soft footfall on the stone not far away, he sat up.

Heinryk motioned to him to stay where he was. He came over and used a long metal key to unlock Frederick's wrist and leg irons, easing them to the floor so they wouldn't make any noise.

"Wait," Frederick whispered.

Heinryk stopped and looked him in the eye.

"I don't want you to do this because I promised you work in Hagenheim. I can't honestly promise you anything. I—"

"I know. I'm setting you free because . . . well, because God spoke to me in a dream last night."

Frederick absorbed this information while Heinryk finished unlocking the shackles.

"So you are coming to Hagenheim with me?"

Heinryk shook his head.

Frederick gave him a questioning look, but Heinryk only shook his head again and stuck his hand into the bag he was carrying over his shoulder. He drew out a long, sleeveless tunic with the colors of the Duke of Grundelsbach, like the ones his guards wore.

"Put this on. It should help you get past the night guards, who are all half-asleep."

"Thank you, Heinryk. I will never forget you, and if I can, I will find a position for you and send word to you."

"Thank you, my friend. I know you will. Now come. Stay just behind me."

Frederick pulled the soldier's tunic over his head and followed Heinryk out of the cell.

How strange it felt to walk out after being there for so many days. And how good it felt not to have to drag the heavy irons and chains behind him. His muscles were weak and it hurt to walk. But he didn't mind the pain. He just needed to focus on not getting caught.

Heinryk started up the dungeon steps. Frederick forced himself not to look around at the poor souls he was leaving behind. No wonder Heinryk was so sad to come to work here. He had to look at them every day, every one of their hopeless faces.

At the top of the steps was a door. Heinryk used his key to open it. Outside a guard was sitting on a stool, his back against the wall. His mouth was hanging open and his eyes were closed, and he didn't wake up as they came out. Heinryk did not close the door all the way behind them. He must have hoped they would think the door had been accidentally left unlocked.

Frederick continued to follow Heinryk as they passed through a narrow passageway, up another set of stone steps, then through a wider passageway.

The castle was eerily quiet. They did not see anyone as they went through a low door that led to a narrow wooden staircase, obviously used by the servants. They went down a flight of steps and passed a young man who looked tired and whose hands were covered in soot. He gave a mumbled greeting to Heinryk, who mumbled back, but Frederick kept his head down and only grunted, as he imagined a guard in the duke's service might have done.

They finally came to a door that led out a small passageway to what was the kitchen, but instead of going to the stone building, Heinryk veered to the right into the darkness of the night, the only light being a full moon and a torch burning near the stables.

Heinryk turned to him. He was a head shorter than Frederick, but he clapped his hand on Frederick's upper arm. "May God give you grace, and may He speed you to Hagenheim."

"Thank you. I can never thank you enough. I shall pray for you."

"Go now, before someone sees us."

Frederick hurried away in the direction he thought was the castle gate. Soon he could see the gatehouse up ahead, silhouetted in the darkness. There were sure to be guards there. Should he have gone another way? But there probably was no other way to get out. If there were, Heinryk would have told him. But what would he say if the guards stopped him and didn't recognize him? Questioned who he was and where he was going?

His heart beat fast. He'd never had any practice at lying, and he did not want to start now. But more than his own neck was at risk. He had to think of Heinryk. He could not get caught.

He walked with his head high and shoulders back, as he imagined a guard would walk, swaggering straight up to the gatehouse. As he drew close, he could see two guards sitting on stools, talking quietly with each other and hunched over a game board, as though they were playing chess or nine men's morris.

As Frederick approached, they both looked up, straightening, clearly surprised to see someone.

Frederick tried to look purposeful, as if he had somewhere particular he was going, and nodded to them as he passed.

His fingertips tingled as he listened for them to call out to him, demanding he come back and tell them who he was. But as he walked farther and farther away, he heard no such order.

Soon he was walking down the road that took him through the town. Houses lined the main street through Grundelsbach. Nearly all the windows were dark. The moon was high overhead, and Frederick kept walking.

He was free.

⁂

Adela allowed the seamstress to lift her arm so she could pin the material in place, ensuring her new dress for the ball would fit perfectly. She had lost weight since Frederick had been gone. For weeks, she'd been too distraught to eat.

Lord Barthold had promised to take her to a small waterfall in the woods that he was certain even she had never seen, even though it was not far from the castle. She had expressed her doubt so strongly that he had offered to be her servant for a day if she was right.

She laughed. "No, because if I lose this wager, I'll have to be your servant for a day."

"I would never force you to be my servant." He looked almost insulted. "My lady, if I win the wager, you will simply have to"—he put his hand up to his chin and stared at the ceiling—"dance every dance at the ball with me." He smiled his wispy smile, so different from Frederick's bold, more enthusiastic smile.

She needed to stop comparing Barthold to Frederick. But she wasn't ready to forget Frederick's face, his mannerisms and expressions, the things he'd said and done. She was so afraid she would forget, and he deserved better than that.

Perhaps she was being unfair to Barthold by letting him think she might care for him.

But then she wondered, might she care for him? Or was he only a distraction from missing Frederick, from the pain of losing him?

These were self-indulgent thoughts. Frederick was gone. She had to stop thinking about him. After all, she and Frederick were not betrothed. Who knew if her father would ever have allowed her to marry him? Or if Frederick would even have wanted to marry her? Not to mention the fact that she had thought, many times, that she could not marry a peasant, a man who did not even have servants.

She carefully wiped the tear from her cheek so it would not fall on the silk fabric. The seamstress would not be happy if Adela stained the beautiful dress before she could even finish making it.

Barthold had become quite an attentive suitor. Her father thought he was a good man. Perhaps she should marry him and let him take her away from the place that reminded her so much of Frederick. Grundelsbach was not that far from Hagenheim. She and her mother could visit each other. Valten and her father liked Barthold. Everyone said he was handsome. She should be happy with him instead of throwing away a perfectly good duke's son and his marriage proposal.

❧

Basina and her daughters traveled on their donkeys and Frederick's horse for two days. At a town, they asked a blacksmith how far it was to Grundelsbach. "About a morning's ride."

The sun was going down, so they went a little way from the town and spread their blankets on the ground in a forest. After tending to their animals, they lay down. Soon Ursula was breathing heavily, already asleep.

Then Basina heard Eulaly sniffing. She laid a hand on her shoulder. Eulaly rolled over and Basina could see she'd been crying.

"What is the matter?" Basina squeezed her daughter's arm.

"Nothing. I'm just so tired and sore." Her face crumpled and she sobbed softly.

"We have never ridden a horse for more than an hour. We are all sore and tired, but we will be in Grundelsbach tomorrow."

"But then we'll just have to ride all the way back to Hagenheim."

Basina couldn't help but smile. "We will survive. And I am very proud of you and Ursula for not giving up. You were determined to come with me, even though you could have stayed in Hagenheim. You are very brave girls."

"We are strong women, aren't we? To survive Father's constant anger and bullying. Especially you, Mother. I'm sorry for how he treated you and Frederick. And I'm sorry I never stood up for you."

"You could not stand up for me. He would not have allowed it, so do not feel guilty about it."

"I do, though. There was one time when he—" Her breath hitched and she pressed two fingers against her lips. After a moment, she went on. "He beat Frederick with his walking stick for trying to defend you. He must have been about ten or eleven, because I was eight or nine. I thought he was going to kill Frederick."

Basina remembered the incident Eulaly spoke of. She had picked herself off the floor and gone to Frederick's aid. By then the man had worn himself out and went out and fell facedown on the ground, sleeping off his drunken fit.

"And perhaps it is a sin," Eulaly said, "but I'm not sorry he's dead. I'm glad he can't hurt you anymore." She wiped at the tears that still flowed from her eyes. "I know I was wrong to treat Frederick badly. I did it because I knew it would please Father and he would praise me for it." She started crying harder.

"You were only a child. You didn't understand, didn't know." Basina stroked her shoulder and her hair. "The important thing is that you understand now, that you are repentant and confess it to God. He is faithful to forgive you."

She sniffed and wiped her nose and eyes with her hands. She nodded.

"Now, go to sleep. We need to get a good night's rest."

Thankfully, it was warmer than usual for early November. But they needed to get to Grundelsbach as quickly as possible and find Frederick.

❧

Frederick walked all night, praying he was going in the right direction. When the first gray vestiges of light crept over the sky, he looked for a secluded place to sleep. Thankfully, this road followed alongside a stream, so he'd been able to drink all the water he needed.

He found a soft spot of grass among some trees, sank down, and soon felt himself drifting to sleep.

When he awoke the sun was high overhead. Strange that he had slept so hard, but it was the sweet sleep of freedom. And of someone who'd been walking all night.

He was soon back on the road. He wondered when they would discover that he had escaped. And how long would it take him to walk to Hagenheim? Four days? Five?

Leaving Grundelsbach was more bittersweet than he could have imagined. He was more curious to see the duke, his birth father, than he'd thought. Did he look like the duke? Would he feel a kinship with him? No doubt the duke would not have been curious to see him and never would have claimed him as his son. Though he did not question that his mother had told him the truth, it was still strange, the thought of being the son of the Duke of Grundelsbach and the half brother of Lord Barthold. He even felt a bit of sympathy for his half brother, since Adela had clearly preferred Frederick.

He'd discovered a bundle of food in the pocket of the soldier's tunic, which he'd taken off and hidden under a rock not far outside the town wall. The food he'd saved for a few hours, but now he pulled it out and devoured it. All the walking had made him ravenous.

The muscles in his legs ached and trembled after doing nothing for almost two months in the dungeon other than trying to loosen his chains. "God bless Heinryk and his wife and family," he said as he ate. Then he said a more formal prayer for his former *gaoler* and friend.

As he walked he said a prayer of thanks to God for how mild the weather was. November could be quite cold, and he had no blanket, no warm clothes besides the ones he'd been wearing when he was captured by Lord Conrat's men.

He thought about seeing Adela again, and his heart became so full it ached. What must she think? That he'd abandoned her?

Lord Conrat was so evil, he may have made her think something horrible about him—that he'd run off with another woman or that he was dead. *God, please let her not think me faithless.* He would do anything to make her marry him, go to any lengths. But could he ever hope to make enough money through wood carving to make her want to marry him? Would she be content to marry a skilled craftsman? Perhaps she would regret marrying a man who was not rich and powerful like her father, the Duke of Hagenheim—or like Barthold, a future duke and legitimate heir.

But he wouldn't worry about that now. Instead, he'd remember how she'd found him in the dungeon and buried her face in his chest. How she'd kissed him.

In the Grundelsbach dungeon he'd dreamed about what it would be like to marry her, wondering about the kind of life he could provide for her. The bishop was paying him quite well. Already he had been paid more than he ever hoped to make. But he also could not earn enough money carving wooden doors and beams to give Adela the life she lived in Hagenheim Castle, though he should be able to hire a servant so she at least would not have to cook and clean. How would she feel about having only one servant? About living in a house instead of a castle?

He would do anything to make her happy.

Adela rode beside Barthold. She was much more comfortable being with him, and she thought it was because he seemed more comfortable with her. He talked more than he used to. He looked at her more. Before, when she thought Barthold cold and unfeeling, it was probably because he was like her brother Valten—quiet and reserved. Some men just didn't talk very much.

She saw that they were riding through the tree-lined avenue where Barthold had been shot and Frederick had come to her rescue.

"Stop." Adela's heart was pounding, stealing her breath.

"What is it?" Barthold grabbed the reins of Adela's horse and stopped both horses.

"I don't want to ride here." She could feel the tears welling up in her eyes. A shudder went through her. She could see Barthold with the arrow sticking out of his shoulder. Could see Frederick pulling her onto his horse and taking her to safety. Could see the guards hauling him away to the dungeon.

Barthold turned both horses around and walked them back the way they had come. When they were out in the open, on the hilly meadow just outside the town wall, he stopped and dismounted, standing by her horse's side.

He held his hands out to her. "Come. We can walk a bit."

She let him help her down, his hands around her waist. But it felt wrong. Frederick was the one who should be touching her. But he wasn't here. Only Barthold was.

She leaned forward, letting her forehead rest against Barthold's shoulder.

His arms encircled her immediately, pulling her close—too close. He was holding her too tight.

She cleared her throat and put her hand up, gently pushing him away. He let go and took a tiny step back.

The two guards who were with them were surely watching, but it was the thought of Frederick seeing her that made her more uncomfortable. Poor Frederick. But that was foolish. Of course Frederick couldn't see her. But he had known exactly how to hold her—not too tight, but close enough to make her feel wanted and cherished.

She hated this feeling of being torn, of feeling bad for abandoning Frederick, but also feeling bad for Barthold because she was constantly comparing him to Frederick.

"He's gone, Adela."

She looked up into Barthold's face, his words stabbing her. "What?"

"He's gone. But I'm here."

Did he dare to bring up Frederick to her? She stared up at him, her hand on her hip as tears pricked her eyes.

"I don't mean to say anything hurtful, but it's true. I'm here, and I want to marry you, Adela. I will care for you and be a good husband to you. I will give you anything you want, provide whatever your heart desires."

She turned away just in time to keep him from seeing the tear that dripped from her eye. What if she let him marry her and care for her? It might stop this pain in her heart, these tears that kept coming even though she tried to hold them in.

"I'm sorry if I made you cry." His hand was on her shoulder, warm and gentle. She could almost imagine it was Frederick's hand. Almost imagine it was Frederick telling her he was sorry he made her cry.

She turned back toward him and buried her face in his shoulder, putting her arms around him. This time he didn't squeeze so hard. In fact, his hands were barely touching her.

Frederick was gone, and she had to accept it. She had to stop grieving. Her mother and father and all of her family were worried about her. Frederick couldn't see her, couldn't be hurt by her marrying another man. He was in heaven, where there was no crying and no pain. But Barthold was here. He was real and solid, and he wanted to marry her.

Marrying Barthold would make many people happy—Father,

Mother, Barthold, and both of their families, even the king, who had sent a letter approving the match, as it would strengthen the regions.

Frederick was dead. She must accept it.

And she just wanted the pain to end.

CHAPTER 23

Basina's stomach was tied in knots as they neared Grundelsbach, and she started to notice a familiarity to the trees, a few houses scattered along the road, then the approach to town. The gentle rise, the bend in the road. Then there was the town gate. The guards' colors. She remembered it all. And she remembered the man she had loved.

She had been so foolish to love him, to let herself fall in love, to give herself to a man who could never marry her. So young and daft. She'd only been sixteen, and he had been young too, only twenty-one. He had taken advantage of her, she could say, and if he'd truly loved her, he would have respected her and not encouraged her to fall in love with him. For he could not have been in love with her. According to Lord Conrat, that is. Lord Conrat, who had told her that the duke no longer wanted to see her, that the duke was marrying the woman his father had chosen for him, and that she was arriving any day. Basina's services as a servant were no longer wanted and she was to leave the castle immediately.

She could still feel the impact of those words, how her stomach sank, how weighed down her body felt as she gathered her things from the servants' quarters and left.

She had not had a chance to tell the duke that she was carrying his child. But somehow Lord Conrat knew. Perhaps a demonic spirit told him. And perhaps the duke did not want her to leave, had not spoken to Lord Conrat about it at all. But regardless, she could not stay when he was marrying someone else, someone it was his duty to marry.

Her heart feeling as though it were breaking in two, she'd traveled to Hagenheim and married the first man she met.

He'd seemed kind enough, a farmer with his own land, and Basina had only one brother and one sister who lived with her husband far away. Stenngle had seemed eager to impress her and make her want to marry him. She'd hoped she could conceal that she was pregnant, but she'd confessed it before the wedding. He had not seemed too disappointed, and she'd been relieved. But as time drew near for the baby to be born, he'd held it against her more and more. Had grown colder and colder. She knew she'd made a mistake in marrying him, but once she was married, it was too late. She could not undo it. Only wealthy men could have a marriage annulled, and she was neither wealthy nor a man.

She'd lain awake at night trying not to think of Reichart. He may have used poor judgment in becoming involved with her, but at least he'd been tender and kind, and she couldn't imagine him ever striking her—unlike her new husband. She loved Reichart so much she even hoped he was content with his wife and that she treated him well. Even though Basina could not be with him, she still wanted him to be happy.

Would she see him today? Her stomach did a somersault at the thought. She dreaded facing him after so many years. Would he think her old and ugly? She was not yet forty, but she knew she did not look as she once had—young and vibrant, without wrinkles or extra weight.

A cold wind was blowing, and she was glad they were nearing their destination, though they did not know where they might sleep tonight.

Exhausted and aching, they neared the gate and passed right through.

The cobblestones themselves seemed familiar as she led the way through the street. The castle was on a hill at the other end of town, similar to how Hagenheim and Hagenheim Castle were situated. Her heart beat faster. Her knees felt weak. But the thought of seeing Frederick bolstered her courage. She would do anything to find her son. Including facing the man who had broken her heart so many years ago. How she'd longed for him to come and find her. At first she'd hoped, but of course he could not. He had a duty to his father, his people, and his wife-to-be.

The castle loomed ahead. By the time they finally reached it, her heart had stopped pounding and her knees were strong again. She had to find Frederick. This was her best chance.

The three women dismounted and led their horse and mules. They approached the guard house at the bridge that crossed the moat to the front door of the castle.

"Halt. You are not allowed to pass unless you have business in the castle." The guard's face looked as if it were carved out of rock.

"I have business with the duke," Basina said, holding her head high.

"He is not expecting anyone today."

"If you will tell him my name, he will see me." Her voice sounded firm. Thank goodness she was able to project confidence.

The guard stared down at her without moving or speaking for so long she thought he was going to ignore her. Finally, he said, "What is your name?"

"Basina Zeringer." Her stomach twisted as she imagined the

duke hearing her name for the first time in more than twenty years. Would he reject her outright and refuse to see her?

The guard, still not cracking his stony facade, said, "Very well." He turned and spoke a moment to the guard behind him. Then he glanced back at her. "Wait here."

Basina nodded, and he turned and started to walk across the wooden bridge over the moat.

Eulaly took her hand and squeezed it. Ursula smoothed her mother's hair and arranged the scarf around her neck and over her shoulders.

"You look very pretty, Mother."

Basina wasn't sure if she should cry or laugh. But a surge of pride went through her at how mature her daughters were being and had been throughout the last several days. Indeed, she had seen an improvement in their behavior—less selfish and self-centered—ever since their father had returned and Lord Conrat had forced them to go back and live with him. They finally understood that even though he was their father, his behavior was wrong and abusive. They saw that their brother was good, had been good to them, and they'd tasted the peace and normalcy of living apart from their angry, argumentative father.

That train of thought distracted her from thinking about how Reichart would react when he heard she was here, wanting to speak to him. Was it possible he wouldn't even remember her?

A pain stabbed her chest. Rejection would be better than him forgetting she had even existed.

"There he is." Ursula's voice was breathless.

Looking back, Basina saw that the guard was returning. Already. Had the duke refused to see her? He must have, to give his answer so quickly.

The guard strode up to her. "The duke will see you. Come."

Her heart skipped a beat. She would see him. Would he think she looked old and ugly? But Frederick was what was important. She was doing this for Frederick.

She followed the guard, then stopped and looked back.

"We'll wait for you here, Mother." Eulaly waved her on with a stalwart expression.

Basina nodded, then continued to follow the guard through the huge, heavy door of the castle.

She could barely breathe as the guard's footsteps seemed to resound through the empty corridor, reminding her that her and her daughters' shoes were so worn and threadbare they had holes and had been patched more than once. And though she had some money, the money Stenngle thought he had hidden away, she feared how soon it would run out.

Reichart. Reichart. Reichart. The guard's footsteps seemed to be echoing the duke's name, her heart beating in rhythm.

The guard suddenly stopped in front of a door. Were they here already?

The door opened, and Reichart was standing in the middle of the room. Staring at her.

"Come in." Then he glanced at the guard. "You may leave us."

The guard backed out the door and closed it. She was alone with Reichart.

He looked the same, except for a bit of gray in his hair. His expression softened as he gazed at her. Her knees went weak, and suddenly she remembered how good it felt to kiss him.

"Basina. Where . . . where have you been?"

"Near Hagenheim. And now I am here to ask for your help to find my—to find our—son."

His lips parted and his expression changed. Slowly, his mouth fell open. Then he put his hand to his forehead.

"A son? Why did you not tell me?"

"Lord Conrat told me you knew and that you didn't want me around when your new wife came." The pain rose up just like it was happening for the first time. Tears even welled in her eyes.

"Basina. I did not know. I did not . . . We have a child?" He put his hand to his head again.

"Lord Conrat took him away—I don't know where. I came to ask for your help finding him."

His brows drew together, wrinkling his forehead. "How long have you been traveling? I'll get a servant to take care of you, to find you a room."

"I don't need a room. I need to find my son. And Lord Conrat is the only person who knows where he is, and he said he would kill him if I tried to find him." Basina put her hand to her mouth to hide the way her lips were trembling.

Reichart's jaw hardened. He stared at her a long time, then said, "I will find him. Stay here." He strode toward her and the door.

"I want to go with you."

He stopped as he drew alongside her and gazed down at her. "Basina. I did not know you were with child, and I never would have sent you away."

The way he looked at her—her breath left her and she couldn't speak. His blue eyes bore into her as if he were wrapping his arms around her. He lifted his hand. Was he about to touch her cheek? But then he dropped it.

"Come."

His voice sent a shiver across her shoulders. Even though it had been more than twenty years since she'd heard it, the years seemed to melt away. She was sixteen years old again and enveloped in a blanket of feelings—love, hope, tenderness—for this man.

But the love, hope, and tenderness were even more overwhelming now, though she was considered an old woman and past emotions like these. After the years of longing for those feelings again, of trying to feel them for her angry, harsh husband . . .

She could not allow herself to be foolish again. And it was foolish to think Reichart could care for her the way he had then, if he ever cared for her the way she'd imagined he did. She needed to focus on finding Frederick and saving him. Reichart was simply a means to an end. At least that's what she would tell herself until she was safely away from him and these dangerous feelings.

She followed him, and he slowed his walk to come along beside her. In glancing at him from the corner of her eye, she caught him looking at her.

"I never would have sent you away, never, and especially if I had known you were . . . You should not have left without telling me."

"I believed Lord Conrat when he said you didn't want me or the child, that you wanted me to go." She said the words while looking straight ahead.

Reichart slowed, as if he wanted her to stop, but she kept walking.

"I wish you hadn't believed him." He spoke the words softly as they encountered a guard along the passageway.

The guard greeted him, and Reichart nodded. They came to stone steps leading down. The steps were steep and narrow, so Basina let him go before her. She stayed close, remembering moments she hadn't recalled in many years. But the joy of remembering them was worth the pain, at least for the moment.

She might soon find Frederick. Was he in this dungeon? Why was this the first place Reichart was looking? Though it made sense that he was here, that this was where Conrat had taken him.

They continued until they reached a floor where several guards were standing around talking. When they saw Reichart, they quickly greeted him and stood at attention.

"Is there a prisoner here named . . ." He turned to Basina.

"Frederick."

"Frederick."

The guards' mouths fell open, and they glanced around at each other.

"He is young, twenty-one years old."

So he had done the calculations in his head and knew how old Frederick was.

"He is tall, as tall as you," Basina said quietly.

"He's my height," Reichart relayed.

"With light brown hair and blue eyes."

"Light brown hair and blue eyes," the duke repeated, his voice sounding gruff, and she saw his throat bob as he swallowed.

"Sir, there was a man of that description here," one of the guards said, "but he escaped two days ago."

"Why was I not informed?"

"He was one of Lord Conrat's prisoners."

"Lord Conrat is not the duke here. I will know everything that happens in my castle and my dungeon."

"Yes, Your Grace."

The guards looked humbled and apologetic.

"Has this escaped prisoner been found?"

"No, sir."

"Then go and find him. You and you and you. Take two other guards and search the roads out of town until he is found. But you are not to harm him—do you understand? Now, go."

The guards scrambled up the steps.

"You, Otto. Show me where this prisoner was kept."

The guard hurried to lead them down the rest of the steps into the dungeon.

Moans echoed from below. The guard led them past several

men chained to the wall. Reichart looked at each man they passed, and his brow furrowed more and more the farther they went.

"This is it." The guard stopped in front of a cell where two shackles and chains lay on the floor.

Reichart went and knelt beside the chains. He picked them up and examined them. "What happened here? How did he escape?"

"We don't know. The shackles weren't broken. He must have gotten a key somehow."

Basina stared at the shackles and imagined Frederick being chained there, alone and abandoned, and a heaviness clutched at her chest. But at least he had found a way to escape.

Reichart was staring at her. Then he straightened and brushed past the guard and walked back the way they had come. Basina followed him.

When they had come out of the dungeon and were above, Reichart called out, "Matthias."

A man dressed in soldier's garb who was at the opposite end of the corridor turned and started walking back toward them. The duke went to meet him. Basina stayed just behind him.

"Matthias, I need you to gather a contingent of soldiers, ten good men, to go with me to . . ." He turned around and his gaze connected with hers. "Where do you think he would have gone?"

"To Hagenheim."

Reichart addressed Matthias again. "To go with me to Hagenheim."

"Yes, sir."

Basina's heart soared. Reichart would find Frederick. *Thank You, God.*

The guard passed him, no doubt on his way to carry out the duke's orders. Reichart was gazing down at her. "Will you come with me?"

She nodded, and he led the way back to the room where he had been when she first spoke to him. He went in and closed the door behind her.

It was a small room with tapestries on the walls, a fireplace, and a desk. But she barely saw it as he stood in front of her, bending to look into her eyes.

"Basina, what I did to you was selfish and careless and cruel, and I—"

"Please, stop." If he told her he was just using her, she could not bear it, for that would mean he hadn't loved her. "Please don't say any more." She held up her hand and turned her head away slightly, unable to look at him because of the ache in her chest.

"Forgive me," he said.

Silence stretched between them. Finally, he said, his voice strained, "I have wondered thousands of times where you were. Were you safe? Were you happy? Did you marry?"

Again, there was silence. Basina could feel her heart pounding. Afraid of what he might say. Afraid of what she might say.

"I loved you, Basina, and in my heart I still do."

She closed her eyes as her heart ached with yearning. How she wanted to believe him. He had always said the right things, sweet things, the exact things she longed to hear. But it simply couldn't be true.

"You can't love me. You are a duke, and I was only a servant, and now I'm a peasant, a nobody."

"You are not a nobody to me. You are the mother of my child." His voice cracked on the last word.

"I did marry. I married a cruel man who treated me badly."

"Please say he did not hurt you."

"He hurt me every day. And he beat me."

Reichart raised a hand to his head as his features twisted, as if he were in pain. "I will kill him."

"He is dead."

Reichart turned away from her. His shoulders moved up and down as he breathed hard. He didn't speak for several moments, and then he said, "You stay here at the castle where you'll be taken care of. I shall return when I've found Frederick, and—"

"I want to come with you."

He faced her again. He seemed to be thinking. "It will be difficult for you to come with me and my men. Did anyone accompany you here?"

"Yes. My two daughters."

"Please, stay here with your daughters. I will come back when I've found Frederick. I want to keep you safe."

She would not let him put her away. She was too close to Frederick to become passive now. So she put her hands on her hips and looked him in the eye.

"I am not a horse that you can leave in the stable."

"I did not mean it that way." He held out a placating hand.

"I am coming with you."

"Very well, but if we are moving too fast for you and your daughters to keep up, I will give you one of my most trusted guards to travel with you and make sure you stay safe."

She would be foolish not to agree to his conditions, so she said, "Very well. I accept."

Reichart suddenly squeezed her hand and stared deeply into her eyes. "I want to speak with you more when we have a little privacy. Please don't disappear like you did before. Because this time I will search for you and find you."

Basina's heart was in her throat. So much time had passed, but it felt as if there had never been a day that she hadn't loved him.

⁂

267

Reichart had arranged for Basina and her daughters to have their needs attended to, with extra clothing to change into and food packed for them, while he left to gather his men for the trip. They set out with Reichart and his men before the afternoon was half gone.

Basina was glad the soldiers moved at a steady pace, but not too fast so as not to exhaust the horses. She, Eulaly, and Ursula had wrapped themselves in the warm woolen blankets they'd been provided in Grundelsbach. They followed just behind Reichart and the rest of his men, with Sir Ulrich, the knight Reichart had assigned to protect them, staying close to them.

Sir Ulrich was quiet but kind, and her daughters seemed quite enamored of him, especially Ursula. It reminded her of how she'd felt about Reichart when she first started working in Grundelsbach Castle.

Reichart had been so handsome, her breath had caught every time she saw him. He was sad about his father dying, and she sometimes noticed him staring out a window, at the floor, or at nothing. Lord Conrat had often been hovering nearby. The man with the pinched face and sharp eyes frightened her, and she never made eye contact with him. But when he wasn't around, sometimes Reichart would say "Good day" to her.

One evening he said, "Lovely sunset tonight. Come and have a look."

She went to the window where he was standing. It was so narrow, she had to stand close to see. The sun was sending out rays of light through the clouds, bright orange and red. It had been just about this same time of year, in fact.

They quietly admired the sunset, pointing out different things about it. Then Reichart turned to stare at her. "Is your father still alive?"

"No, Your Grace. He died when I was five."

"Oh." He kept staring at her face. "My father died."

"I know. I am very sorry. You must feel very sad."

They had been simple words, but they were heartfelt nonetheless. Reichart's eyes were intense as he leaned toward her. "You are a kind maiden. You always smile while you work. What makes you smile?"

She might have argued with him that she did not always smile while she worked, but he was the duke, so she didn't contradict him.

"I suppose I smile because . . . I am pleased to have this position in the castle," she replied truthfully. "My family needs the money my job provides. And I am pleased to serve you, my lord." What young peasant girl, desperate to keep her family from starving, would not want to serve such a handsome lord, and one with kind eyes who was never harsh?

"I like your smile." He leaned even closer.

Basina had felt a warning, almost like a bell sounding, and she moved away from the duke, sidestepping and saying, "I must get my work done before the mistress comes looking for me."

Hurrying away, she looked over her shoulder at him. The wistful look on his face made her heart clench.

After that, she would see the duke nearly every day. She realized now that he had been very young, but at twenty-one he'd seemed much older than her sixteen years. She'd fallen in love with him instantly. And he'd taken advantage of that.

At least that's what she'd always told herself. But what if he had loved her? Yes, it had been wrong of him to seduce her, and she'd been foolish to allow it, but now that she knew he had not sent her away, had not told Lord Conrat to tell her that he didn't want her, she couldn't help but wonder.

And the way he had looked at her when he found out he had

a son, and when he heard she'd been married to a man who beat her—she could almost imagine he still loved her.

Ach! She was being foolish again. Of course he didn't love a peasant woman, one who had been previously married, someone who could never represent him well among his own class of people.

But at least she was free. Stenngle could no longer hurt her, and Frederick would finally be free as well. Perhaps he'd even be allowed to marry Duke Wilhelm's daughter Adela, the girl he cared about so much.

It wouldn't matter that Basina still felt as if she had never been loved, could never be loved by the man she still cared for, though that love had been buried during all the years of her marriage to Stenngle. All those years she'd told herself she didn't love Reichart, that he had treated her badly, had taken advantage of her and cast her aside. He didn't deserve her love. But the moment she had set eyes on him in Grundelsbach Castle, her heart had come alive with all the old feelings of love and longing. It was as if she were sixteen again.

She shook her head. She must stop herself from going down that road. She was much too old for such things, and now she was even a widow. What would people think if they knew of her childishness?

She rode atop the gentle mare, with her daughters on either side of her. Sir Ulrich turned to look at them. "Only about a half day's ride now."

Eulaly sighed loudly. "I'll be so glad to get off this horse. I don't know how you soldiers do it, living in the saddle all day every day."

Sir Ulrich shrugged. "It's a good life . . . if you enjoy it. And I do."

Sir Ulrich was clearly a man of few—and simple—words.

Basina often caught a glimpse of Reichart among his soldiers ahead of them.

Two soldiers emerged from around the bend in the path, approaching them at a fast gallop. Reichart rode up to meet them. After a few moments, Reichart broke away and headed toward Basina.

Her heart fluttered. When he reached her, he turned his horse around to ride alongside her.

"I sent some fast riders ahead. They found Frederick in Hagenheim. He was in the Cathedral speaking with the bishop when my men located him."

"Thank God." The breath rushed out of her, and she felt herself smiling, a laugh bubbling up inside her. "He is well, then?"

"Well and safe."

Basina let out the breath she was holding. "Thank You, God." Her heart swelled with gratitude as she allowed his intense gaze to capture hers. "And thank you for searching for him."

"Of course. It will not be long before we will all reach Hagenheim."

Eulaly and Ursula were staring at them. Her cheeks warmed as her daughters kept glancing at her with raised brows.

For a while all were silent. Then the soldiers began to talk among themselves, and Eulaly and Ursula were talking with Sir Ulrich.

"I wanted to tell you I'm sorry for what Lord Conrat did." Reichart's horse was very close to hers, so close his leg brushed against hers. "And I'm sorry you were alone and with child."

She turned to look at him. His head was down and he was leaning toward her. Remembering those days, leaving Grundelsbach, knowing she and her baby were alone—a lump formed in her throat and she couldn't speak.

He lowered his voice even more. "I was young and selfish, and I took advantage of you."

The heat rose into her cheeks again, and she suddenly found her voice. "Don't insult me. I know that. I know you did not love me."

His eyes went wide and his mouth opened. "I did not say I didn't love you. I loved you."

The men around them quieted suddenly. Basina's breaths seemed to come only in short gasps.

Reichart sat taller and addressed the soldiers. "We are going to take a short rest now." He took hold of Basina's horse's reins and led her off the road. The rest of their group followed, but he kept going until he entered a small stand of trees. He dismounted and looked behind him, then seemed satisfied that they were far enough away from the others.

Basina's heart was thumping hard against her chest. She stayed on her horse while he approached her. He placed his hand on her wrist as he gazed up at her.

"I loved you, Basina. I never should have treated you the way I did. That is not what love is—taking advantage of someone who has no choice but to obey."

"I did not love you because I had no choice," Basina said quietly. "You always gave me a choice."

"But it was unfair, and I . . . I knew I had to marry Mathilda."

Basina could feel the tears as the pain stabbed her, the same as it had twenty-two years ago when she learned he would marry the well-born daughter of a wealthy count. But she would not cry in front of him.

"I wanted you," he said. "My heart broke when I lost you."

"Am I supposed to feel pity for you?" The words were out of her mouth before she could think.

He sighed. "I just want you to know that I did love you. And I'm sorry for all the pain I caused, for the hardships. Did you get married before Frederick was born?"

"Yes."

"But he was not good to you or to Frederick?"

"No. He was not." The tears pricked her eyes again. She turned her head away, suddenly aware of how Reichart was holding her wrist, caressing it. When had anyone ever touched her that way? But she could not let him seduce her again. She pulled her hand from his grasp, keeping her face turned away so he could not see the tears streaming down her cheeks, running down until they were wetting her neck. She at first refused to wipe them, because then he would know she was crying. But they tickled her neck, so she pulled out a small cloth from the pocket in her sleeve and wiped her face as regally as she might imagine a count's daughter would do.

"I'm sorry, Basina. I want to make amends for . . . all you've been through. But it's more than that. I want . . . I still care for you. I want to marry you."

"How can you say that?" Basina turned toward him, forgetting her vow not to let him see her cry. "You can't marry me."

"That's not true. You're the mother of my child, a beautiful woman with a kind and loving heart who took care of my son—"

"I am hardly of noble birth."

"That does not matter to me. And now I can marry whomever I want, and I want you."

He held up his hands toward her. She turned her body toward him and let him help her down from her horse, hardly knowing what she was doing, only knowing that she wanted to be closer.

His hands lingered on either side of her waist as he brought his face within a hand's breadth of hers.

"Marry me, Basina." His voice was gruff and low. "Say you will."

Surely this was a dream. But even in her dreams she'd never imagined this. His eyes were so clear as they stared into hers. His face was so near, his lips so tempting as they hovered over hers.

273

"Say yes."

"Yes."

He closed the gap and kissed her.

He kissed her gently, then with more longing. Her heart soared, and she slid her hands around to his back, holding on as he pulled her in.

When he moved away, she laid her head on his very real shoulder, her lips still tingling from his very real kiss. Reichart was real, not a dream. And he wanted to marry her.

And just then, in the blink of an eye, her long, dark night was over.

CHAPTER 24

Frederick was footsore but in high spirits as the town wall of Hagenheim came into view. His destination beckoned to him—Hagenheim Cathedral. Its spire rose tall and straight, and Frederick headed toward it as soon as he passed through the gate.

Going in search of the bishop, Frederick found him in his private study area.

"Frederick!" The bishop's eyes went wide. "Where have you been? They said you were dead."

"Who said I was dead?"

"I thought the duke's men had found your body, mauled by wolves. Lord Conrat, one of the men who came from Grundelsbach with Lord Barthold, was the one who was supposed to have found your body."

His stomach sank. Adela did not think him faithless and inconstant—she thought him dead!

"Duke Wilhelm has been searching for you, but no one knew where to look. You and your family had disappeared."

Frederick ran a hand over his face.

"Come. You look weary. I shall have the servants take care of you. From where have you traveled?"

"Grundelsbach."

"Grundelsbach?" The bishop looked surprised again.

Frederick explained what had happened, what Lord Conrat had done to him and why. "And I only hope my mother and sisters are safe."

"Frederick, I do not wish to hurt or discourage you, but Lady Adela . . ."

"What? Is Lady Adela all right?" His heart skipped and pounded inside him. *God, please.*

"Lady Adela is well, but the people are expecting her to marry Lord Barthold."

His heart sank into the pit of his stomach.

Just then several voices sounded outside the bishop's door. Thomas knocked and entered.

"Pardon me, but two soldiers from Grundelsbach are here and say the duke is searching for Frederick. Should I tell them he is here?"

The bishop frowned. "Yes, but inform them that my guards, as well as Duke Wilhelm's guards, will fight to prevent them from taking him."

"I will relay your message, but I don't think they want to take him anywhere. They said he is the son of the Duke of Grundelsbach, and they just want to make sure he is safe."

Frederick's lungs filled with air. The duke knew he was his son?

Thomas nodded, then looked at Frederick. "It is good to see you, Frederick."

"And you as well, Thomas."

Thomas smiled and left.

Frederick's mind was spinning, but the bishop was speaking to him.

"Lady Adela doesn't know you're alive, Frederick. You must tell her. And you must do it tonight." The bishop's eyes opened a little wider, and a slow smile spread across his face.

"Tonight?"

"The Duke of Hagenheim is giving a ball tonight. Lady Adela is expected to formally accept Lord Barthold's proposal of marriage, and the duke is expected to approve it."

Frederick's heart squeezed painfully. Had he escaped only to lose the person he wanted most in the world? But perhaps he should leave her alone, let her marry someone of her own station.

"Lady Adela needs to know you're alive before she accepts Lord Barthold. But you don't have much time."

He realized he wasn't unselfish enough to let her marry Barthold. He loved her too much. Besides, he didn't know if Barthold could make her happy.

"What should I do?"

"You're going to the ball."

❧

Adela awoke feeling unsettled. Then she remembered the dream she'd had.

She'd dreamed of Frederick again.

If she was supposed to marry Barthold, then why could she not stop dreaming about another man?

A tear dampened her eye. She could not be crying. If she was going to marry Barthold, she needed to be happy and stop thinking about Frederick.

She broke her fast with her mother, eating in the solar and discussing the ball.

"The singers are practicing now if you want to go listen to them," Mother said.

"I might go later."

Adela stared out the window. The wind was blowing the trees, the leaves waving back and forth. The weather must be turning colder.

"*Liebling.*" Mother placed her hand over Adela's.

Adela turned to look into her mother's eyes. "What is it?"

"Darling, if you're not happy and at peace, then you don't have to agree to marry Lord Barthold."

Happy? At peace? "Do I need to be happy and at peace to marry someone?" Adela laughed, but the laugh seemed to change quickly into a half sob. She pressed her hand over her mouth. She quickly controlled herself. "I'm well, Mother. I want to marry Barthold." But even as she said the words, she doubted them.

"I am well, truly." If she delayed the announcement, how would that help? "And I don't want to hurt Barthold."

"Darling, you shouldn't marry a man just because you don't want to hurt his feelings."

"Well, that's not the only reason I'm marrying him." She tried to laugh again, but it died before it reached her throat.

"I just want you to be sure before you say yes to him."

Truthfully, she believed Barthold was a good man. How was she going to find a better one? One her parents approved of, who lived so near to them?

"Mother, I do want to marry him. I am the last daughter, and it's time for me to marry, to have my own life." To stop worrying everyone.

"Don't marry him because you think it's time to marry. Marry him because you love him. Do you love him?"

"I think I do." But the tears that stung her eyes told her something else.

"If you are not certain . . ."

"No, Mother. I want to marry him. I am certain."

"Very well. If you are certain."

"I am." She would not be some spoiled duke's daughter who thought her life should be perfect, who thought God would change life and death just for her.

Mother wrapped her arms around Adela.

"I'm well, Mother. I have everything I need." Had God not been better to her than He was to most people? Had He not given her loving parents and met all her needs, including sending her a wonderful man to marry, even though the man she loved had died?

She was crying, but it was only because Mother's kindness always touched Adela's heart.

❧

Frederick stood as the bishop and two of his priests squinted at him. Soon they were discussing Frederick's clothing and appearance in voices too low for him to hear.

"I don't need fancy clothes," he told them, but they barely glanced at him and continued their conversation. Then the two priests strode away with purposeful step.

"I have shoes for you." The bishop was staring at Frederick critically. "And a hat, very stylish."

"No. No hat." Frederick had seen the hats that the wealthier townspeople wore—like giant multicolored mushrooms—and he wanted no part of them.

"Very well. No hat."

The bishop bid the servants draw Frederick a bath. Frederick saw the stalks of dried lavender floating in the water but decided not to take the time to pick them out; he just stepped in the water and grabbed the square of soap—which was visibly infused with lavender and other herbs. There was no way for him to escape smelling like flowers. At least lavender was a more masculine scent than, say, roses.

After he was bathed and dressed in some clean clothes the servants provided, the bishop lectured him on the etiquette for a feast at a duke's table. Most of it was either common sense or the good manners his mother had taught him.

The bishop also tried to explain some of the dances that were performed in the wealthy aristocrats' homes. Frederick listened politely, then said, "I know a few country dances, but I don't think I will be dancing." Would he be in a position or a temperament for dancing tonight? It all depended on how Adela reacted to seeing him.

The bishop smiled his acceptance of that.

"I will attend the ball as well," the bishop said, "so that I can explain to Duke Wilhelm what Lord Conrat did. He will not wish to have that man under his roof when he hears of his treachery."

Just then the priests returned with some clothing—fancier clothes than he'd ever seen anyone wear. They told him he had to try them all on, but Frederick refused. He picked out the least outrageous of them—a long tunic with gold buttons down the front, embroidered cuffs on the sleeves, and a fine woolen mantle fastened at the shoulder with more gold buttons. The young priests approved.

By now the sun was sinking low, the wind was blowing, and the temperature was dropping, as if winter was finally setting in.

"You should go. The ball will have started by the time you get there. Just remember." The bishop placed a hand on his shoulder. "You are also the son of a duke."

"Illegitimate."

"Frederick, God is your Father, and in His eyes, you are legitimate."

Frederick nodded. He might be rejected by everyone else, but Adela was the one who mattered to him now. And God. God had helped him get free. God was the only one who would never forsake him. Even Adela had believed he was dead and decided to marry someone else. Could she truly forget him so soon? How could she marry Barthold? He never could have forgotten her so soon.

But he wouldn't think like that. He would believe she cared for him until she told him otherwise.

The bishop's guards mounted up and rode with the bishop and Frederick the short distance to Hagenheim Castle. One of the guards at the gatehouse locked eyes with Frederick and his brows rose. Did he recognize him?

As they rode across the castle yard in the half-light of evening, he could already hear the musicians and singers performing for the crowd inside the castle. In a moment he would be face-to-face with many people who believed him dead—or wished him dead. Not least of which were Lord Barthold and Lord Conrat. But the only person whose reaction he truly cared about was Adela's. Would she be glad to see him? And would his sudden appearance be enough to stop her from wedding Barthold?

∼❧∽

Adela allowed Lord Barthold to take her hand and lead her onto the floor where several couples were dancing. Her parents had invited their relatives and friends from near and far. Nearly everyone whom Adela knew, and many people she didn't, were invited to the ball. Her sister Elsebeth had traveled from Keiterhafen. Her brother Gabe was there from Hohendorf, and the two of them were deep in conversation with each other. Everyone was dressed in their finery—silk and fine linen in beautiful colors and patterns. She

didn't know why, but she kept glancing at the door, watching the guests arriving. Who was she looking for?

Frederick was not coming. Had she not accepted that?

Barthold took her hand on one side, and a stranger took her hand on the other. They danced the Carolingian in a circle, moving to the left, then to the right, forward and then back, raising their clasped hands high in the air. Barthold was smiling. Everyone was smiling. Adela smiled too, but the insincerity of it made her face hurt.

Her mother and father were looking very pleased. Her brother and sister-in-law, Valten and Gisela, seemed happy. All the guests looked well supplied and comfortable. Even the singers and musicians appeared joyful, probably because Father paid them so well.

But Adela's heart was heavy, her mind sore.

This was a ball and a feast, a festive time with music and dancing. Was she so self-focused that she could only think of the man she had lost?

The song was still going on. She had to at least hold back the tears while they were dancing, did she not? She could not ruin the night for her mother and father and all their guests. And Barthold. How selfish would that be?

She heard some commotion near the door as someone entered. The song was just ending, and while the stranger let go of her hand, Barthold kept hold of her other one. He stepped quite near to her and said her name. She looked up at him, but something made her turn to see who had just come in.

The crowd suddenly hushed. Adela had to take a step away from Barthold to see around the people. Near the door, standing beside the bishop, was a young man. His gaze flitted around the room, as if he was searching the crowd for someone. He looked so much like Frederick that she gasped and disentangled her hand from Barthold's.

Her heart thumped hard. She devoured the man's face and body with her gaze. She did not recognize the clothing, and the body was thinner than Frederick's familiar shape. But the eyes, the nose, the lips were just like Frederick's. And when his gaze came to rest on her own, their eyes meeting and holding, his expression changed.

She ran toward him. He strode to meet her and caught her in his arms, lifting her feet off the floor, hugging her to his chest.

"You're alive. You're alive." Her words came out like a croak, her throat so tight she could barely speak.

"Adela." It was all he said, but it filled her up inside, dispelling the ache that had been there only a moment before.

She buried her face in his shoulder, holding him, reveling in the way he was holding her. She never wanted him to let go. He was alive, and her arms around him proved it. He was here, solid and real.

Thank You, God, thank You.

The room was quiet as a man began to speak. The voice sounded like the bishop's. But she was more interested in the way Frederick was breathing, fast and shallow, as if her nearness affected him as much as his affected her.

But when the bishop said the name *Lord Conrat*, then *Frederick*, his arms suddenly loosened their hold on her, and he pulled her to his side. She followed his gaze to Lord Conrat.

CHAPTER 25

Frederick could have held Adela in his arms forever, but he needed to face his enemy. He gently moved Adela to his side, keeping a protective arm around her.

"Lord Conrat," the bishop was saying in his deep, imposing voice, "wrongfully abducted and imprisoned this innocent man, Frederick."

"I knew nothing of this." Barthold glared at Lord Conrat, his mouth open as he stared at his father's trusted adviser. "You lied about Frederick being dead."

Lord Conrat held up his hand as if to ward him off. "I was mistaken. I did not—"

"He did lie, and he seized Frederick and sent him to the Grundelsbach dungeon." The bishop took another step closer. "Frederick was the church's wood-carver. He had done nothing to deserve such ill treatment. Lord Conrat's motives were jealousy, control, and misplaced loyalty. He wanted to make sure no one discovered who Frederick's father actually was."

The bishop paused. No one spoke, but they all had confused looks on their faces.

Lord Barthold was still glaring at Lord Conrat, who stood

about thirty feet away. Frederick had caught a glimpse of Barthold dancing with someone when he came in but had not recognized the woman beside him. He now realized it had been Adela. A pain stabbed his middle at the thought of Adela dancing with Barthold when she thought Frederick was dead, hardly cold in his supposed grave.

But for now he had to focus on the bishop and Lord Conrat.

"These are lies!" Lord Conrat's voice cracked as it rose to a high, shrill note. "I never abducted or imprisoned this man."

"Yes, you did, Lord Conrat," a voice boomed from behind Frederick.

He looked over his shoulder. An older man, probably about twice Frederick's age, walked forward, brushing past Frederick's shoulder.

Conrat's face turned red as a few soldiers, wearing the colors of the Duke of Grundelsbach, quietly came in the door behind this stranger who'd just walked in.

"Lord Conrat, you will no longer serve me or Lord Barthold. And you will never have another opportunity to harm Frederick, my other son." The Duke of Grundelsbach turned around and looked straight at Frederick.

"Father!" Barthold took a step forward. "What are you saying?"

"Before I married your mother, Barthold, I loved another woman. I believed Conrat when he said she had left me of her own accord. But it was a lie. Conrat sent her away, knowing she was with child. And I am very sorry I never knew."

Frederick's heart raced inside his chest. He had not been unwanted. He had only been unknown. A breath of air rushed into his lungs.

The Duke of Grundelsbach turned back to face Lord Conrat. "You have been wrongly imprisoning people in my dungeon. I should have appointed someone to oversee you, should not have given you so much authority. I regret trusting you."

The Duke of Grundelsbach motioned with his hand, and his guards moved forward and took hold of Lord Conrat, escorting him out. Lord Conrat said not a word, but his face was hard and his eyes even harder as he glared straight ahead.

"What is going on?" Barthold looked angry, his brows lowering as he stared at his father.

The duke walked toward Barthold and spoke in a low voice that Frederick couldn't hear. But it gave Frederick the chance to look down at his reward for escaping the dungeon and walking all the way back.

She was gazing up at him, a slight smile on her face, her blue eyes shimmering.

"I'm so glad you are alive." She turned slightly so she could put her hand on his shoulder and bring her face closer to his.

His chest ached as he stared at her lips, longing to kiss her. But kissing her might not be a good idea, since so many people were staring at them, including her parents. And her fiancé.

She hugged him, then buried her face in his chest. Did she feel sorry for Barthold? Even Frederick felt some pity for him. He'd lost Adela and discovered his father had a son older than he was.

Frederick held her close and kissed the top of her head as the duke spoke to Barthold. Barthold gestured angrily with his hand, then glanced at Adela, who was still in Frederick's arms. Barthold turned and stalked away.

The crowd parted for him as he headed straight for the door that led out of the Great Hall.

Adela looked up at Frederick and spoke in her soft voice, so that he had to lean down to hear her. "I'm so glad you're here. And so sorry you were treated badly. Are you well? Did they hurt you?"

"Not too much." Frederick smiled. "Nothing your smile wouldn't make up for."

Her smile was a watery one, as her eyes filled with tears. She hid her face in his chest again. He put both arms around her, not caring who saw them. How could he care what other people thought, people who had nothing to do with his happiness? He couldn't, not while Adela filled his arms—and his heart.

꩜

Adela breathed deeply as she pressed her face into Frederick's tunic. She wasn't sure where he'd gotten such rich and beautiful clothes, but it didn't matter. She didn't care what he wore, only that he was alive and here holding her. After all the pain and sadness, her heart felt so good and so light, it might float her right up to the timbered ceiling.

Poor Barthold. She hoped he wasn't too hurt. How fickle she must seem, switching her devotion from one man to another so quickly and easily. Though she had begun to like him and care about his opinion of her, she had not felt the passion and love for Barthold that she had for Frederick. Their marriage could have been cold and lonely, and surely no one wanted that, not even Barthold.

Frederick had been seized and greatly mistreated. He was making light of it, no doubt. "What did they do to you?"

"Don't worry. I will tell you all about it some other time. Right now I just want to hold you and take in your sweet, beautiful face." He smoothed her hair back from her cheek, making her breath catch at the touch of his hand.

But she had to at least know something of where he was and what had happened. He'd been gone so long. "Were you in a dungeon in Grundelsbach?"

"Yes."

287

"And the duke is your father?"

"That is what I am told."

"Do you need to talk to him? Have you even spoken to him?"

Frederick smiled slightly as he gazed into her eyes. Their faces were so close he was a little blurry. "No, it is well. He is talking with Duke Wilhelm at the moment. I will speak with him later." He seemed to be glancing back and forth between her eyes and her mouth.

She was thinking more and more about kissing him. He must have suffered so much. But he'd risked coming back here and encountering Lord Conrat and his guards, the same men who had snatched him away and locked him in a dungeon.

"How did you ever escape?" Her voice sounded breathless from being so close to him, from thinking about kissing him.

"The *gaoler* helped me. I hope I can return the favor."

"The *gaoler* helped you escape? But I am not surprised. I would have helped you escape as well. You have such a trustworthy and lovable . . . temperament." She almost said "face."

"As do you." He brushed his hand over her cheek again, as he had done when he moved her hair off her face. Only there was no hair now to brush back.

Her skin tingled at his touch, and she sighed. She could still hear the men talking, could see her father and the Duke of Grundelsbach conversing, looking very serious.

"But how strange that your father is the Duke of Grundelsbach." Barthold was the heir, but would the duke give Frederick an inheritance? He had not been married to Frederick's mother, so that meant he could either choose to acknowledge Frederick as his son—which he had just done—or not. And he could grant him some kind of favor, such as a position, or he could give him money or land or property that wasn't already to be inherited by the heir.

Perhaps her father would approve of her marrying Frederick after all.

"My mother only told me recently. She had kept it secret for a long time."

Adela had always attributed her brothers' integrity and good character to having a father who taught them well. But Frederick was proof that a man could choose to have good character even if he hadn't had a decent father to teach him how.

"I am sorry, Frederick." The Duke of Grundelsbach was approaching them.

Adela loosened her hold on Frederick and turned to face the Duke of Grundelsbach, but Frederick kept an arm around her.

"If I had known of you, I never would have let you grow up without my provision or without my presence in your life. I am sorry things happened as they did." The wrinkles around the duke's eyes were deep for a man his age. But Frederick did resemble him—his chin and jawline were the same, and their hair was similar, though Frederick's was a bit lighter brown.

"I pray you can forgive me. And that your mother can forgive me."

"Where is my mother? I was worried after Lord Conrat forced her to leave Hagenheim."

"She and your sisters came to Grundelsbach looking for you. She asked for my help in finding you, and I discovered you had escaped from my dungeon. They are on their way here and are just behind me. A few of my men and I rode on ahead."

"I should go find them, make sure they are safe."

"No need. My trusted guards are with them. They will not allow any harm to come to them. Nevertheless, I will go and escort them the rest of the way."

Frederick seemed to be studying the man's face. "Perhaps I should come too."

"You may if you wish. But as God is my witness, I will neither harm nor coerce your mother. I will respect her, as she deserves."

Frederick's jaw twitched, but he said nothing.

"You should know that your stepfather, Stenngle, is dead," the duke said, pausing before going on. "In a rage, he stumbled and fell into the well, striking his head on the way down. He either drowned or broke his neck and died on impact."

This was enough news to overwhelm anyone. But Frederick seemed to bear it well. His expression hardly changed, except that he clenched and unclenched his jaw. Then he nodded.

Adela wished she could comfort Frederick, could hear his thoughts and feelings, but with so many people around, all she could do was stand close beside him to let him know she cared.

❦

Frederick's mind seemed to go numb with the shocking news. His father—stepfather—was dead.

At least Mother would not be terrorized by him anymore. That was certainly a blessing from God, even though it seemed wrong, somehow, to thank God for a man's death.

The duke took another step forward and placed a hand on Frederick's shoulder. "You are my son, and I will do right by you. I will not forsake you again."

Should he thank him? Frederick just gave him a quick nod.

"And now I shall go and meet your mother, sisters, and my guard. I will make certain you are informed when they arrive." He looked Frederick in the eye, then patted his shoulder and left.

Frederick looked down at Adela. She was staring at his face with wide eyes.

"What are you thinking?" he asked her.

"I am thinking how glad I am that you are alive."

The people around them were talking among themselves. The music had ceased when the duke came in, and now he saw the duchess, Lady Rose, motion to the singers to begin again.

Duke Wilhelm came toward them.

"Father," Adela said, "Frederick is alive."

"Yes." Duke Wilhelm actually smiled at him. "Welcome to Hagenheim Castle. Will you not join us for the dancing and feasting?"

"Of course he will." Adela slid her arm through his. "He shall sit beside me."

He could feel the eyes of all the people in the room on him as they walked toward the table. A few people began to dance to the music again, and the noise in the room rose as the party recommenced. Had newcomers entered the room at that moment, they might not have realized that several people's lives had just been changed at this ball a few minutes before, especially his.

❧

Barthold would not wait another moment. He gathered up a few of his things and departed Hagenheim.

Perhaps it was peevish of him, even a bit dishonorable, to leave without thanking his host, Duke Wilhelm. But he was in no mood to be grateful. He'd already left the ball that was supposedly given in his honor. Or should he say, in his dishonor?

The image of Adela's beaming face as she hugged the usurper was imprinted forever on his mind. How could she prefer that peasant wood-carver over him? How could she humiliate him in front of all those people? And then his father coming in and announcing that he had an illegitimate son with another woman.

The only way it could have been worse was if his father had

announced that since this wood-carver was older than Barthold, he would be the new heir.

But his father wouldn't do that to him, surely, not after all the training he'd been through, both for battle and for diplomacy. Besides, he was his father's only legitimate son.

And Lord Conrat—Barthold had always known Conrat was a strange man, cold and even cruel to anyone who was not part of the Duke of Grundelsbach's family. But to have Father renounce him and haul him away to the Hagenheim dungeon . . . Barthold still was unsure whether Conrat had done anything truly wrong. But no. His father must have proof that Conrat had seized Frederick and imprisoned him in Grundelsbach Castle, and he had told everyone that he was dead.

If only he *had* been dead. But that was an ungracious thought, and surely it was beneath him. At least his mother wasn't there to hear about it all.

As he mounted his horse, he thought of Adela, of her beautiful blonde hair and blue eyes, her bright smile. He should have kissed her when he had the chance.

But he knew she wasn't in love with him. He'd always imagined she'd love him when they were married. And now that he thought about it, perhaps he hadn't been in love with her either, because he was more angry than hurt at her choosing Frederick over him.

Frederick. His own half brother. What a revolting thought.

He galloped out of the gate, sending a few townspeople stepping to the side. He would not have run them over, but they probably didn't know that.

It was getting late, and he had been traveling only about an hour when he came upon a group of people traveling toward him—several of his father's guards and three women.

One of the women was quite young and lovely, with long brown hair that fell over one shoulder and eyes that looked him straight on without glancing away.

His father's guards looked surprised to see him.

"Your father is in Hagenheim," they said. "He rode on ahead."

"Yes, I've seen him."

They all looked uneasy. No doubt they knew that Barthold's father's errand was to find his illegitimate son that Barthold had no idea existed until an hour and a half ago. Everyone slowed to a stop in the middle of the road and stared at him.

One of the guards asked, "Are you on your way home to Grundelsbach?"

"I am." He looked again at the pretty woman and decided he was willing to face the hurt his father had just inflicted on him. He said, "On your way to Hagenheim? I will ride with you."

The guards glanced at each other, then rode on.

Barthold maneuvered his horse to ride beside the prettiest woman. One of the soldiers did the introductions, letting him know that the older woman was named Basina, and her daughters were Eulaly and Ursula. Eulaly. That was the one giving him the side-eye. The other sister, Ursula, was pretty too, but she seemed to have her eye on Sir Ulrich, one of Father's favorite knights.

The way Eulaly was looking at him was a balm to his wounded pride. Adela may not have wanted him, but other women would.

While Sir Ulrich was speaking with Ursula about the weather, he started a conversation with Eulaly. Thankfully, she took over and did most of the talking. Soon he was admiring the way she thought. She probably didn't know how to read, but she seemed intelligent and well-spoken, even so.

They rode at an easy pace, and by dark they were passing through the town gate.

Eulaly smiled at him. "Our house is this way. Good night, Lord Barthold."

"Good night, Fraulein." He rode on back to Hagenheim Castle. He only hoped the Duke and Duchess of Hagenheim had not given, in addition to their daughter, his bedchamber to Frederick.

Chapter 26

A dela walked beside the guard who carried her picnic basket to the hill outside town. As soon as she began setting out the food, she saw Frederick walking up the hill toward her, smiling.

Every day her father allowed her this midday meal with Frederick, as Frederick was meeting with his father, the Duke of Grundelsbach, every evening when he was finished with his work on the Cathedral doors.

When Frederick reached her, he hugged her and kissed her forehead as the guard watched, and they sat down together on the blanket.

Frederick said, "Do you remember me telling you about Heinryk, the man who helped me escape the dungeon?"

"Of course."

"And that my father sent orders that Heinryk was to be given any position he wanted?"

"Yes. And did he choose a job?"

"He did. He had Father's scribe help him write to me all about it. I shall show you the letter. He sounded very happy."

"Oh, that is such wonderful news." Adela hugged Frederick's arm.

"I have something else to tell you," Frederick said.

Adela felt her smile fade at his sober tone. Would he say he'd decided to move to Grundelsbach with his father?

"Why do you look worried?" He reached out and brushed her cheek with his finger.

She forced a smile. "No reason. What do you have to tell me?"

"My mother and father just got married last evening in the chapel at Hagenheim Castle."

"They did? That is wonderful!" Adela clapped her hands.

Frederick laughed. "I'm glad you think so."

"Don't you think it's wonderful?"

"It is good. I am pleased. But they left this morning to travel back to Grundelsbach."

"Oh?"

"My sisters went with them to Grundelsbach."

"And did you wish to go with them as well? Did your father want you to? I'm sure your mother wished it."

"My father did ask me to go with them. He wants me to learn diplomacy and become knowledgeable about all the leaders and noblemen so that I can advise him. He wants me to take charge of the steward and other officials in Grundelsbach and take over Lord Conrat's duties."

"Will you do it?" Her heart was in her throat. Where did she fall in his plans?

He shook his head and took a bite of the meat pasty he was eating. After he swallowed he said, "I don't want to learn diplomacy or take charge of anyone. The only thing I've ever wanted to do was be a wood-carver, to make things with my hands that will give people joy." He looked intently into her eyes. "But you were not born to be a wood-carver's wife, Adela. You might come to resent me if you married me."

"I would be very content, as long as I was with you." She squeezed his arm. "I know you must think I'm too spoiled to be your wife, but—"

"I wish you would not say that you are spoiled. No one thinks you're spoiled."

"You must think I'm spoiled, or you would not say that I would resent you if I married you."

Frederick frowned, but there was a gentle light in his eyes now as he gazed at her. "I know you have dreams and hopes too. You wish to travel, to paint, to improve your skills as a portrait painter. But I will be living here in Hagenheim for several more months, carving these Cathedral doors."

"That is all very well. I can learn a lot here in Hagenheim."

"And after I finish the doors, I will only be a wood-carver, creating wooden figures, carving timbers and panels and doors for people's houses. I may even have to travel in order to get enough work."

"Oh."

"But you can travel with me and paint the way you always wanted to. And I plan to buy the house from your father, so that I shall always have a home for my family."

"Yes?" Adela leaned toward him, holding her breath.

Frederick leaned toward her and took her hand in his. "If you are certain you do not mind being a wood-carver's wife, and if you think you would like to travel with me, then I beg you, Adela, to marry me, because I love you and I want to adore you for your whole life."

"Yes. Yes, I will marry you." She leaned the rest of the way, and their lips met in a long kiss. He didn't care that a guard was watching them, did not care who saw them, as long as he was able to kiss his future bride.

EPILOGUE

*I*t *is a miracle."*

Adela walked to the Cathedral with her mother's words ringing in her ears. She'd had to wait six months to marry her Frederick, but every one of her siblings had been able to come back to Hagenheim for the wedding.

Miracle. Yes, that was the word that kept coming to her mind as she walked down the cobblestone street beside Frederick, who held her hand in his as they made their way to the church to say their vows. So many people were crowding the street, watching them, the guards had to keep shooing people out of the way.

They could see the bishop waiting for them, waiting to lead them in their vows, which they would say in front of the crowd, before God and man.

There at the bottom of the steps stood her family—all of them. She hugged her brother Gabe and his wife, Sophie, with their five children. She hugged Valten and Gisela and their six children, even though she saw them almost every week. Tears filled her eyes as she embraced her sister Margaretha and her English husband, Colin, having traveled all the way from their home in England with their four children. She hugged her sister Elsebeth and her husband, Sir Gerek, who, with their four children, had traveled from their castle in Keiterhafen.

Next she embraced her sister Kirstyn and her husband, Aladdin, who had traveled from Lüneburg. She embraced her brother Steffan and his new bride of less than a year, Katerina, who was just showing her first pregnancy. Then she hugged her brother Wolfgang and his wife, Mulan, who held their one-year-old in her arms.

She turned to her little brother, Toby.

"I suppose I'll have to get married next," he said, giving her a sad half smile.

"You're the last one." She hugged Toby's skinny frame. When she pulled away, she saw that Toby had tears in his eyes.

"You should be happy," she told him, blinking back her own tears. "I'll be staying in Hagenheim with you and Mother and Father. At least for now."

He nodded. "I am glad."

"And you'll have to sit for a portrait so I can practice."

His eyes got big. "I never agreed to that."

Adela just smiled and shook her head.

She hugged Mother and Father, then said, "Why do you two look so happy? Ready to get rid of me?"

"Frederick isn't taking you far," Mother said. "And if he does, he'll bring you back."

"That's why we're happy," Father added.

She hugged Frederick's mother and father next, and settled for a small wave at his brother, Barthold, who gave her a wincing smile.

Frederick was by her side again, squeezing her hand. He kissed her briefly, and then they walked up the steps to the bishop, who was waiting at the top.

Their eyes met, and Frederick's look made her stomach flutter. He was everything she could want in a friend and husband, and she leaned into him, ready for whatever adventure they found for themselves, creating art—and life—together.

ACKNOWLEDGMENTS

The character of Heinryk was inspired by Enrique "Henry" Nazario (April 9, 1979–March 23, 2015) and all the men and women with good hearts who work at correctional facilities, who do this thankless but necessary job to keep the rest of us protected. Every honest job is noble work when one works to provide for his family. And love is the greatest of all virtues. I appreciate Henry for doing a difficult job out of love for his family. May Henry rest in the arms of Jesus, and may God bless his family. A loving and noble heart is worthy of the love he inspires.

I want to thank my agent Natasha Kern for all her kind support, encouragement, and love she shows for me. She's always there for me, and I'm so grateful.

I want to thank my editors at Thomas Nelson, Kimberly Carlton, Julie Breihan, Jodi Hughes, and others who help keep me from looking as scatterbrained as I am, for helping me clean up and improve my characters and plot, and for keeping me from missing opportunities to make my stories better.

I'm so thankful for my friends and family who let me "talk out" my stories, for brainstorming with me, and for encouraging me, especially Faith and Grace, Aaron, Terri, Kristin, and Regina.

ACKNOWLEDGMENTS

Finishing this book, since it is the last one in the Hagenheim/
Fairy Tale Romance series, was extremely difficult. I've gotten very
attached to these characters and this story world, so it's hard to say
fare well. But I pray the stories have meant something good to
my readers and encouraged them in some way, as they have me. God
bless you all.

DISCUSSION QUESTIONS

1. At the beginning of the story, what was Adela expecting married life to be like? What did she hope to accomplish first before settling into "dull" married life? Do you have any similar goals?

2. Adela felt an immediate attraction to the handsome peasant, Frederick. Why did she think, at first, that she could never marry him? If you were the daughter of the Duke of Hagenheim, would you have felt the same way? Why or why not?

3. How did Adela's feelings about marrying Frederick change over the course of this story?

4. Adela did not fall in love with her suitor, Lord Barthold. What qualities did Frederick have that Barthold did not possess? Do you think Adela chose wisely by choosing Frederick over Barthold? Why or why not?

5. Frederick's father and uncle had the same father, who was angry and violent. What might have caused Frederick's father to follow in his own father's footsteps and become angry and violent, while his brother did not? Why might

one sibling be abusive, like his father, and the other sibling become a good, gentle person?

6. Why did Adela keep her identity a secret from Frederick? Do you think they still would have fallen in love if she had been honest with him from the beginning? Why or why not?

7. Why did Frederick's sisters treat him the way they did? Why did their behavior start to change by the end of the story? Change is not easy. What does it take to change one's behavior?

8. When the Eselin brothers attacked Lord Barthold and Adela, why did Frederick feel guilty? How could he have prevented it? What did Adela feel guilty about, blaming herself for Frederick ending up in the Hagenheim dungeon?

9. When Frederick went missing, how did Adela use her talent to try to help find him? Was it a good plan? Why did it not work?

10. How did Frederick deal with being imprisoned in the Grundelsbach dungeon? How can taking action help bolster your spirits in a bad situation?

11. How was Frederick a "Cinderella" character? Aside from being a boy, how was he different from your ideas of Cinderella?

12. Does having money contribute to a happy marriage? Why or why not? Do you think Adela and Frederick will be happily married? Why or why not?

From *New York Times* bestselling author
Melanie Dickerson comes a reimagining of the
Wild Swans—and the first book in a new series of
fairy-tale retellings set in medieval England.

AVAILABLE JANUARY 2021

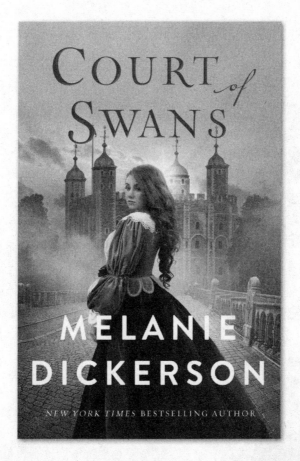

THOMAS NELSON
Since 1798

For the first time ever these three beloved tales from Melanie Dickerson—including the *New York Times* bestseller *The Silent Songbird*—will be available in paperback!

The Orphan's Wish –
coming August 2021

The Golden Braid –
coming March 2021

The Silent Songbird –
coming September 2020

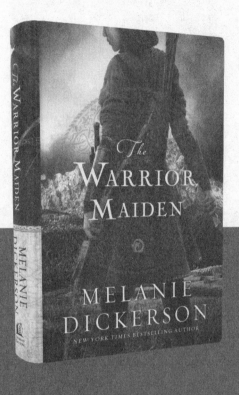

She lost everything to the scheme of an evil servant. But she might just gain what she's always wanted . . . if she makes it in time.

Available in print, e-book, and audio!

About the Author

Jodie Westfall Photography

M elanie Dickerson is a *New York Times* bestselling author and two-time Christy Award winner. Melanie spends her time daydreaming, researching the most fascinating historical time periods, and writing and editing her happily-ever-afters.

Visit her online at MelanieDickerson.com
Instagram: MelanieDickerson123
Facebook: MelanieDickersonBooks
Twitter: @MelanieAuthor